I HEAR YOU CALLING

I HEAR YOU CALLING

R F DEANGELIS

R. F. DeAngelis

I would like to say a special thank you to everyone who has helped me and my family out; from Lynn, to Jane, to Daffyd, to Ethan, to August, to everyone at Callahan's Crosstime Saloon on Facebook.

I would also like to thank Photo by FRANCESCO TOMMASINI on Unsplash for the background to my cover.

Prologue

I don't know where things went wrong. I was raised, well like most young women were. I was about 12 when I first started thinking something was wrong, that I was wrong. I started off by trying to tell my mom... that went about as well as expected. It took a couple of days, but eventually I was accepted as gay.

Navigating my small town was a little harder.

My mom didn't tell anyone, but somehow the girls at school found out. I went from being on the cheer squad in Junior High to an outright pariah by High School. Small towns everyone knows you, and I was already known as the weird kid even before it came out.

Then after what my mom eventually told me was several years of talking and fighting back and forth that I was completely unaware of, I was kicked out of church. I cried for a week, started having nightmares, visions of hell dancing in my head.

That was my ninth-grade year.

Tenth grade was different.

I got tired of the small minds, and the net, with its world beyond, made things a lot easier, my mom helped. On the first day back to school I walked in ready to own everything, my brown hair was cut short and dyed black, my brown eyes were replaced by wicked violet contacts, and my clothing, though well within dress code, was made to shock everyone. Goth hit my school that day and by the time I was a senior, Goth was in. I had never been so happy to be named Lydia in my life.

Hit college, got drunk, had a kiss, had a girlfriend, had a fling, went wiccan, then pagan, then agnostic. By the time I was a junior in college I was hooking up, going out, and living the life I always wanted. Senior year was a rip all over again this time with classier friends and more well-read peers. I heard about BDSM and so much more.

Then, school was over, and the bill as they say, came due. I had thought I was a bitch, I had nothing on student loans. Jobs evaporated just after I graduated, and I found myself unemployable. No experience, no prospects, no money. Depression hit hard, I grew my hair out, put up the contacts and got a real job.

Then of course, I lost it.

Downsizing to a smaller apartment made things somewhat better, but rent kept going up and the pay for whatever I could find didn't. Then, thankfully I ran into an ex-girlfriend from college. She had inherited a little bit of money and a coffee shop, a place for people like us, that her uncle had built. She offered me a job and what's more, a room. I took her offer.

That was five years ago.

Chapter 1

My life is routine. I wake up, work most days, and go back to sleep. The official work uniform is whatever you feel like so long as it's legal and you can put a black apron on. Mine is a pair of faded blue jeans and whatever band shirt I happen to grab that morning. My morning's start whenever I get up, and I rarely get up before noon.

Shuffling out each morning requires coffee to get me going, dark shades to avoid the day star, a quick drive in a car that rattles as it rolls, and settling into the shop usually around 2 pm. At one point I had a life outside of work, I gamed, I dated, I went to clubs. Then, well things happened, let's just say I have bad luck with women.

Saturday night is game night, I don't play anymore. Why? I'm at work Saturday night.

It's ok, I have something most don't.

Saturday night is Writer's Night, not that this place isn't filled to the brim with people clacking away at their keyboards, but Writer's Night is when a few of them will hit the microphone we turn on and let some of their poetry or other prose shine. It's a hot mess and I love it.

I look forward to my Saturdays.

Today is not Saturday.

I get two days a week off, one is Sunday, the other floats. This week it's Wednesday.

Cleaning day.

My day doesn't start any earlier, is just gets a whole lot less exciting. Elizabeth, Beth to her friends, is a hell of a businesswoman, smart, savvy, wonderful, creative, everything you could ask for in a boss. Kind, considerate, and always willing to get things done and work with people. Beth the person is a walking talking disaster area.

A weeks' worth of dishes was nothing to wake up to on cleaning day, laundry was always backed up, the game room a.k.a. the dining room, often still had pizza boxes in it. Beth always helped and she was always grateful. It may not be ideal, but what is?

Chapter 2

The buzz of the alarm, an ancient creature with built in tape deck that my mom got for me when I was 8, lets loose with its ghastly cry. I would get rid of it, but I have a Pavlovian response to the thing and no other clock seems to work. Beth swears one day its dying speaker will result in an incantation that will wake Cthulhu.

Jeans, t-shirt, rinse repeat... get in the car.

"RrRRrrRrrrrrrr..."

"..." I tried it again to the same sound only lower and winding down. "Don't start with me." As if threatening it would work. I turned the key again and it ground just a little slower. "Look, I need to get to work," I bargained with my steering wheel. "If you crank, I promise, I will wash you my next day off."

Counting to 10, I turned the key... the car roared to life. "Good girl, thank you. Trust me, I'll get you something. Just please keep running for me."

We, me and my car, throttled off down the road with my little bug doing its best impersonation of the little engine that could from my childhood. I had gotten her as a lark in collage, a vintage beetle. I saw her for sale and had to get her. Back in college I kept her tuned and purring. Now? I made good money working where I did, well it was more than minimum wage anyway, but if I wasn't living with Beth? My sweet one got what I could give. This wasn't the first bargain I struck with her; it wouldn't be the last.

Slide into work, throw the backpack down, and into my apron, something so practiced it might as well be one move, I was almost face to face with Walt. Walt is, what you would call our problem child, an honest to god online troll in the flesh. He sits all day, clacking away at his keyboard, usually giggling to himself about something, as he literally trolls websites to piss people off. Right wing, left wing, whatever.

This wouldn't be so bad, if he left it on the screen. No, he wore whatever he felt would offend the snowflakes more. When the holiday cup from a rival, and frankly much bigger store came and went, he was happy holidays-ing everyone who would sit still while wearing an ugly Christmas sweater that said the same thing. When people started getting offended about a candidate's words, he ran around with a shirt that he had to have custom made with a pair of arms ending in comically small hands that were picking up a cat with a word bubble saying, "because I'm rich." Today it was a red hat and an old beat-up looking t-shirt that said, "socialism for all". He was also demanding to know from the new girl if he had 'triggered her'.

"Walt, I swear to god. you will bounce when I toss your ass out of here if you don't back off."

"She was staring."

The girl, Rita, who he had been harassing burst out with, "Oh, you poor snowflake, you dress like an asshole on purpose then get offended when you're stared at. Fuck off pendejo."

I watched as Walt's face lit up. "Oh, I like her."

"Walt." I sighed, it was already a long day thanks to this asshole, and I wasn't even 10 minutes into my shift. "I don't care what you like, I doubt she does either. Go troll someone who will happily argue with you on whether or not seafood and an egg custard work together." His face lit up even more and he strode off with newfound purpose.

It took twenty minutes to convince Rita not to quit and I let her know she didn't have to take any of Walt's shit, ever. That no she wasn't in trouble for cussing at him, and that yes this wasn't corporate, but no we couldn't just throw him out because he hadn't done anything illegal.

The ebb and flow of the walk-ins with its never-ending variety of people out shopping somewhere else in the plaza was only punctuated by the denizens of the regulars as they shuffled in, crab walked, plugged in and drank enough caffeine to jumpstart whatever kept them clacking away at their keyboards. The tide of the rush came and went and around eight I took my break.

Pop out back, have a few puffs on my vape, a large black coffee, and a few moments of peace with my headphones. I do the big over the ear ones so guys leave me alone but keep my left ear out so I can hear anyone coming up. It's supposed to be fall, we're into late September but none of the leaves have changed. It's too warm even after dark, and the dumpster is a little too full. Someone got a shipment. Thankfully we're the only ones who do anything like food, and then it's only sandwiches and a few sweet breads, so there isn't a huge smell.

I love me some Siouxsie Sioux and the rest of the old school stuff, but honestly most nights like this I find myself listening to something hard, loud, and screeching. Arch Enemy is good, a little Lorde and Lordi, basically anything that makes me feel. Johnny Cash did Hurt better, Trent and I will both die on that hill.

Honestly it's why I went Goth all those years ago. I was already an outcast, I like the darker side of life anyway, kind of felt called to it to be honest, and I got to decide what was goth to me. That was the key. Now my music was the only thing I had left. The highlights of my days were dealing with assholes, entitled shits, and others. Retail of any kind quickly gives you a low outlook on humanity. It's hard to remember that the people on the other side of that counter are people and not all the same when you can spot a bad customer by hair style. We're in an age that's taking a hard look at its prejudices and here I am slowly getting more and more flinch every time a 'Karen' walks in.

That name for them kills me, my mom is named Karen... Of course, she missed her calling as a hippie.

"I miss it." As soon as the words were out of my mouth, I felt a chill. No one was there to hear me, no one was listening. Not quite true, I was. "God help me I miss it. I miss feeling, I miss being me. I miss the world of magic I used to live in."

I wiped my face as I headed inside.

It wasn't the first time I had started crying for no reason, it wouldn't be the last.

Chapter 3

The sound of pots clattering in the kitchen woke me up. I glanced at the alarm clock, 11:20 am. I didn't have to be up till one. Beth shouldn't be up either. Wouldn't be the first dream that woke me up this way, my dreams can get... odd.

The crash from the other room let me know that it wasn't a dream that woke me. Stumbling out of bed ready to kill Beth, I lurched forward down the hallway only to stop dead in my tracks. There, picking through our pots and pans, crashing around in the cupboard like a bull was a man, tall, dark long hair flowing down his back, and stark naked. He was, by most modern definitions, handsome, and I had no fucking idea who the hell he was.

For a moment I was too stunned to move, a naked man was rummaging through my kitchen... MY KITCHEN!

He turned, a look of shock on his face to match my own, broke me out of my trance. "What the fuck!" The look on his face was shock but quickly turned into something more. "Let me rephrase, who, the hell, are you?"

His lips spread wide and his grin was that of a man who was all that and so much more, so much into such a smooth package. He checked me out, starting at my bare feet, then slowly up my 5-foot frame, over my tattered band shirt and breasts lingering for just a second on them before finally making it to my face. He liked what he saw, and it was excruciatingly obvious in his current state of undress.

"I'm Ferris, Allen Ferris, and you?"

I'd known men like him since I was a kid, hit on for the first time by one very much like him at a gas station when I was nine. He liked my eyes and my pretty smile, and I was treating my ice-cream cone right proper according to him. I was creeped out then, disgusted when I learned later what he was speaking of. This Allen was bringing up the same slightly coated in oil feeling.

"Calling the cops." I started backing away. Beth kept a few things littering the house that could be called decorations, if you just saw the edges. We had dated for four months, and honestly, she was my most stable relationship. We broke up when we realized the only thing we had in common was chucking dice across the table and pretending to be orcs. She was big into SCA, as such she had quite a few blades around that were more or less live steel. One such weapon was hanging on the wall 2 steps down the hall I just came from. If I was quick, I could get it before he could even drop the pot he had pilfered from the void under our sink.

He seemed to finally remember he was naked as he covered himself with a pan lid he pulled from the counter, where I'm betting he put it while rummaging. "Um, look, this isn't what it looks like." He was about to go on when I reached the sword.

To be clear, Beth is the swordswoman, Beth is into SCA, Beth is into H.E.M.A., I'm just a geek. Geek or not I know one thing, keep the point at the attacker's face. The sword I found myself holding was just a sword, straight, double edge, cross guard, etc. It was much to my chagrin also nearly as long as I was. The message was received loud and clear.

"Liz? Liz! Your roommate is going to kill me." His words were a bit hysterical especially considering I wasn't advancing on him, but his tone was one of amusement, as if me hurting him were somehow hilarious.

Also, Liz?

Beth came out of her room mostly naked, by mostly I mean she was wearing pleather boots, cuffs on her wrists, they were still joined together, and a ball gag. I had to admit she wasn't exactly pleased with me. When we'd been together oh so briefly, I had been the one wearing the gag, now it looked like I was interrupting her fun.

The look she gave me was enough to let me know this person was as on the up and up as slime balls get. I looked from her, to him, rolled my eyes and headed back to bed. Flopping down on it I heard them talk, not what they were saying just tones.

His was amused, hers was contrite.

I think I might throw up.

Movement through the house ended with the front door closing followed by footsteps that were heading straight towards me. Sitting up before the door opened, I waited for what was going to be a fun encounter.

My room is, well, it's me, especially right now. It's a mess, but an organized functional mess. Under that mess was my old life, old makeup I hadn't worn in years, a few club things, some art, a few RPG books, some art supplies and more. Under the mess was the college kid who moved into a friend's, to have a life again. She did, for a while. Now everything was clean, just not straight. Things were piled up, books were stacked, clean clothing hadn't made it out of baskets let alone into drawers. Only my childhood bear didn't have something stacked on him. It just seemed disrespectful. Yes my waste basket was overflowing, no nothing was in it but papers, and no, I hadn't thrown anything into it since...

I really need to get back to writing, or drawing, maybe painting? Maybe one day I'll care again.

Beth entered with a, "You know, you could have at least put on real clothing." The gag was around her neck, the bright red ball resting on the hollow of her throat, nothing else had changed.

I looked her in the eye, took a deep breath, "Liz?"

One word, and any argument was gone. Beth blushed a deep crimson. "Well yeah, he likes it."

"This from miss never change for a guy?" I stood and went over to her. "Beth you hate when people call you Liz." She did, I'd seen her get into fist fights over it.

"Yeah, but he says its cuter than Beth." Her tone was almost a whine. "And it's not like I'm getting any younger."

Beth was staring down the big 30, and to be honest I wasn't far behind her.

"What happened to don't settle for anyone, guy or girl?"

She smiled at me, "You got it easy..." I looked at her strangely until she spoke again. "Mom called last week. Vicky is getting married, she's pregnant."

Vicky was her cousin, a miss perfect that never seemed to do anything wrong. No matter what Beth did, somehow Vicky always seemed to do one better... at least as far as Lisa, Beth's mom, seemed to be concerned.

I put my arm around her and pulled her close. "Come on, you look ridiculous." I took her into the kitchen and started water for tea.

"Beth, you're ok, you do great."

"Lydia, you're sweet, but I want more than just an ex-goth ex-girlfriend roommate."

"I am not an ex-goth."

"Hun, you know I love you, but when was the last time you went out? Or hell even got made up?"

Chapter 4

Halloween, also called Christmas for goths, much like Christmas we tend to start the season a bit earlier every year, also we never really stop wearing the spooky stuff. That's the stereotype anyway. In truth it's part harvest festival, part new year's celebration and more. A few years ago, I was all about Samhain, took part in a ritual and, well, had fun. Now it's just good to see the decorations going up.

Work was fun, I got to deck things out how I liked and Beth was always up for pushing things just a bit more. The spider webs were up, the cheesy clings were over the windows and cold case, we had a skeleton in the corner named Jack and are selling pumpkins under him. I was kind of proud of that.

In the center of the room was a fireplace, we didn't have it put in, it was a leftover from when this place used to be some kind of barbecue joint. Beth loved it so we kept it. During the winter we even burned wood in the thing and in the summer, it was just decoration. It has a gas line that ran under it, but we didn't really bother. It has all kinds of iconography strewn about it, it was as close to a true hearth as I had ever seen, and I loved it.

I wasn't the only one, a lot of regulars love to sit at the tables that crowded around it, including Creepy Chick. News update if you've never worked retail. If you are in regularly enough for us to remember you, we probably have a name for you.

In our place we have; 'Mom', an older black woman who always comes in and does her best to help out anyone she can, she's sweet, kind, caring, and always has a story of one of her grandkids. She's a half-caf, full pump of vanilla, and Anna was the name on her cup.

Neck Beard, everyone has him, a slightly to way overweight guy who always seems to have two to three days' worth of scruff, glasses optional, who is either a great big teddy bear or an asshole. Ours is both. Yes, he has threatened to kill our troll Walt more than once. I firmly believe that is how Walt will die, pissing off the wrong person. He always gets an americano. Travis is what was on his cup.

Oingo and Boingo, a set of really cute twin girls who come in for copious amounts of caffeine, bounce all over the place and always have headphones in. Whatever the drink of the day is until fall then its pumpkin spice. Their names were Nissa and Lissa.

Dexter, really cute guy even by my standards but painfully plain in dress and everything else, serious serial killer vibes. He always gets a flat white and his name was actually Dexter, frighteningly enough.

Doc, always got to have a Doc. Our Doc is a nurse from the local hospital who is always giving out 'I wish you would' looks to the antivaxxers that we seem to attract. He's about six nine and got the name from his love of Doctor Who. He recently switched to cold brew. I think Doc fits him better than David.

Walt... the only good thing to say about Walt is he's never targeted anyone for being in the LGBTQIA+ family. I'm pretty sure he's gay, though I've never seen him with anyone. It's just, him being that much of an asshole and a misogynist and never once hitting on any woman? He drinks tea. I swear everything he does is to troll people.

That brings us back to Creepy Chick.

Walt won't go anywhere near her. Not after he said something, and she just looked at him. I'd call her goth, but most of her aesthetic seems to run the gambit from homeless to hand me down. She barely wears any makeup and I know she's trans because some days she doesn't shave. Yet, I would never mistake her for anything but a woman. She's just tired, worn, almost wrung out. She's my black with room for cream and sugar and she never sits anywhere but one spot on the east side of the hearth. Her name was Isabela, but her cups always said Izzy.

It was a real shame too, she had some of the most amazing eyes I had ever seen. Steel blue one day, green the next, ever flowing like that. Sometimes she looks at you with chipped emeralds, sometimes they would be sapphires, sometimes a cloudy sky, but mostly they were these flat blue grey storms whose outer edge was black and right up next to the iris was this dark rim. Her hair was always this wild nest of curls, mostly brown but occasionally you'd see red or even blonde flash through it when the light was right. The grey she was gathering was at her temples and formed two witches' streaks and the colors as they descended were just as wild as the rest of her. If she had tried, she would be a force to be reckoned with. I could see it in her every once in a while. Flashes of something fierce just beneath the surface. That's what Walt saw that day, what everyone that tried to bother her saw sooner or later, something old, dark, wild, and frightening.

To me she, like all of them, were a comfort to have, even Walt, god help me.

I wasn't going to let him ruin the mood tonight, it was Saturday and we were two weeks to Halloween, and that always brought out the fun on Writer's Night.

We got odes to the dead, someone reads the Raven in its entirety, we had the normal emo stuff that seems to come out no matter the time of year. One hit me to my core, I think it was Oingo who recited it, but I'm not sure.

I was behind the register when she started. "Don't scream." Her voice cracked a little. She cleared her throat and continued. "You will hurt their feelings. Don't scream, it will get better." I walked over to the edge and looked at her, tears were flowing down her face. "Don't scream, you will undo all your work." She slowly held her chin slightly higher, defiant. "Don't scream, it won't matter anyway."

There was some scattered clapping as she descended the three steps and made her way back to her sister. It goes to show, you never know what people go through. It was odd. For a moment the world seemed clearer, as if the air had been slightly dirty and dingy and now everything was a little brighter. In that moment as I watched her she left little wakes behind her as she moved. Then just as quickly my world snapped back into the slightly out of focus I was used to.

It took a few moments before anyone was ready to try to follow that up, but eventually things got moving again. As things progressed through the night, I noticed something odd. Creepy Chick was not typing away. Instead she was staring at the microphone and occasionally, when someone was done, her body would tense. Izzy, it seemed, was trying to build up the nerve to perform.

After three more false starts, she finally got up and headed to the little nook with its unforgiving light. As she moved my world snapped back into that focus. Oingo had left eddies in her wake. Creepy Chick? She left a disturbance in her wake that grew larger as she got closer to the dais.

Normally there is some kind of intro from the artist, a little I wrote this when, I hope you like this, even before ripping my heart out Oingo had said "this is very personal to me." Izzy just stood there for a moment.

Her eyes took everything in, every person there, then locked with mine. "My hands flex, blood drips from them." Her voice was husky and, like her eyes, tended to change from time to time, now it was rich, thick. It flowed out of her and touched everyone. "I look up." She paused. "They mistook me for human." With those words a growl entered her voice. Not something as crude as her actually growling, more like a well-practiced grind. "I look up. They run." As I watched, the shadows behind her seemed to slowly start to uncurl. "I try so hard to be what I am not. For so long I did this." A dark frustration lifts off this worn woman and the lines crafted by my mind continues to unfurl, giving her wings, horns, making her impossibly large in such a small space. "With you." She was looking right at me. I could feel it. "I want to be me. You make me, me. Let me do the same." Her words, my heart. Around me I could see more, people were reacting. Women were leaning in, men were smiling that smile that showed they were uncomfortable.

"Dance with me in eternity. Walk with me in pain and pleasure. Leave behind what was. And together we will be." The invitation was so clear, I could see this being so well, this demon, this dark goddess laid bare before me. I watched as small gold orbs slowly floated off each person and made their way to her. Then just before they reached her, the vision was gone again. Reality had reasserted itself and I was back in the here and now.

Izzy simply walked off stage and out to the parking lot, purse in hand. For a brief moment I thought it had just been the way the work and her voice affected me. Yet as she brushed past, a smile graced her face and she didn't look quite so tired.

Chapter 5

"Rita, watch the front." I needed a minute, hell I needed an hour. I hit the back grabbed a bottle of water and went outside. The sound of the door hitting the wall shook me, it shook me more when it slammed shut. It took several deep breaths to calm myself.

What, the hell, was that?

Sure, when I was a kid, I used to see stuff. I mean who didn't as a kid? College was college, you take stuff, do stuff, explore. I never did LSD, but I got slipped psilocybin once. Rotten thing to do to someone who's not expecting it by the way. I saw, well I saw stuff like that. Lines of energy connecting people, places, things, wakes behind people like they were moving through water.

It took me weeks to figure out what happened to me, I never did find out who did it.

But this?

"Nice night huh?"

I snapped out of my thoughts and looked around. Off to my right was a man, I didn't know him, hadn't seen him before, and worse, I hadn't heard him come up.

"Yeah, uh, nice night."

He kind of smiled and came closer. "You saw it didn't you, you saw it feed."

My heart stopped. "Excuse me?"

He took out a knife, it was long, long enough I don't think it technically qualified as a knife anymore. "Now did you see because you saw, or did you see because you're one of them?" He started slowly moving towards me, trying to cut off my escape, but approaching me like I was the one who was dangerous. "I kind of need to know."

I reached back for the door, remembering just before my hands hit it that I heard it slam. Back doors don't have handles, you need keys. Keys! I waited for him to get a bit closer then I turned as if to run, flinging my arm out, with my keys in hand. Ten years of gaming, anime culture, bar hopping, and retail had left me with quite a collection of things that were on my key chain. I aimed for the eyes and wasn't disappointed.

I ran for the front, down the well-lit alley. As I approached the lights, the lights snuffed out. First starting at the far end, then slowly coming towards me. Even with the lights going out I should be able to see the far end, it was less than 100 yards to the well-lit promenade. Yet nothing, just blackness. My mind froze, something deep inside me would not go down that way no matter what, and that darkness, no, The Darkness, was coming towards me.

I became aware of three things at the same time. One, my pursuer had caught up with me, and like me, he too was completely trans-fixed. Two, the cherry of a lit cigarette was coming towards us both briefly burning brighter from a long drag. And three, he was both more aware of what was going on than I was and far more terrified.

"Shit, fucking bitch." He'd dropped the knife and pulled out... a cross? "Fucking vampire bitch. I'm protected from you. I got you." He started running towards her, I assume her. As he did the dark-ness enveloped both of us completely, I heard sounds, small voices, children of some such laughing, dogs, large ones growling, and then, the sound of someone hitting pavement.

"You've certainly have had a busy few moments."

The world snapped back to reality. There, halfway to the mouth of the alley was my attacker, slumped against the wall, unmoving. Beside me, smiling a sad worn smile was Creepy Chick, cigarette still in hand but down to the butt, lip stick ring around its white filter.

Carefully she picked up one of her feet and put it out on the bottom of her shoe.

I looked from him to her.

She looked back, then turned to me and smiled. "He's alive. Probably will wake very confused but alive."

"You...You're a Vampire?" The words were shaking as badly as I was.

Her laugh was rich and deep, it curled within me and had none of the sting I usually associated with the sound. "Oh lord, heavens no. I'm as human as you are and I'm certainly not undead." She held out her wrists. "Care to feel?"

My hand trembled as I reached out, her skin was warm, almost hot to the touch, but it was soft, softer than mine. As I checked her pulse it was strong, rapid, unhealthily so, but it was there. Slowly I withdrew my hand.

"What happened?"

She looked from me, to him, to me. "Well, I heard what sounded like a scream, and keys hitting the pavement. So, I came looking to find that poor dear coming at me screaming something about me being a vampire. He even had a cross out. When he went to stab me with it, I stepped in, barred his arm, let his momentum carry him into my hand and wound up throat punching him." She reached into her purse and took out another coffin nail and lit it. "Looks like he'd already been in a fight, his face is all scratched up."

"Me, he pulled a knife on me back there."

"Really? And you did that?" She looked at me, really looked. "Good for you."

"So, what now?"

She seemed to pause for a second. "Drunk or not, he pulled a knife on you. I say we call the cops."

I snorted. "Think they'll believe me?"

She shrugged. "He pulled a knife on you; tell them he was trying to rob you. It's far easier. Got cameras back there?"

I chuckled dryly; she was right. "Yeah, we do."

Chapter 6

She didn't bolt, she stayed, talked to the police, acted like everything was normal, so normal that I started to doubt what I saw. Two things stuck with me; you're one of them, I'm as human as you are. I did learn a few things. Her name wasn't Izzy nor Isabel. It was Yssabaue, Meredith Yssabaue Dorcha.

When everything was said and done, and yes Beth had to be called. I was left alone with her. I had questions, and I hoped she would be in a sharing mood.

"So, why do you go by Izzy?"

I watched her pale face flame crimson. "God that mouthful..." She shook her head. "Ok, story time. So back in the late 90s, I was in my early 20s and had just started transitioning." She took a moment then sighed. "I was goth, newly so. Well not really, turns out I was goth before I had ever heard the term. Anyway, so I wanted a kick ass name. Well, some quick and rather inaccurate searches on the internet turned up what I thought was Queen Elisabeth the Dark only spelled to be kick ass."

Did you ever just hear something so honest you were floored? From my own days being goth in college I had heard some truly cringe worthy edge lord names, but no one who would so blatantly come out and say it.

She locked eyes with me and smiled. "And that just made all the cringe worth it. Thank you."

"For what?"

"That smile."

I could feel my face blooming crimson. I took a deep breath and looked at her. "So?" Nothing came to mind.

"I'm sorry. I wasn't trying to make you uncomfortable." Her smile faded a little and I was sorry to see it go.

"No, it's ok. I just." How did I put this? "I haven't had anyone flirt with me in a while."

A rich, throaty chuckle escaped her upturned head. "Oh no, no my dear. I'm not flirting. Me flirting is much more..." She broke off looking for the words.

"Subtle?"

She snorted. Not a lady-like laugh, a snort. "God no. I'm awkward, direct, and don't really care that much about how I'm perceived."

I nodded, then took my chance. "So... As human as me huh? Seems to be he thought I saw something and accused me of being like you."

People, we move, we twitch, we breath. Watching her stop all of that was frightening, but tonight? I had a knife pulled on me, her staying still only registered as weird. We were locked in a staring contest, her not moving, me not budging. Finally, she relented and looked away.

"Forget what you saw, what you heard. It's better that way." She started turning away.

"Hell no." I grabbed her arm. "Look." At which point I did. I looked around and realized we were very exposed. Still holding on, I dragged her off away from the alley, away from everything. "Look. He came after me, if you know something." I waited and saw her chew it over.

"Fine. I'll make you a deal." She took a deep breath. "Go home, get some sleep, think about what you're asking, really think about it. The price of knowledge is the knowing in this case." She looked around. "On my honor, I will be here tomorrow, same as always. If you still want to know, need to know. Ask again."

I don't remember letting go, she just wasn't there anymore.

Quickly making my way back over to the shop, I was in time to see the police leave with the guy who had tried to rob me. Beth looked uncomfortable as I came up.

"How are you holding up hun?" she said as I drew close.

I shrugged. "Not the first time some guy came at me with a knife." Sadly, it wasn't.

"Look, go home, I'll close up." She came over and hugged me. "Do you want to take a few days off?"

I thought about it for a moment. "Want to? Maybe, but my credit card doesn't." She nodded. I looked around. "So... where's my keys?"

She blinked at me. "The police took them; you didn't get your car keys off of them?"

Perfect end to a perfect night.

Chapter 7

How wrong I was.

Allen took me home. He was the one who drove Beth up there, they had been having a date. He took me home because she asked him to. He didn't say a word to me the entire drive and was grinding gears the entire time.

Once he dropped me off, I went inside and texted Beth.

Foxbutt987:: Your boyfriend seems a bit upset::

RougeRogue13:: Yeah, he's mad we got interrupted::

Foxbutt987:: Sorry to inconvenience you::

RougeRogue13:: It's not like you planned it::

Foxbutt987:: No, I most certainly didn't plan it::

RougeRogue13:: He's just been kind of concerned lately with the stress I'm under and all your Drama::

Foxbutt987:: My Drama? WTH?!?!? I barely leave the house except to go to work::

RougeRogue13:: That's actually his point. We hardly get to see each other without a chaperone. I'm thinking of spending a few days over at his house::

Foxbutt987:: So? Go ahead. I'm not your mom. Have fun::

RougeRogue13:: I don't want to leave you alone. And besides with you stuck without a car what else can I do but babysit you::

I looked at the text. What in the hell was happening?

Foxbutt987:: Go::

Foxbutt987:: I'll take care of me, just go.::

RougeRogue13:: How are you going to get to work?::

Foxbutt987:: I have spare keys, both for the car and the store.::

RougeRogue13:: Thank you!!! 😊::

I looked at the phone. "Fine whatever."

I went upstairs and took a quick shower, letting the water run over me, feeling its heat. The water pounding against me didn't exactly make it all real, it was more a signal that it was ok to feel. All of it started playing in my head like a series of bad clips. The flash of the knife, the guy coming towards me, the feel of my keys hitting him. The sound of my feet pounding away at the concrete as I tried to get away.

Every sound throughout the house came into sharp relief, the sound of the water from the shower first and foremost, with its white noise drumming away at my skin and the tile of the wall. Next was the tic of the clock just outside the door. Though battery powered, the movement of the second hand was still one of those that did it in a start stop motion and as such there was sound to it.

I couldn't believe I could make that out.

Next came this odd hum. To start with I couldn't make it out. After the fourth time I realized it was tires on the road just outside. I was upstairs, in a shower and I was aware of the traffic outside in our little suburb.

The sudden squeak of metal-on-metal right on top of me made me jump. I looked down at my hand. It was on the faucet and I had turned it off. I actually remember wanting to do that, but not moving to do it.

Moving the curtain, I jumped when I saw someone staring back at me. I then slapped the mirror. "Get a grip." Telling myself that didn't help. I grabbed a towel and dried off, rubbing myself all over trying to run off something, though I'm not sure what. Towel drying my hair is not my normal go to, but I didn't want to do more than that right now.

I went to my room and crawled into an old Invader Zim sleep shirt and curled up on my bed. Reaching over to set my alarm I noticed my phone. "I thought I left you downstairs."

I picked it up and plugged it in. I had a new message.

RougeRogue13:: I need you to open for me::

I looked at it for a few moments.

Foxbutt987:: Sorry just got out of the shower. What's up?::

RougeRogue13:: I need you to open for me tomorrow::

Foxbutt987:: OK. Why?::

I waited for a few moments. Don't get me wrong, I could do it. But just an hour ago she was asking if I need to take tomorrow off.

RougeRogue13:: Lydia this isn't a request. I can't come in tomorrow I need you to cover for me::

Foxbutt987:: Beth, are you ok?::

RougeRogue13:: It's Liz, I'm your boss and your landlady, do as you're told::

RougeRogue13:: Look, I'm sorry. Somethings come up. I need you to do this for me, please?::

Foxbutt987:: Sure Liz::

Ok that was weird.

So, there I sat, alone, just me, the dark, and nothing else.

Chapter 8

Getting to work was fun. I took the bus, but being well aware of them from my pre-car college days I knew to take the early one. It was a good thing too, because things had not improved. It was nearly 15 minutes late.

Once the ride was over, the ride itself was fairly good all things considered, I wound up at work about 40 minutes before I was due to be. Turning off the alarm early would get me a call from the security company, so I went to the back popped open my car and waited. My vape, along with most of my life was in this car, so me, my music and a little relaxation in the daylight was well in order.

"Hey, you ok?" I looked over right into the face of Walt.

"I'm fine." I didn't have the ability to deal with him right now.

"Look, I know you got robbed last night. I just wanted to make sure you were ok."

I looked at him like he grew a second head. As I did, it dawned on me. Walt, like most people in my life, were a series of cut outs. I didn't actually know what he looked like. Sure I knew he was blonde, kind of tall, and a bit of a jerk. But if you had asked me I don't think I could have described him. Recognize him? That I had no problem doing, but describe him? Not a chance.

I looked at him, really looked at him. He was tall, but then to me most people are. No, Walt was way over 6 foot, skinny but built, kind of rugged in a way. I'd say he was handsome, but his brown eyes were off ever so slightly, the left one looked a little over to the left and wiggled ever so slightly as he looked at me. His facial hair, which he was obviously trying to grow, came in in fits and spurts, all patchy. While he did look built, he was also lanky as if his arms were to long for him despite his height.

His clothing was all new, fashionable even, but he wore it badly, it hung off him as if he didn't quite know how to put it all together right. Then there were his shoes. His shoes were old, converse from some time before now, with the plastic of them needing a good scrubbing. The red was filthy and the laces needed replacing. Here was the biggest jerk I knew, inquiring if I was alright when my best friend went from caring about me, to throwing me on the bus.

"I'm trying to decide who the bigger jerk is, you or me?"

Walt looked at me funny. "Why?"

"Because you've been coming in for years, I've threatened you with bodily harm, and I've never really seen you before, not you anyway."

He threw his head back and laughed. "God I'm not that big an asshole. I know you see like a million people a day. I'm just another face."

Laughing, I slowly got out of my car. "So? I'm not the bigger asshole because you're not enough of an asshole to think I owe you knowing about you?"

He chuckled, this sound that was half barking laugh and just a little too much giggle. "I call it the asshole paradox. I am so much of an asshole I know it, but it also means I know how much of an asshole I am not. Therefore, you not seeing me is perfectly normal as I am just customer number 197 on any given day. You're normal. Our minds aren't made to see that many people, we don't do it well. I might be part of your tribe, i.e. regulars, but because you constantly see so many people outside your tribe you never see the people within it." He looked at me triumphantly. "It's why diversity isn't our strength and groups should stick with each other, it reduces stress and will keep us from killing each other."

Standing, I looked at him. "Dear god do you actually believe that?"

His grin just got bigger. "It doesn't matter. The facts speak for themselves. My belief in them wouldn't matter one way or the other. Besides that's not the point, keeping the conversation going and people thinking is."

Today, a woman that might be something more than human was coming to talk to me about that, if she didn't back out and leave me hanging. Yet here, right now was something that might be even more strange. A chance to talk to a troll and find out why.

"Walt..." I had to do this right. "Why is keeping the conversation going important?"

He shrugged. "It's simple. Most people, especially on the left, they're feeling not thinking. Every time they come to some conclusion, be it drugs, guns, what have you, they might have some truth to it. But it's like a blind squirrel finding an acorn. So, what if you found one?"

"Doing the right thing for the right reasons matter."

He nodded. "It does. But if we let people just do whatever, soon we wouldn't have anything. Like it or not the world is a cruel place. You need to be able to justify everything you do." Again, he shrugged. "Most people can't, they just want to get their way, and while I'm fine with that, you can't take mine. Humans are evil at heart; we'll take everything everyone has. So, we better protect what we got at all cost. I'll take care of me and mine, you take care of you and yours and as we have that conversation we'll move forward with the right people in power, not just the ones that make us feel better. Do this and we'll actually get somewhere. Gay marriage didn't happen overnight and the push for trans people to be included has almost cost us everything. We have to go slow, or we will lose it all."

"If the world is so cruel, shouldn't we be, you know, nice?"

"Nice." He snorted. "That and five bucks will get you coffee. No one is nice unless somethings in it for them."

I could feel something strange, a cold predatory smile pushing up the corner of my mouth. "So, you just came to check on me to? Get what exactly from me?"

He shrugged again. "Companionship. It's still a transaction."

Chapter 9

Opening went well, so did the breakfast rush. Noon rolled around without incident, and when I was supposed to come in and no one did, I realized I would be covering both shifts. The day dragged on the way only a double can and when four came around I started waiting to see if she would show up.

There was always a rhythm with these things, people who are regulars come in at regular times. Normally I see her before the after-work rush. Walt, it seemed was always here. By the time the day slaves were supposed to hit the line, I still hadn't seen her, to make matters worse the rush was late. Thirty minutes into the rush that wasn't it hit me; it was Sunday.

It's not unusual for me to forget what day it was, working retail things tend to blend, but I didn't work Sundays. I replayed the conversation with Beth from last night in my head. She had offered me a few days off, and I was so shaken I had said I would work. She didn't correct me; she didn't remind me I had tomorrow off. No, she roped me into pulling a double on my day off.

I stood there in shock.

"You ok?"

I looked at Rita and it took me a second to recognize her. Shaking myself awake I put on my best customer service smile and said, "I'm fine."

She rolled her eyes and gently taking my arm led me away from the counter. "Bullshit someone else chica, you got attacked last night and are back in here today, today of all days, like nothing happened.

I figured you were one of those try hard white people who just had to get right back up. Now you just zoned out. You are not ok."

I could feel myself deflating. No, I wasn't. What's more she was right, I had insisted on working, had to keep moving so I didn't think.

Taking a deep breath I looked at her, "No, I'm really not. But this place needs me."

"Why Beth not here?"

"Something came up."

She gave me a long look but nodded. "You're a good friend Lydia, don't let no one tell you otherwise." She looked around. "Sunday is slow. Not a lot of you guys come out on church day, too many pendejos. I got this; you go take a break."

I looked at her funny. "You guys?"

She grinned. "The Gays." I kept looking. "Chica, I'm as straight as they come, a real Cis-Het. But I'm also the daughter of Dreamers whose parents brought them here in the 80's. I ain't got shit against anyone who pisses off the conservatives." She smiled and pushed me gently towards the back. "Take a momento, get your breath. Just don't leave me hanging too long, no?"

I nodded and headed out back.

As I hit the back door the late afternoon sun hit me full in the face. Its rays turning red as the great orb raced towards the tree line. I stopped and took a deep breath. Closing my eyes and thinking about everything I found myself shaking slightly.

"So? You ready?" I didn't recognize the voice.

Have you ever moved, just that twitch reaction kind of move, but you did it so fast you heard a popping? For me it was my neck. The slap as my back hit the propped door and my arm snaking in to bolt to safety also let me know I was way more strung out than I was letting on.

While my body was on the fast track to anywhere not here, my eyes and mind were trying to decide if it was warranted. What I saw was an Elder Goth. Someone poured her into her pants, the makeup was spot on, everything was blacks and reds, one eye was inhuman the other one was achingly so with a bloody tear trail. The lips were black and red, not the simple two tone of red with black lip liner, but full black kissable at the edges with the red blooming at the center and the two colors bleeding into each other as if the blood hadn't been completely wiped off her lips. A black leather, or pleather, skirt was over those way too tight pants, and a long coat with both spikes and buckles and straps was opened wide. Knee high stilettos polished to a shine graced her feet with their platformed toe making the heel at least seven inches. Its silver skull buckles shone in the fading sun. Her top was a faded, battered tee of a band I hadn't heard of, but it had to be vintage. Her hands were gloved, but the tips of the fingers were cut off to allow blood red dagger point nails to shine through and on each was a black skull. Had I met whoever this was in college I would have fallen at her feet and begged.

But college was a long time ago.

My heart slowly started regaining some of its natural rhythm when this creature of night spoke again. "Oh, god I'm sorry Lydia, I didn't mean to scare you."

It hit me, this goddess was Izzy.

"Wow." I took her in. I'd never seen her made up before, not once in the two years she'd been coming in. Once upon a time she would have been a dream come true, my heart rate agreed as well. For a brief moment, intimate things ran through my mind. Times I had done things, wanted things, fantasized about things. This strange apparition was the star of such fantasies. "Where were you when I was 20?"

She laughed, that warm rich laugh I had heard every once in a great while. I gave that to her this time. I felt myself warm from that laugh and found myself wanting more. Then reality slapped me in the face and I realized what I had said. Embarrassment and humiliation ran through me, heating my face even more.

She smiled, stepped just out of reach and brought her hand close to my face, I leaned into this caress. The feel of her gloved hand on me felt good, inviting, and strangely like home.

"You never have to be embarrassed with me. I never want you to be anything but you. I love honesty and find it refreshing." I stood in her warmth and for that moment, nothing was wrong. "Ready to go?"

Reality came crashing back in. "Go?"

"Out? I promised you if you were here, I would answer your questions. I thought it would be nice if I, you know, took you out to eat?"

A groan escaped me as I slid slightly down the partially opened door. "I can't, I'm sorry. Beth had something come up and I covered for her."

She looked at me and smiled, no disappointment showing. "That's fine, you're worth the wait... if you still want to that is."

I felt myself nodding, a smile spreading across my face. "Yeah sure. It's Sunday, we close about 9. I should be out before 10."

I slid inside and made my way back to the front with that grin still plastered on my face.

Chapter 10

As the night wore on, I watched as Izzy sat over in her normal spot and seemed to draw the attention of everyone in the room. Even Walt gave her a second glance, but I suspect that was because she sat in her normal spot looking remarkably unlike how we all knew her. She'd been a fixture here since we reopened, and never once had I seen her dressed up. Most nights she ordered coffee and nothing else, only occasionally did she order food. The woman could be vegan for all I knew.

Most nights she just quietly tapped away on a laptop that was only a few steps above a word processor, seemingly completely unconcerned with the world around her. That thing was anachronistic with the rest of this place and stood out. To start with I thought she was a technophobe until I saw her smartphone. While older it definitely worked, she also had a fairly nice tablet.

"I can see it." Snapping out of it I looked over at Rita.

"See what?"

"You, her. She's hot, in a Dia de los Muertos, bruja kind of way." She looked at me and nodded. "A goth girl is good for you."

I looked at her, "What do you mean?"

She shrugged. "You need some color in your life, and I think darkness is that color. I think goth suits you, might be a good look for you."

I couldn't help it, a chuckle escaped. "Rita, I am goth."

She turned, looked at me and raised an eyebrow. "I thought you were grunge. I was gonna introduce you to my cousin till I figured out you like girls." She made this odd gesture with her hands. "Why do you not dress up?" She looked me up and down. "One of the things you told me when I started was I could dress how I wanted so long as I didn't do my nails due to food regulations. You going to tell me that boss lady of ours doesn't let you dress up?"

I shook my head. "No, she would, I just don't. I don't really feel like it and who would care anyway?" I mean, I look in the mirror and just can't.

"I would for one chica, I think you'd look good all deathed up."

I looked at her funny. "You would? I thought you were straight."

"I'm straight, not dead. Besides I learned long ago when people dress as themselves, they always happier." She looked me dead in the eyes and crossed her arms. "Why should Halloween be the only time you dress like you. You suppose to dress as people you ain't."

I had to admit she had a point. Here this woman was, younger than I was by a few years, and she is chastising me for not being myself.

"No offense, but like, why do you care so much?"

She thought it over and looked at me. "You white girls have that mom friend thing going on, you know that one girl in your group that kind of looks after you?" I hadn't thought about the mom friend since I left college. "Well think of me as your Abuela friend."

"Doesn't that mean Grandmother?"

She snorted. "Abuela means more than that, Abuela is the woman who made you, your parents, who stands firm, gives advice, looks after you, spoils you, makes sure you know what's what."

"Oh, so you're going to spoil me now?"

"Damn right, we're friends, aren't we?"

I felt a huge smile spread across my face, "Yeah we're friends."

"Good. Now I expect you to be Gothed up next time you work."

I chuckled and we got back to work.

The rest of the night was ok for the most part, but the conversation and I guess date, loomed closer with each cup of coffee made, each thing sold from the bake case, and each and every swipe of my cloth on the counter. My nerves and stomach started to bunch, and I wasn't sure which I was more nervous about.

Closing time saw a few more people sneak in for one last cup, and of course the people who seemed to think one minute till we closed meant they had all the time in the world to order.

We got the last one out at 10 after.

Registers came out right, the orders were done, and the cleaning went smoothly. Yet, I found myself dragging my feet just a little bit. Did I really want to know I was, was what? She said, 'I'm just as human as you.' Yet... I saw her suck golden light orbs out of people, sort of. I saw darkness and horns and more.

Then after getting attacked by someone who realized I saw it and having her just there. I mean, she saved me, but really if I had just made it back around, he might not have caught me, and I knew a thing or two about basic self-defense. Yet, this darkness just filled everything.

He had said vampire. I saw her feed, saw her look better after.

"Good god Lydia, get a grip on yourself. A goth vampire? You'd have been all over that shit just a few years ago, not even think about it, take me and make me you. Hell, I have slash fic on that very subject." What? D was my jam.

That was fantasy, this? A knife wielding maniac just moments after seeing her for who she is. This was reality, and that reality had consequences. Nervously I ticked down the last of my duties, readied the deposit and locked up. I quickly walked down to the drop box and slid away what should have been the most pressing thing on my mind.

I headed back and began my date.

Chapter 11

Just outside the store, under one of the faux old fashion street-lamps, in the midst of the late evening, she stood waiting for me. I definitely had to give her style points. I felt like the reluctant bride in a vampire novel walking towards her, and she? She offered her arm as if she were the gentleman. Smiling I took it, but unlike the ridged stance most men used for it, hers was softer, her arm angled differently, somehow, she made this gesture feminine, dominant to be sure, but not masculine.

"So? Where to?"

Her smile let slip a flash of fang, and I suddenly couldn't remember if she had them before, if they were store bought, or her own. "Are you hungry?"

I smiled. "Starved actually."

"I know a place that will be open for a few more hours, it should be plenty of time for us to speak." She looked at me. "You can buy me dinner."

I raised an eyebrow. "Oh, I can, can I?"

"You cannot if you wish, I can take you out on a date instead, or we can part ways here."

I looked at her a bit confused. "Um, ok. I'm not sure I'm following." I watched as her mouth worked, as if she were struggling to say something. Then, as if she managed to get around something large, she nodded and smiled at me once more.

"It's simple. I believe we have three options open to us. One; we part ways, you do the simple thing and realize I am a crazy old crone and that the individual last night was a random freak who you will most likely never see again."

The look I could feel myself giving her at that suggestion clearly got the point across as she continued. I just made the choice to go through with this.

"Two, I buy you a lovely dinner and feel quite nice doing so as I will have had the honor of a date with a lovely young woman I've had my eye on for a while, but didn't know if she would be interested in a renegade like myself." She swallowed. "Or three, I fulfill my part of last night's bargain and let you buy me dinner in payment for the information you want."

"Can't we like split the bill?"

Her face turned very serious. "I'll not have you starting off owing me. I don't want that type of power over you until you understand."

Something in the way she said it made me feel like this, in and of itself, was part of the information. If I just took the date, I could probably have a good time with her, but I wouldn't be any closer to what I wanted to know. Then, what she said hit me. She was, in a strange way, asking me out on a date. Moreover, it was something she had thought about before.

I looked at her, then past the haughty mask she was wearing. I could almost see the edges of it. She was scared I would say no. She was scared I would leave and she didn't want me to but she didn't want to try forcing me to stay.

"How long have you wanted to ask me out for?"

Her chin, a very round thing, went up slightly. "The first day I came in, you still had blue glitter in your hair. The style, your build, you were the woman I had seen at the club the night before. I could feel you. Then before I could say something, your girlfriend came in and you were obviously very happy."

That had been shortly after Beth reopened the place. I had been dating a woman calling herself Shadow. "That was years ago. Have, have you been coming here all this time because of me?"

She shook her head. "No, I wrote off the idea of asking you out when I saw the two of you together."

"God why?"

She raised her left eyebrow, then her face fell. "Because." She swallowed. "I'm... unable to afford certain things that would make my life easier."

She sounded ashamed. It was the only word I had for it. I didn't get it, but I knew that tone no matter how controlled the person who it came out of was. I reached out and touched her arm, she looked up with tears on her lashes. For a brief moment I saw a lady, a high court lady who had been stripped bare to skin and shamed in front of the entire world. Yet still naked she stood, chin up and brazen. I would call what I saw pride, but that wasn't right. It was defiance, pure and simple. It made me even more ashamed that I didn't get it.

"I'm sorry, I can see this hurts. If you don't want to talk about it I get it. But I honestly have no clue what you mean."

A sound from the tree above, just out of the light, caught my attention just before a croaked and cracked voice spoke. "She's still got a dick, bit bitter about it if you ask me."

She wheeled on the voice, forgetting me entirely for this new interloper. "That will be quite enough out of you."

The leaves rustled and a limb shook then into the light came a raven. It came to rest on a branch that left it more or less eye to eye with her, if a little above.

"And you're being pretentious as hell with the slip you been pining over for years." It cocked its head to the side, still staring at Izzy. "You going to scare her off for her own good and then go mope for a week?"

She slapped at the bird. "She needs to know what she's getting into, and kid gloves aren't going to help her."

"Of course, your highness. Not like you're tired of bleeding or anything."

"Watch your tongue."

"Prefer watching yours, it's all pink and flappy, reminds me of my last meal."

With that she hissed at the thing. Full on, fangs out hiss. That broke the spell of a talking, intelligent bird. The absurdity of it hit me all at once, then I realized, he was a familiar.

"You're a witch." Both of them looked at me, then back to each other. As one, they both started laughing. Seeing a crow laugh I had to say did wonders for my nerves over all of this, but hers was this music. Some of them were these little he-hes and ha-has but it was more than that, she really loved to laugh, and it showed she didn't worry too much about it. Then she snorted, the hand went over her mouth only to have her do that again.

"She's no witch love." The big black bird croaked out. "She's a fairy."

Chapter 13

"Like, with wings?" The idea of this woman with huge wings flashed through my mind.

With a sigh, she shot the bird a look that might mean it had a future as a stuffed bird to look forward to. "No, no wings and fairy is... over simplified."

"Says you." Croaked the bird. "Look, you like her, she ain't run off when I opened my mouth. How about you take her to dinner, you both pay whatever, and she buys you a dessert. Poor girls bank account probably can't handle your appetite anyway fat ass."

Pursing her lips and shooting the bird a death glare she looked at me. "I'm not sure that would be equal exchange, but with my buzzard here blowing the punch line, I think that would work."

"I'm not a buzzard." Came its offended reply.

"And I'm not a fairy."

"Yeah, but I bet she knows more about what that is than what you are. It's a good start."

Watching them, it was impossible not to see they had been together for a while. With her being a fairy or whatever, it made me wonder exactly how long a time that was.

"How old are you?"

She looked back at me again, her attention going between me and the bird, then asked. "Do we have a deal? You buy me something for dessert and I tell you what's going on?"

That's when it hit me, she needed the deal. This was definitely worth dessert. "Deal"

She held out her hand and I took it, shaking on it seemed a bit childish until I felt a claw tip on my wrist. It was a quick scratch. I snatched my hand back out of instinct and watched as she brought the tip of that wickedly sharp nail up to her mouth and licked it.

"Done" With that the wind picked up and blew behind me, forcing me a step towards her.

She offered me her arm once more and escorted me to a nice sit-down restaurant right here in the little shopping arcade. Inside was country and western, more or less, much more of an emphasis on country with its deer heads and other mounted animals including a buffalo.

The woman waiting to seat us obviously knew Izzy. "This her? Oh don't you two look good together." She grabbed two menus and gestured for us to follow. "Right outside, you won't be disturbed and Becky or Whitney will be with you in a minute." With that we were led back out into the night air.

Outside it was dark, very few lights shown and only one was turned on for us. There were tables, most with umbrellas, only one of which was open. It was about as far away from everything as you could get with two chairs, one facing us as we came up, one slightly off to the side but with its back to a wall.

Izzy took the one where she could see everything while giving me the one where my back had something to lean on. Once we were seated the woman stopped, looked at us, smiled and went off happily humming to herself.

"So." I scooted my chair further into the table. "Come here often?"

She smiled with a bit of a shy look about her. "Yes, but probably not for the reason you think. I'm allergic to wheat. I can eat it, but if I do, I'll get sick." She turned a little red under her makeup. "It's not pleasant. They have enough here I can eat and are used to me. I come here for lunch."

Thinking back to the decor. "And they treat you ok?"

"The staff? Sure. They're all right." She looked out at the night. "The Patrons sometimes..."

"So, do we wait till after or?"

"We have a deal, as long as you buy me desert, we're fine."

"Ok so..." I tried to think of something to ask but nothing was coming to mind. What did you ask someone who was a fairy? "How old are you?"

That laugh of hers erupted from her lips, and when it did I could see the delicate fangs inside her mouth. They were top and bottom, though the bottom ones were less pronounced. The top ones however were very much there, and they were double, the canine, and then a slightly larger set for the teeth just behind.

"I'm 43."

I blinked and looked at her. "I, I thought you'd be older."

"Disappointed?"

I thought about it, thought about all the tales, all the stories like this. Some ancient thing, person, and a young girl. A fifteen-year difference seemed, so mundane. "I just thought you'd be, I don't know, older."

She leaned back in the chair and looked towards the door to the patio just before it opened. A leggy rake thin girl came walking towards us. "Hi, I'm Whitney, I'll be your server. What can I get you?" I blushed realizing I hadn't even looked at the menu.

"I'll have a Pepper, and an order of hot wings, traditional, mild, with ranch."

The girl looked at Izzy. "I know what you want, I was asking her."

I looked up at her. "Does she ever get anything different?" Lord knows she never did at the coffee shop.

"Sometimes, but she knows enough to say so first. Normally its Dr Pepper, hot wings, and a bloody steak with steamed broccoli and mashed potatoes."

We both chuckled and looked at her. "What's she get for dessert?"

"Nothing, all of our deserts have gluten in them."

I looked over at my date, she just shrugged. "Today I'll be getting those grilled shrimp."

Whitney looked at her. "For dessert?"

"Dessert is a treat at the end of the meal, in this case I want shrimp."

Our server nodded, shook her head then looked back at me.

"Um, I'll have a coke and, well." I glanced over the menu. "Potato skins will be fine."

She nodded and walked off.

After the door closed, Izzy cleared her throat. "I am, what you would call a Changeling."

Thinking about it for a moment, it made sense, she was only in her forties because she was young. "So, you were swapped out as a child?"

She shook her head. "That was the assumption people have always made, but that's not how it works. Souls are immortal, yours, mine, everyone's. But Fae are immortal... until we aren't. When one of us is killed something of us comes back, born into a human. As we age some of us, well we tend to act oddly." She looked slightly uncomfortable. "Since we can go from behaving normally one day, to not the next, the thought was that Fae were like cuckoo's, letting mortals raise our children."

I thought about it for a moment. "So, all those autistic kids?"

"Are autistic. They're nothing new, and we both got saddled with the changeling moniker. But those kids are just kids, normal humans, and deserving."

"So, some of the odd kids are just kids and some of them are like you?"

"Yes." With that she sat back again and looked once more at the door.

Sure enough, Whitney came back with our drinks, smiled, told us our appetizers would be here soon and left.

"How do you do that?"

"Simple, I have a better view of the door than you do."

Of course. "So, not magic."

She heard the disappointment in my voice. "No, not magic. Observation, understanding and patterns. Magic is real, it's been used since the dawn of time. There are stories of witches, sorcerers, other world beings, peoples made not of earth but air and fire, daemons whispering secrets on the wind, and so much more. Yet the simple truth is there is a reason science reigns." She reached out took her drink and sipped. "Because science learns, not repeats."

"What do you mean?"

"Take a wizard, the real deal, flinging fire and ice, calling the wind and rain, forcing demons to build temples to his god. He's a great wizard and his knowledge is terrible. So, he teaches his apprentice what he thinks the lad can handle. That wizard dies, but with him part of his power dies to. Soon its generations later and even what is written down in books is lost because no one alive remembers the key to make eye of newt work in a spell is to use mustard seed. Some poor amphibian gets killed or mutilated and all for a potion that doesn't work." She drank again. "What's more is thought becomes rote, rote habit without thought and soon anyone who tries something new is branded heretic."

She sat the glass down and continued. "Meanwhile science? It's surrounded by mad boys who want to know what's beyond the next horizon, men and women who imagine impossible things then try them out again and again until they have the how of it. Then rather than hide such knowledge, they crow like cocks at false dawn. Soon every tongue of these mad men wags either in support of this new idea, providing they can me it work, or in condemnation of it if they can't. No idea is too out there, too ludicrous, too insane."

She looked at me, sadness written on her face. "So, we went from steel to splitting the un-splitable, to crashing even the parts of atoms together in a mad dash to find the next horizon, and men of war went from swords to bombs to horrors. That is the price of such knowledge being common. But the reward? Monitors that help mothers know when the baby stops breathing. The library of Alexandria in the palm of your hand and safe from one man burning it. The moon with the footprint of man on her face and mirrors so we know she slowly fades from us and the knowledge to keep her there if need be."

"So what good is magic?"

She looked at me, nodded, then smiled. "Exactly. You'd be much better off, much safer if you ignored all of this and prayed for a nice, safe life."

Safe? I'd been safe. Was I anymore? "So, even though I'm like you, you're telling me to basically go away because it's too much for a little girl like me?"

"No. You're not like me, not yet. Just because you have a soul that wasn't human, it is now. You can choose to live life as a human. Do human things, if you do so you will only have to worry about human concerns."

I could feel it, it was tangible. "What aren't you telling me? No, better question. If magic exists, has existed all along. Why haven't we seen it?"

The sound of wings alerted me to the return of the bird. "Because she lost the war."

She gave the bird a look that said clearly, 'You're living on borrowed time.'

After death glaring at the thing for a heartbeat more. "Yes well. To put it simply there was a discussion on whether we should help humans or control them. I had my opinions, some others had their own."

"Wait. So let me see if I get this." I took a moment and gathered my thoughts. "You are a human born with a fairy's soul."

She rolled her eyes. "Fae, fairy is a type of fae. I am not a fairy."

"Fine, whatever, a fae soul, and you remember before?"

A derisive sound came from the bird. "She wishes. Doesn't work like that. Who she was is dead, who she is now is what matters. Sure, she gets flashes but that's it. Feelings, impressions. Oh, your wings are coming."

Once more the door swung open and our food arrived.

Looking at our server, "I'll have the chicken and rice." She, however was looking at the bird.

It cocked its little black head at her, "Nevermore." When it spoke, there was a quality to it, one of meaning. This was an echo of that, it was mimicking.

"I still don't get how you taught a wild crow to do that." The bird hissed at her. "Especial one so ill tempered."

"She's a Raven, I call her D'eun."

"Dune huh?"

"Something like that."

She nodded at both of us and moved on.

Izzy looked at me. "Where were we?"

"Just means bird, don't know why she bothered naming me if she was just going to call me bird."

"Hush you."

"We were talking about why I've never seen magic, why it doesn't show up in history."

"Right." She picked up a wing and stripped it bare. "We had some disagreements, a split, one side wanted things direct, the other wanted to be subtle. They wanted to be seen as good guys, and the 'good guys' won." She was waving the bone around to emphasize her points. "The thing is, they aren't good. They look good and that's all that matters to them. As such they manipulate things." She picked up another doomed wing and tore into it. It was a wondrous thing because despite the almost savagery she used; she wasn't making a mess of herself. "Think of it as the difference between a comforting lie and a hard truth."

"Like, nihilism vs altruism?"

Izzy's eyes snapped up and locked with mine. "Uh-oh." Came a quiet squawk.

Slowly, with an icy tone, she spoke. "Something like that."

I set my chin and met her gaze. "You can teach me or be mad with me, the choice is yours."

A predatory smile spread across her lips. "Good, very good." She reached down and towards her plate, claw tipped fingers extended and yet another wing disappeared. "Let's take your example." Between the time it went into her mouth and the stripped bone came out without messing up her makeup, and the time she spoke was shorter than one would think. "Nihilism tells us that nothing we do matters. There is no heaven, no hell. No one to judge us, and in a few years, no one will even remember us. Life is, at its heart, useless. That is a hard truth. Altruism of course, doesn't really exist, because everyone is good for a reason, be it a belief in heaven, the praise they receive for doing their good deed, or even that warm fuzzy feeling they get from doing it. As such nothing is ever Altruistic." She smiled. "This is another hard truth."

I found myself nodding. I didn't agree with the statement, but it didn't make them, at their heart, any less true.

That predatory smile crept back onto her lips. "Only both are a lie. A lie made by the illusion weavers to control you, me, all of us."

"How are these lies?" I mean I wanted to believe it, I wanted to believe in altruism.

"Simple, when nothing you do matters, no judgment, no one remembers, no nothing, then the only thing that matters is what you do. Altruism is real, if it wasn't no atheistic soldier would ever throw themselves in the line of fire to save another, especial not to save people who didn't, and will never, know them."

Just like that, I went from a world where this very morning it was pointed out to me that people are only nice to you, friends with you, so they won't be alone, to having that point shredded by a person not believing in god or anything else but life, dying for people who would never know or realize it. One seemed real and logical, well-reasoned, the other was emotional and illogical... it also actually happened in real life.

"But how does that keep us in line?"

That would have to wait, the food had arrived.

Chapter 14

Her steak was bloody, the outside barely charred. She used the mashed potatoes as a condiment for them, taking a small bit of the white mush on her fork then the bit of meat she had just cut off. We had decided to hold off on the rest of it, give me time to think while we ate.

This was weird. Other than the bird, and seeing a little last night, I hadn't seen her do anything supernatural. Honestly, I wasn't completely sure what I did see.

"So, what was with those gold orbs flying off everyone and going to you?"

Apparently, I have waiter timing, she was mid chew... and choked.

"You saw that?" The look on her face was a priceless one of shock and amazement.

"Kind of hard to miss, what with the room getting darker, you were growing wings and horns and all."

"Told you she was the one." D'eun rasped.

She regained her composure, took a swallow of drink, then, "Glamour. It was glamour. Think of it as raw emotion. It's a form of energy people produce."

"And you feed on it?"

"To an extent. I can feed on any raw energy and magic, leys, well springs, nexuses, but glamour is the easiest to come by." She took a breath, "And feed on it is a bit of a misnomer as well. I can live without it, or I should say exist without it."

"It's not real glamour, it's more like raw magical essence. All living things produce it, so it flows all over the world." The bird squawked. "Hence ley lines and stuff."

She shot the bird another dirty look, I was really beginning to like her and her crazy pet. "Ok so, why hasn't magic shown up? Like vastly influenced world events, that kind of thing?"

The two of them looked at each other.

Finally, after another long pull on her drink. "It has. But once I tell you, you won't be able to unsee it."

"I'm sitting here with a fae of some sort and a talking bird. Trust me I'm not going to look at anything the same way again."

She shrugged. "A short, brown haired, mousey, Austrian man with brown eyes, and a stupid mustache, convinced the German people that blonde-haired blue-eyed Nordic and Scandinavian people were the master race."

I sat there, blinking at her. She had just uttered that sentence so matter-of-factly that the absurdity of it seemed laughable. "Hitler was a fairy?"

"Crawww!!!" came the angry reply. "No Hitler was human. He just used fairy magic to make his stupidity believable."

"To be fair, Jews, Romani, Homosexuals, the Disabled, etc. were easy to other without it, it was the master races isn't you and yet somehow is that took magic."

"But they were just words."

She smiled at me. "It's never just words." She took a breath then looked me dead in the eyes. "Here's the short of it, roughly 2500 years ago there was a war of competing ideas. The races you would know as the fae were divided. Humans had exploded and they were becoming more advanced. Iron was on the horizon with some places already using it. So, the question was what to do with humans. Some shrugged it off and thought you were too dangerous to yourselves and would never get very far, some liked you, wanting you to go further, to become brothers and sisters to us. Some felt you needed to be tightly controlled. Some didn't care."

Her eyes got a faraway look as she continued. "That war turned bloody. One side knew if they could control the way you saw the world, they could control you. One wanted you to grow to become equals." Her look slowly went to pain. "We lost."

The bird spoke up again. "And the lords of light shaped you, made you, hid the magic in everything you do, made it mundane. Where do you think spells came from? Spells were just that once upon a time. Spelled words on pages to deliver their magic to the masses."

She nodded. "Every word you speak is power, it is magic. Put a little glamour in it and it moves, flows become more. Put a lot and you can make a rock look like gold." She took the last bite of her bloody steak scooping up the remnant of her mashed potatoes with it. "Illusion you call it now. That's only one type but with it you can make a fool appear wise."

Words. Words were power. Every kid learns this in school, from the pen is mightier than the sword to sticks and stones. Granted she was saying words did more damage than either of those... if I was understanding correctly.

"So your telling me all magic is, is words and the ideas they carry?"

"Isn't that enough? The atom itself has been split by those words, the moon walked upon, Mars didn't need robots, but it has them." She sat back once more. "But no, there are more powerful magics. But words are unlocking those as we speak. Alternate dimensions, both higher and lower, worlds built from 1s and 0s that daily become more real. Knowledge is power and words are the spells that move that power."

There it was, laid out before me. Words of power spoken, written, invoked. I saw it every day. "But it's meaningless. I can say 'I win the lotto' but it doesn't happen."

"And how many other people say the same thing?" She sagged. "By making it mundane and stopping people from thinking of it they flood the world. Your word used to be more than gold; your word used to carry the weight of you behind it. Now oaths are exchanged like water and are far less meaningful."

I promise, till death do us part, more and more, on and on. She was right.

Still... "Ok but how did you do that thing in the coffee shop?"

"I used words to paint a picture, then as it weaved..." She hesitated slightly, shifting, uncomfortable. "I laid in the spell to find my mate." Her cheeks burned red under her makeup.

Slowly what she said penetrated the fog of my thoughts. "What?" Was the only thing I could think of to say.

The bird started laughing.

"You put a love spell on me?"

All of the color drained out of her face. "What? No, oh god no, never."

"She's not even capable of thinking that way, none of her kind is. They'll make deals with you all day but none of them will so much as give you a hand up if you don't agree."

I blinked at the bird, then looked back to her. She looked as if I had just accused her of eating babies or something.

"What then?"

"Spell was meant to see if a person hearing it could see her is all. It was a revealing, not a compulsion." Was its squawked response.

She reached over but stopped just before she touched my hand. She turned hers holding it out, offering. "Understand this. One side, they believe in light, illusion, manipulation. They will weave spells to seduce, distract, or outright compel obedience. They cloak themselves in it; the proper way, for the greater good, that's just how it is, you should behave, and more to get you to act and react in predefined ways to stimuli. They train you to obey without thought." She waited hand still offered.

I moved the last little bit and took her hand.

"Lydia, my Oath. I will never, ever violate your free will."

She was so sincere, so honest, so earnest, I couldn't help but smile. At the same time, I knew she wasn't what I was looking for. "I appreciate that."

"Then why?" She squeezed my hand. "Do you sound so disappointed?"

Oh god how to explain? This woman, so much, she looked and felt so much like what I wanted, she awakened things I thought long buried. I had tried, I had played. I had gotten hurt every single time. I didn't really care about it anymore... not really. It was a fantasy, but one she awoke. For a brief moment I had hoped she would be my fairy godmother in this.

"Nothing, nothing important."

"Those are two different things, and I think both of those are not truth." She squeezed my hand again. "I don't know if this is going to be a this, but if it is, if it ever is... we can't lie to each other, not even pretty lies."

There wasn't going to be a this, an us. It was a fool's dream. Still, she was warm, sweet, and hot. Hot did count for something. She'd shared some of her secrets, and would undoubtably share more if I asked. She had asked... could I tell her?

"When I was in college, I wanted to be a sub and be poly. But I gave that up. It was childish." I rolled my eyes and looked away. "Then with you not going to force me into anything... well for a moment, you kind of fit my bill as the perfect top. And I don't even know if you have a clue what I'm talking about... what the hell is so funny?" The bird had fallen off its perch and hit the ground it had been laughing so hard.

Izzy for her part? She held my hand tight and a look of pain, pride, anger, and regret flowed over her face. "Then I must apologize for not finding you sooner."

Chapter 15

I sat there, at the restaurant, annoyed by the fact that a 'stately raven' lay on the ground having what can only be described as a laugh attack that had developed into giggling hiccups, holding the hand of a woman who had to be the oddest person I had ever met, all while she peered out of shadow darkened eyes and told me she was sorry she hadn't found me sooner. The entire thing was surreal.

I took my hand away and looked at her. "What do you mean, you wished you had found me earlier?"

The bird, her literal wing man, woman, thing, whatever, answered as it rolled over. "She's got harnesses and whips and all. She's been a top since she was 20, and trust me, she's no spring chicken."

She reached down picked it up and set it in her lap. It was huge, yet she petted it as if it were somehow so much smaller than her. "Yes, I'm a top. Yes, I have seen you in the store, and yes, I was interested in you. Have been for years."

She took a breath and continued. "You were, as I said, a lesbian and I wrote you off, so to speak. Being friends of a kind with you, seeing you, bantering from time to time was more than I wanted to give up if things got awkward."

I relaxed a bit. She had said as much earlier. She hadn't acted due to a worry of her downstairs being... was there a polite way to talk about it? I mean I would like to think it didn't matter, but I'd never seen one. I liked her sure, but even my BOBs were all sleek bullets with nothing even remotely accurate about the shape. I couldn't blame her for being stand-offish. She was one of my regulars and I did enjoy her. I hadn't asked her out either.

Why hadn't I?

"Ok, but what about the spell."

"Well you see..." The crow began. Gently she placed her fingers on her beak and closed it.

"I needed to know." She swallowed hard. "Things aren't going so well for me right now." She looked off into the distance. "Moving is an option. It doesn't feel right, not yet, but it's an option." She turned back to me. "I had to know." She shrugged. "So, I took a poem I wrote for you, one I wrote shortly after seeing you for the first time, weaved a spell of recognition into it. If you were one of us, or if you..." She paused, hesitant. "Would be receptive to someone like myself. Well, you would see."

You're as human as I am. She was fae. Didn't I remember something about them being very literal? "If I was merely receptive, I'm guessing I would have just thought it was pretty." She nodded. "You wrote that for me?"

"Yes well, I'm a bit of a romantic."

She started to say something else, but life it seemed had other plans.

A large amount of water fell out of the sky and doused her, the bird, the table, and me. From the roof came two figures, both clad in brown leathers. One struck a bell that shined bright in the dim light. Its silvery tone pierced my mind and made everything split into a million pieces. Migraine attacks are common for me, I get them, at most once a month. This sound brought one instantly to me.

Rainbows slowly slid into my vision, each and every light source had one of the jagged things. I don't know when I hit the ground, but someone was on top of me. Worse this sound, deep, rumbling, primal, was coming from somewhere nearby. It was an impossible sound, far too low, felt more than heard. As my senses cleared, I saw a boy, he couldn't have been more than a teen, and he was holding me down on the ground, but he was watching something else.

His leathers were fairly basic, more something patched together from other things than armor made to be armor, at his waist I could even see it ride up. What's more on his waist, still sheathed, was a hunting knife. My uncle had had one just like it. He wasn't paying attention to me, he was looking elsewhere. The question was, could I do it?

"You stole it from a church?" It was Izzy's voice, loud, clear, in pain to be sure, but it was also part of that low sound earlier, the rumble was there just under it. That was all it took. Maybe I could, maybe I couldn't if it was just me, but it wasn't.

The oiled knife slid easily out of its sheath and just as easily into what I hoped was his kidney. He screamed, but at that moment I didn't care, I shoved at him, shoved him off me twisting as I went.

He, for his part, tried to get off me as fast as he could, but for some reason his legs didn't work so well.

Too bad.

I got to my feet and looked for my friend.

There she stood, arms down, hands out facing the man in a proper pair of leathers, upon his head was a brown version of what I always thought pilgrim hats looked like. In one hand was the bell, in the other was a cross bow, sans arrow thingy.

I looked back to Izzy and to my horror I found where the bolt was. It rested deep in her shoulder, its flat feathers biting into her. I quickly checked to see if she was ok, and that's when my mind made sense of the rest of her. Horns sprouted out of her head, two large ones and some small, they curved gracefully back from her head and looked as if they were polished black glass, the small ones formed a crown on her head. Her shoulders were extended up and pointed, her arms hung down much lower than normally possible and ended with hands far too large, the end of each finger was also tipped with that same inky blackness, just as every non-human part of her was.

On her back were wings; huge, black, shadowy, smoky wings with a tail that curled and whipped behind her which was tipped with a flat fan of feathers. She hissed, roared, both? Showing off a mouth far too large, with teeth meant for a creature whose bite would crush stone.

The twisted pilgrim turned to me, looked at the boy and lost all his color.

Izzy spoke, I heard her, he did as well but something tells me nothing else on earth did. Nothing else on earth.

"Take your son Jacob, take him and run. The boy won't remember. Some boys made fun of him; one drew his knife. You were never here. Take this oath and harm not me nor her ever again and I will give you his life. Fight me and the boy dies before you can get to him, and all for the crusade of another."

The man strode towards the boy, I took a step back as he did. The mewling and whimpering of the boy finally penetrated my brain and it made me sick to my stomach.

He looked back at her, then to me, "How do I know you won't come for retribution demon?"

"I'm no demon Jacob, and you know it. Otherwise, you wouldn't have brought the bell. The holy water didn't burn, not me, not the púka. You made a mistake. Don't make another and I will not hunt you."

He nodded. He knew more than I did at this point.

I let him take the boy, but when he reached for the knife, I jerked back.

"He lost it Jacob. It will keep him out of the life but consider this. A púka not yet awake took him. Save his life Jacob, let it go."

He raised the boy up, nodded and ran off.

The shadows that had cloaked the area followed him, they were flowing, almost like a living thing. Shortly it left us exposed. As they left so did her inhuman features.

She walked towards me slowly. "Lydia, hun. I'm going to need that." She reached towards me.

"Are you ok? You have an arrow in you, of course you're not ok." She wasn't, I could see the blood blossoming around the wound. I pointed at it for emphasis.

"Yes dear, and we'll get that taken care of in a moment. Right now, I need you hand me the knife, ok?"

Looking down at the end of my arm I could see that indeed I still had the knife in hand. It, my hand, both were covered in blood. I looked back at her then returned my gaze to the hand. My knuckles, what I could see beyond the red of blood was white.

"It won't let go."

"I know hun, just let me take that from you."

I looked and realized she wanted the knife, so I gave it to her. Her hand shot out grabbing my wrists, as her body turned slightly to the side. A quick squeeze and my fingers went numb.

"Is she ok?" The feminine voice shocked me. What woman was here with us? I turned and our waiter stood there with a look of horror on her face.

"No, we were attacked. Two white guys, they had masks and were talking about devil worshiping faggots. She got the knife from one of them and cut him. The other one took the first and ran off."

"God you've been shot?"

Izzy looked down at herself. "Yes, yes I have. But let's take care of Lydia first. I'm fine."

"I'm going to call the cops."

Izzy went to say something but stopped before she could. She looked at the woman and spoke. "You know what, I think that's a good idea." With that she slowly sank to the ground.

Chapter 16

The hospital was its usual cacophony of smells and sounds. They prayed for the rhythmic, disturbances in that rhythm meant something was wrong. The doctor checking me out said it was just shock. They let me see Izzy for a few moments before they took her off to surgery. She told me to tell the cops the truth but keep it simple.

So here I sat, a police officer and his partner looking at me. "Care to tell us that again?"

"I went on a date with a girl from my work. It was going great when these guys dumped water on us, then they rang a bell? It was loud whatever it was, and I was laying on the ground. I don't really remember much. But the guy on me had a knife and I stabbed him with it."

"A bell?"

I took a deep breath. "Yes, a silver bell. He rang it and the next thing I know someone hit me in the head with a sledgehammer."

The partner patted his arm and took him off. "Docs say the other one has some kind of ear damage. Probably some kind of flash bang or something."

His partner looked at him as if the flash bang idea was dumber than my bell. "Dude, its either that or a tin bell caused that trannies ears to bleed."

At that one word I flew hot. "Excuse the fuck out of you?"

They both turned and looked at me... and I realized they were far enough away and whispering, that I shouldn't have been able to hear them. Right now, I didn't give a fuck.

"I've got good ears, get the hell over it. Now what the hell did you call her?"

I watched two men get really sheepish really fast. "Sorry ma'am."

"You're damn right you're sorry. Is there anything else or would you like to complete the insults and call me a dyke or something?" Honestly, I didn't mind being called a dyke. I wasn't one, but hey all the women I knew who called themselves that were kick ass. The thing is he didn't get to say it. He certainly didn't get to say...THAT!

The two exchanged looks. "No, I think we've got everything. We will call you if we need anything else."

I tracked down a doctor, but as I wasn't family, they wouldn't tell me anything.

So, I went to the waiting room.

People were there, waiting. Go figure. As I sat however, I became aware each of them was glowing, only slightly but it was there. As I looked around me, suddenly all these little things started happening. The walls kind of melted while staying upright. One rippled like water when something large comes close to the surface but doesn't break. A table leg reached up and scratched its head.

Leaning back, I took a deep breath and closed my eyes.

Upon opening them again a child, young, blonde, blue eyed, and slightly dirty was less than a foot from my face. "Don't worry, I saw it too."

Outside, outside was nice.

Once I was out, it occurred to me that it was late, and I might need to do something about that. I took out my phone and saw that Beth had called. 12 times.

****"Hey Hun, letting you know it hit me you were supposed to be off today. Thanks for covering for me. Call me when you get this."****

****"Hey Hun it's me let me know when you get this ok?"****

****"Lydia, I'm getting ready to go to bed, please call me back."****

*****"Bitch I'm worried, call me."*****

*****"No one's at the house, call me damn it."*****

*****"Ok I called around, someone said something happened at one of the restaurants? Did you get attacked again? You better not have gotten attacked again."*****

*****"Lydia, god damn it. Where are you? Call me, this shit isn't funny."*****

I sighed. I bet the rest of them were like that to. That last one came in at 1:25, my phone said it was now 4:38. Shit, five more calls? The last one said it was just 30 minutes ago.

I took a deep breath and dialed the phone.

"My god where are you and what happened?" That was the Beth I remembered, it felt like I hadn't seen her in a few weeks.

"I'm fine, I'm at the hospital."

"How the fuck are you fine if you're at the hospital?"

"I'm not the one hurt." I thought about it for a moment. "Look could you bring me some clothes? I'm kind of covered in blood."

"Yeah, where are you?" She sounded tired, not that I could blame her.

I looked around. "North entrance of St. Brigid"

"I should be there in an hour."

We hung up together, there was nothing more to say, really.

The sound of something hitting pavement by me made me jump and as I looked, I realized it was Izzy's purse. I looked up at the light above and saw something flit off into the dark. Picking it up I went a ways off and found an out of the way, dark spot to sit.

As soon as I was settled, the bird was beside me. "How is she?"

I looked back. "They haven't told me anything. I know they took her into surgery."

A low hiss came from her. "She's going to love that. Bet the bolt head was iron too."

I shrugged; I had no idea. "What does it being iron mean?"

"Means she can't use magic to heal it." He cocked his head up at me. "Burns like a bitch too."

I looked at the thing, really looked at it. She was, well large. Some three foot from tip of beak to tail feathers. Her plumes were black, but they had this blue and green shine to them. Other than that, she looked like a normal bird.

"You're beautiful."

It cocked its head towards me. "Thank you."

Silence stretched on for a moment longer than was comfortable. "She'll be fine."

"Oh, I know. Not the first time she's gone and got herself shot. Honestly bullets are better. They're lead, she can deal well with lead. Knives are a bit of an issue."

I looked at the bird. "What does she do?"

She turned and looked at me. "In life? She fixes computers. Her boss lets her 'dress like a girl'." Those last three words were a perfect imitation of one of my least favorite customers, a guy that only came in because he worked in the plaza. "But he won't let her dress up." The creature yawned. "It's why she doesn't do a lot of dressing up these days."

Made sense. She came to work and did her job, then came to the shop after. Most days she stayed till after traffic, sometimes longer.

"So, what's going on that she's thinking of leaving."

Her feathers fluffed. "Not sure I should tell you."

"Personal huh?"

"Extremely."

"Well, I'm thinking of dating her, so I probably should know."

"If you date her, she'll tell you. Otherwise, nothing doing."

It was worth a shot. "What if I pay you?"

I watched as the bird twitched. "Depends... What you got?"

I reached into my purse and pulled out a few things looking for a bit of jerky. I knew I picked it up at the gas station with some other snacks I got for the day.

"Akkk." Came the loud response to my digging. "That'll do."

I looked down at the pile of stuff I had pulled out to see the bird restraining herself but only barely from a half-eaten KitKat.

I looked at the prize then the bird. As a scavenger I was fairly certain she could eat anything. "I don't know... are birds supposed to have chocolate?"

"You want the info or not?"

I handed over the treat. "Spill bird."

"She got fired." It broke off a piece of the confection. "Jerk ass hit on her and groped her ass, she throated him."

I blinked. "Throated?"

"Yeah, you spread your hand open then catch the guys Adam's Apple with the hard part of your hand between your thumb and forefinger." She whipped her wing out and struck my arm with it. "Ahha."

I shook my head. "So, he won't let her dress up, but he harassed her anyway?"

Its little head bobbed up and down. "Stupid ain't it?"

"So, why am I seeing the world like I took a hit of acid?"

"You're waking up."

That was a bit of a relief, at least I hadn't been slipped acid again. "Will it stop?"

"Eh, ignore it long enough and you'll forget. You all see the realm as children but grownups telling you there's nothing there makes it fade after a bit."

That's a charming thought. "So magic is real, it's all around us, we use it every day and no one knows?" I thought about that for a heartbeat. "That's kind of wild."

"Really? Wild you say?" The bird cocked its head. "Here's a story for you. One day while out walking The Truth and The Lie met up. The Lie looks at the Truth and says, 'Fine day isn't it?' The Truth is confused, after all the sun is shining, the weather's mild. So, she says 'Yes, yes, it is.' They walk together for a bit, with the Truth trying to figure out what the game is. Finally, they come across a pond. 'The waters nice, good day for a swim, join me?' The Truth reaches out and feels the water and sure enough it's nice. So, she takes off her clothes and goes for a soak with The Lie. As soon as she's relaxed, The Lie jumps up, takes her clothes and runs off. She chases after him as he puts her clothing on. The townspeople see she's naked and turn away in disgust. Soon The Lie gets away and dressed as The Truth the people welcome him. The naked Truth on the other hand is so shunned she goes back to the pond and crawls in."

"Appearances versus the ugly naked truth." It was a different, maybe even better way of saying what the divide was and what happened. "All right, hit me with an ugly Truth."

The bird finished off the last of its treat. "You didn't buy her dessert."

Chapter 17

"Crap." I felt deflated. I didn't know exactly what breaking a deal would mean, but it couldn't be good. "I didn't mean to, crap happened, does that count?"

The bird cocked her head. "To her? Definitely. To the oath? Not so much."

"What do I do?"

"Well, technically you agreed to pay for dessert which would be after the meal. She chose shrimp because she's not that big on sweets. But..."

"You're enjoying this."

"So what if I am?"

Come on. Damn it, I mean here was a woman who liked me, who I was starting to like who also happened to be something more and I had now seen that twice.

"Out with it feather duster."

She ruffled her feathers and took a step back. "You really are one of hers." With a resigned squawk. "Fine. Go buy her a candy bar and make sure she gets it before she eats anything else. It's a sweet treat after a meal."

"But you just said, she doesn't like sweets."

"I said she's not big on them. There are a few she likes." The thing then leaned in and leered at me. "Unless of course you want to make yourself dessert, she'd like that a lot."

An image flashed before my eyes, me on a table, legs splayed, her at its head, bent slightly eyes looking up at me as she enjoyed her meal. "I think I'll pass." The bird cocked her head to the opposite side. "For now, anyways." I stood and started walking towards the hospital. "Got to be a vending machine around here somewhere." I took a few steps. "What's she like?"

"Besides sweet moans? Chocolate and caramel, better together. Don't forget her purse." With that, it flew off.

Snatching up the black leather pack with its worn look I noticed it was one of those backpack types. Older but well taken care of, it shone from a recent oiling. As I started walking in I heard a familiar horn.

Sure enough my VW Bug sat in one of the spaces. I was torn. Still Beth had come for me and had driven my car to do it. While I waited, she made the choice for me and got out and came running over to me.

"My god what happened? Why are you in scrubs?"

I looked down at myself for the first time. Basic blue nursing scrubs greeted my eyes. "Um, I think the cops took my top."

She came into view under the light. "And you're pants from the look of it." As she did, I noticed the make-up on her cheek, make-up to cover a bruise.

"Yeah they probably had the pricks blood on them. Jesus Christ Beth, what happened?"

Her hand went up to the cheek before she could stop it. "It's nothing."

I took her hand and moved her out of the light. "If he's hit you?"

She angrily snatched her hand back. "He didn't, we were playing, and things got, a bit much."

"Jesus, what happened?"

With a roll of her eyes and a blush she continued. "I was ass up and he thrust and I fell off the bed into the side of his dresser."

I couldn't help it, I put a hand over my mouth.

"Damn it Lydia, now you're laughing at me." She turned away and walked off a step or two.

"I'm sorry, it's just..." The mental image of him hitting it like a stud bull and her bouncing across the room filled my mind. "I've had a bad night and that was... are you alright?"

She turned back. "Yeah, it's just so embarrassing."

"As embarrassing as the time you went to go down and I literally farted in your face?" I had been mortified by that and she never let me live it down.

"Well no, but scarier, and far less stinky."

"We good?"

"Ya, we good." She came over and hugged me. "So, what happened?"

"I had a date tonight and we got jumped by a couple of guys." I shrugged and tried to play if off. The bruise was obviously the reason for me having to cover for her today.

"Wait you had a date?" She got back in front of me and held me at arm's length. "With who? Why didn't you tell me? Was it nice? You know before? How did it go?"

I could feel myself smiling, this was the Beth I knew and loved. "Izzy, because I was still in shock from last night and wasn't sure it was a date till she showed up. She's great, and it went fine till some assholes dumped water on us."

She blinked at me several times. "Izzy? From work? Oh lord, you liked the poem."

"Wait you knew about that?"

"Yeah, that girls been pinning over you for years."

"How the hell didn't I notice?"

"Because both of you are too cool for school goths who have to ignore each other."

"You know she's goth? She never comes in dressed up?"

"Neither do you, but have you seen what she writes? If she's not goth I don't know what is." She was giving me this sappy, soppy smile. In that moment our years together came full circle. I leaned in and hugged her.

"So, start at the beginning."

"Well, I was at work when she showed up and she was dressed to the nines. Full kit, makeup, everything. She understood I had to cover, waited on me and well we went out to eat. Dinner was good, we did some small talk and got to know each other." She told me she was Fae and so was I. "Then before dessert, these guys showed up, attacked us, shot her with a cross bow, I stabbed one, and they ran off." It sounded so weird when I said that last part out loud, I mean who shoots someone with a cross bow? "Crap, dessert."

With that I grabbed her hand and dragged her inside, all the while my best friend put up with it. Once inside I went on the hunt. I took her from one place to another, all the while I felt like we were 10-year-olds on a mission, and it felt glorious.

"Lydia, what are we doing?"

"Got to find a vending machine."

"Ok, why?"

"Got to buy a chocolate bar."

"Why?"

"Because I promised a fairy I would."

That brought me to a halt, I can't believe I said that out loud.

Beth looked at me, then smiled. "You really like her, don't you?"

The blush had long since creeped up my face. "Yeah, I think I do."

"I've seen her dressed." I turned and looked at her, Beth knew this woman so much better than I did. "Relax it was once, Allen and I ran into her a few weeks ago. Both of us got serious Fairy Queen vibes from her. She does her makeup well."

I stood there not knowing what to do. Was she serious, did she know?

Beth rolled her eyes, "Come on silly." She pulled me. "There's a machine this way." And just like that we were back to two girls giggling and running down the halls.

Shortly, a bar of chocolate goodness with its caramel center was procured, and with a few well-placed questions to the annoyed nurses, we found out where she was. So, there we sat, sisters in our fashion when she looked at me.

"Lydia, it's good to see you smile again. I really missed that."

I felt myself smiling. "Yeah, I missed it too."

"So, tell me for real, what's up with the chocolate bar?"

What had she said? Tell the truth, but let them make the words their own or something like that?" "Um, well I had promised her I'd buy her dessert." I shrugged.

"You like her, don't you."

I opened my mouth and stopped. I did like her; I liked her a lot.

"Lydia, what's wrong?"

"I like her."

She took me over to some chairs and sat me down. I'm glad she did as I felt like I had hit a brick wall. "Hun, what's up?"

The night came rushing back, both nights really. The knife, the darkness, the wings, the crossbow, all of it. All the weirdness hit me at once, just before Beth got here, I'd been talking to a bird. A bird, carrying on a conversation with it, taking advice from it, all of it like it was the most normal thing in the world.

"It's just been bizarre, you know? The guy with the knife, the attack. On top of that she's..." How did I complain or even talk about the rest of it without sounding like I was mad? I let out a defeated sigh. "She's just really intense." And she was, but that wasn't all. "And odd, she's definitely odd, like not normal odd."

Beth looked at me. "Are you talking about?" She brought her hand up and limply dangled her forefinger down and gave it a bit of a wiggle.

"What? God no." Then I thought about that too. I had never really even seen one, well not one that wasn't on the internet or from some sad sack sending a quick pic of his pride and joy, the sad little thing it always was. "That hadn't even really come up." As soon as the words were out of my mouth, I realized what a poor choice of words I had used.

Beth grinned. "Oh, it hasn't?"

I slapped her shoulder. "No!" She giggled and shook her head. Yet I had to admit, high ideals aside that was another complication. I honestly didn't know how I would react.

Beth took my hand. "But for real though, I know two attacks in two days is rough, but it's not like they were her fault."

Only, it kind of was. Not that she did it on purpose... well she did. She cast a spell that would 'find her mate' or some such and that's what got these guys attention. What's more is I only had her word it wasn't a love spell that way. True she didn't lie, she just told the truth in ways that would let others lie to themselves. Was I doing that? I liked her; I really did.

Maybe I liked her too much too fast, maybe there was a reason for that.

Beth put her hand on my shoulder. "Lydia, hun, it's been years since I've seen you smile like this. Hell, you haven't played fairy stuff since you were a kid."

I looked at her; one eyebrow raised. "Um, what?"

"Don't get mad. Your mom and I talk a lot, have since we dated. She loved telling me about all the stuff you got up to as a kid..." With that she trailed off. Then, slowly she took my hand. "That is until you came out and well, she said you just weren't the same."

I thought about it, thought about it hard. I had been a kid, just an ordinary kid. Granted I kept waiting to be interested in boys like all my friends slowly seemed to be, not that I had many friends before I came out, I certainly didn't have many after. Boy just never stopped being icky. Well jerks, they never stopped being jerks. I hung out with some of the boys I grew up with, but by sixth grade all of them had hit on me and didn't take no for an answer. By eighth I was miserable. Worse, I started seeing other girls the way those boys saw me, but I'd be damned if I ever acted like that.

Beth wrapped an arm around me and dragged me into a hug. "Lydia, its ok. Look, you enjoyed your date with her didn't you?"

I thought about it for a moment, it wasn't really a date but I had. "It was just dinner, but yeah, I think I did."

"And you were having fun till just a few moments ago when my big mouth broke the spell."

That may be more literal than she knew, but still. "Yeah, I guess."

"Then take it slow, we'll keep an eye out for her being a creep, we already know she's a bitch, and we'll go from there."

She was right. I was just being gun shy because of the last time. Odd or not it was still the most fun I'd had in a while. "Come on, let's go check on her."

Chapter 18

A quick stop by the nurse's station let us know that indeed, Izzy was out of surgery and what room she was in. We headed up to the appropriate floor and as we got off the elevator Beth's phone rang.

"Crap give me a sec hun."

I looked at her but nodded. She took it off to the left, as I turned right. The door numbers climbed up higher with each passing room. As I approached 365 I heard the doctor's voice.

"The shaft didn't hit anything major, but the muscle will be useless as you heal." I stopped at the doorway to give them privacy. "Now I have to ask, do you have someone to help you?"

I could hear the smile in her voice. "Yeah doc, don't worry, I have someone who will be glad to help, they are an awesome person."

I felt my heart grow, it was almost painful. With a smile on my face I stuck my head in, "How goes doc? She about ready to go?"

He looked at me, then turned back to her. Both of us saw her face, it was free of makeup, looked a bit bruised, she definitely had some rosacea as well as something that would be a birthmark had it been darker. Yet still, the way she blossomed upon seeing me made that ache in my heart grow even larger. For all the strangeness of the last few days, I saw before me a woman who was truly happy to see me.

In my life, I've only had a few people look at me that way; my mom, Beth, a guy from grade school that was crushed when I came out, and now her. I walked over to her, almost passively, and reached my hand out. She took it and smiled.

"I take it this is who you meant?"

She just smiled, and in that moment, she was my world. The details would work themselves out.

She spoke to the doctor without ever taking her eyes off me. "I think we can work something out."

"I'll get the paperwork, let's see if we can get you two out of here."

As soon as he was out, I slipped her the candy bar. "I hope that works."

She looked at it, then blinked. "Crap, dessert." She chuckled, it was a warm sound, something she was obviously used to doing, and she did it well. "I completely forgot." Squeezing my hand, she spoke. "How did you? D'eun. Of course."

"She came to my rescue, yes."

"She likes you."

"Who does?" Beth's words proceeded her into the room.

"My raven. She her own really, but I feed her, look after her, give her a place."

"A free loader huh?"

"Not really, she brings me things."

"Roommate then, not pet. I got one of those."

"Hey." I reached over and pushed her.

Beth turned in and looked at us both, then at Izzy. "So what happened?"

"The cops are calling it a crime of opportunity. After all who brings a crossbow complete with iron tipped bolts to go gay bashing?"

"God, who goes gay bashing these days. I mean that's so last generation." Her face fell. "I keep thinking we'd be passed that by now."

She shrugged. "There will always be those who don't get it, but we have to live our lives, be ourselves."

"Preach girl." She looked at both of us, "So, what now?"

"Well, I go home, live my life. I can do my job one handed if need be."

Beth gave her a look I knew all too well, it was her patent pending cut the shit look. "Iz, I know you got fired. Seriously, now what?"

Her face fell. "I'm paid up till next month, got about 2k held back..." She looked at me. "I was going to move, start over. Now I got something here, so I'll find a job."

"You're a techie, right?"

"Well, yeah. Mostly I work on old computers, but I build decks."

"Decks huh? How cyber punk." Beth chuckled, to be honest I didn't know what cyber punk was. I knew punk, and I knew cyber goth, but what rigs had to do with what I knew of cyber and punk, it didn't add up. "Look Iz, I need the café rigged, top to bottom, Wi-Fi needs updating, and I could really use someone who knows what they are doing. I can afford you, and I know if I was to tell you I want to Neuromancer my place up, you'll get it."

She shook her head. "And you got all that from me calling it a deck?"

"Who else calls them that?"

"All right chummer, you got a deal."

Beth grinned. "Great!"

"What the hell are you two talking about?"

They quickly exchanged glances, then laughed. They spent the next 20 minutes explaining to me what was going on, what cyber punk was, and somehow, we wound up with a game out of it. Turns out Izzy is a game master.

***

The doctor came back and let her know it was ok to go. They gave her antibiotics and pain pills. We all went out to the parking lot, Beth looked at her. "Hit me up when you've rested, we'll go over things then."

"You know I'm going to be unable to actually start work for a bit, right?"

"The big stuff sure, but the conceptualizing, the ideas? That we can get started as soon as you're ready." A horn blew and we all looked over. Allen was waving for her to hurry up. "We got a month and we'll figure it out. Lydia, get her home and in bed, I'll see you later." With that she trotted off.

As they sped away Izzy's face fell ever so slightly. "What's up?"

She looked at me as if she'd forgotten I was there, her smile returned when her eyes met mine and a blush creeped up her cheeks.

"Nothing, not really."

Riiighttt... "I'm not buying that, I saw the same look on your face before."

Her eyebrow slowly creeped up and her gaze turned appraisive. "Oh really, when?"

"When you looked at the guy who attacked us."

With a purse of her lips, she nodded. "I've... heard things. Nothing I can prove but I don't like him. He's..." I watched her search for words.

"He's a creep." I shrugged remembering how we first met. "A bit of an ass, but she's happy."

"Yeah." She returned my shrug, only to realize her mistake as her eyes showed the pain of such movement. "I just hope she stays that way." She looked around. "So, how do we get back to our cars?"

Reaching out I took her good hand. "Come on, Beth drove my car here probably after mister charming dropped her off at it."

She smiled at me. "Fair. Come on, drive me back to my car."

"You drive standard?"

Her face fell. I watched her realize she wasn't driving anywhere. "That's what I thought."

She looked at me. "How could you tell?"

I decided to be truthful with her. "I couldn't, didn't. Look driving one handed especially when it's your right out of whack is bad enough, but of the two it would be easier to convince you that you weren't doing it with a stick. Sorry, you strike me as a hard head."

That chuckle escaped her again. "You got that right." She looked around. "Alright my valiant knight, take me to your steed."

She took her bags, what was left of her outfit and the few other things she had and climbed in. I handed her her purse and she said her thanks, and we were off.

My little car is light, unlike my foot, as such I soon had her reaching for the strap hanging down. Given it was with her bad arm, I quickly slowed down. "Sorry, not used to people riding with me."

She looked at me, confused. "Um, compared to my brother? He once took my mom's van up on two wheels. Until you drive more nuts than my older brother, we're good."

Keeping my eyes on the road, I kept glancing over at her. Yep, her face was pained, but she still had that arm up and her hand wrapped around the strap. "So why are you holding on to the oh shit handle?"

"You I trust." She gave a frantic glance around us. "Them I don't."

I looked around us. "You don't take the freeway?"

"No."

"How do you get to work?"

"Back roads, side streets... no early morning rush hour."

It was true, sunrise had happened long before we got out, now it was after 8 and the road was still packed. Granted movement was flowing, no slowdowns, but that meant cars were close.

"Wait, you drive stick, but you take side roads?"

"I learned on stick; it was cheap. I don't like driving to begin with." She sighed as she relaxed a little. "Talking helps." I could hear her counting something under her breath. "I got into a wreck shortly after I started driving. Wasn't a huge fan anyway."

"But you were ok?"

"Oh, I was fine. My 'new' car wasn't. Chevy Custom classic pickup. I flipped it."

"You flipped a truck, and weren't hurt?"

"Not a scratch. Put my head in a windshield once when I was a kid. Seatbelt didn't engage. Had a red spot but it didn't even bleed."

"So, like, is this like your first time being hurt? Like your powers make you superhuman tough or something and its only iron that harms you?" What was I saying? The bird had already told me she'd been shot.

That laugh erupted from her again. "God no. I'm a little tougher, maybe. I bruise, I cut, I bleed. I just also am usually just to the left of it being worse, or the right. I'm lucky."

I thought back to what the doctor had said, nothing major had been hit. She had an honest to god cross bow bolt hit her just above her right breast and it missed everything but muscle. I found myself nodding. "I can see that. So it's like plot armor?"

I could feel her gaze upon me. "What? I'm a geek, ok?"

That chuckle came back. "No, no hun. I'm sorry someone made you feel that way, but no, that was adorable."

I shifted uncomfortably. "So yeah, like in that movie with the Governator, a gunshot wound that should be fatal is just a scratch?"

"Something like that. I've always thought of it as a probability field, something that keeps me safe but flubs me when it's not life threating."

"Kind of a balance thing."

A sigh crept forth from her. "It doesn't feel like balance."

I thought about it. "I guess not. You've lost a lot, haven't you?

"That easy to see?"

"You're a trans woman, you're a goth." I shrugged. "Doesn't take a Holmes to figure that out."

"A Holmes, not a Sherlock?"

"Shit his brother was better at it than he was."

"True." She sat in silence, then, "You know a lot of stuff, and not just pop culture, how did you miss cyber punk?"

I turned off the ramp and headed onto the road that would take me back to work. "I knew of the genre, just not the name. Honestly, when I hit my stride with it, Tolkien was huge. I got into fantasy first. Then some anime, then a lot of anime, Evangelion, Akira and the like. When I hit college, I made a friend or two and got into a role play group on campus. We did D20, BESM, WoD, stuff like that. I've been goth since I was a kid, so Vampire really spoke to me." Beth still played, and it's not that I didn't want to. "I fell out of it after a while, I know Sherlock because my mom bought it for me."

"I can see that."

"What about you?"

"Tabletop was the first time I got to be me, then... I realized I needed to be more like the woman I made. She wasn't scared of anything. A huge fighter, she stood up for what she believed in. So, I came out."

I pulled into the parking lot and threw it into neutral. "Didn't go well?"

"Mom cried, dad flipped, then it was like it never happened. I preferred girls, so I wasn't 'gay'. I stuck to gender neutral clothing, grew out my hair and they supported me, more or less. My brother tried, asked what I wanted to be called. Then he flipped on it. Never figured out why." She looked at me as she unlocked her hand from the strap and slowly lowered her arm. "Then stuff I thought I left behind as a kid started happening again."

As the sun rose, she moved, and her hair created this halo of light around her head. "I started pulling shadows to me, the first was to escape a group at school. I was tired of being 'corrected' by my peers. That first time they saw me, but I got better at it. Soon I could disappear in a well-lit room, just be overlooked by everyone. One day a guy came and in front of everyone dumped my lunch on me. Said things I won't repeat, and it was too much. The shadows that hid me wrapped around me and I beat the ever-loving shit out of him." She took a deep breath. "When the lights came back on, I was bleeding, but not as bad as he was. I was suspended from school for bringing a weapon despite the fact the police never found one. My parents stepped up and pitched a fit about the teachers letting this happen and with all the weirdness surrounding the incident every-one was happy to sweep it under the rug. One guy, Doug, started following after me. I wasn't dumb, I already knew what a chaser was. So I confronted him. He told me I was one bad ass goth bitch and wanted to know why I didn't wear it to school."

She smiled at me. "You should have seen his face when I said I didn't know what goth was."

"Oh lord, if you didn't know, why did he think you were goth?"

"He said he pegged me to start with, but me screaming about 'bathing in a river of his blood and using his skull as a cereal bowl' clenched it for him. He was from L.A. and was a metal head. So, in my half horse high school he knew what it was like to be the outsider. He and his mom took me under their wing, she was an old hippy complete with dancing teddy bear tat on her wrist. They helped with my parents, and inside a month, the Goth Queen of Bone and Blood hit my small-town high school."

"I remember the push back from when I hit. It must have been interesting."

"Witch, devil worshiper, deviant, you name it I heard it. It really pissed the local pastors off when I quoted the bible back to them but the whole passage not just the one thing that agreed with them." She sighed. "That's when I first ran into one of the hunters."

Hands slapped the top of the car startling the hell out of both of us. "You haven't got her home yet?"

I looked out to see Allen, his grin was something of a jarring thing to see for some reason.

"What are you doing here?"

He looked at me and I could almost see the drop-down menu as he chose his answer. "Um, you've been up all night, you two were attacked, Liz is taking your shift. I mean, you took hers for her after the accident." He looked in and nodded to Izzy. "I don't get why you two are here."

"Got to pick up my stuff from my car, things like my house keys."

"And why not? Look." He turned back to me. "Look, Liz is crashing at my place for a while, why don't you just take her to your guy's place so you can keep an eye on her." He leaned in and whispered. "Let you two get to know each other better without us around."

"Still need my keys, give me a minute Lydia." She opened the door got out closed it and leaned in the window. "I'll be back in a few."

Without missing a beat Allen straightened up. "Come on I'll walk with you, make sure nothing else happens." The smile she gave him looked like a snake sheading its skin, slow and purposeful, it was lost on him. "Besides I want to go over game ideas with you." With that he started walking off with her. To his credit he kept a polite distance and soon they were both in deep and animated game debate. No doubt going over whatever wet works and neural wear or whatever.

I slipped out of the car and went into the shop.

Beth was already working away at something. "So, you really going to turn this place into a cyber punk cyber-café?"

Without looking up. "Well, I think it's a good idea even if no one else does."

"Whoa, step back a sec. I just asked."

She looked up glaring at me, red ringing her eyes. "Maybe it's the way you asked."

"Geez Beth, what the hell?"

"Nothing, sorry. It's not you."

I knelt down. "No, not nothing. What's up?"

She let out a sigh, and with it a tension left her body. "Nothing, I told Allen about it and he." She stopped. "He pointed out I could lose money, customers, that it was a big risk."

"Hey no, I get it. You were so excited. I was just wondering if this was something you just came up with or?"

"Lydia? It's what I first thought of when I heard the term cyber-café. I love this place, I do. But it's my uncle's, he was an early adopter, his Wi-Fi wasn't made for a building like this, we got ghost spots and dead spots throughout, not enough plug ins and so on." She shook her head. "I want it to be mine, to be ours."

"Ours?"

"Lydia, you're my best friend, and I couldn't run this place without you. You keep me sane, you keep me going. And if you think this is a bad idea, I will respect that, but I want you to do this, I want us to do this, I want to open a cyber punk café and have you dress goth or industrial or anything else and I want it to be ours."

My ass hit the floor, it was a good thing I had already been squatting.

"Say yes, please say yes. I've been thinking about it forever, hell I already have the paperwork, I meant to ask you like last month but Allen said I should sleep on it, but I don't want to anymore." She looked at me with her big tear-stained eyes and smiled. "Please say yes."

"Yes!"

Chapter 19

I cried. She cried. We hugged. We called her mom, her mom cried. Honestly, we probably would have just kept that up if everything had been equal. Sadly the knock at the back door changed that.

Beth reached over and opened it, outside was her boyfriend and the woman who I hoped would soon be mine. My girlfriend that is, if it worked out in a way, I guess I would be hers? I mean she didn't seem like she was adverse to BDSM, hell she seemed like she was into it. At least until we got interrupted.

Beth all but purred, "Allen, you two get things worked out?"

His thin lips split into a grin that reminded me of car salesmen on a cheap lot, "Yeah, I'm going to be playing a Street Sam."

She grinned. "Good, I'll see you tonight. I have a few more things to go over with Lydia," she turned to me, "then you two can get out of here."

"Sounds good."

"Iz, why don't you come in and have a look at the equipment, get an idea of what you're up against."

She nodded, came inside and Allen turned to walk off, but as he did, he looked back over his shoulder and gave Beth the same look that Izzy had given me at the hospital. It made me think better of him.

While the future tech guru wandered off with her gimp wing to see what a disaster she had gotten herself into, the two of us headed in to do the paperwork necessary to make this all work.

"So, what now?"

"Well first and foremost, your pay is going to change. As an owner you have a choice, take a salary or a percent."

"What do you do?"

She sighed. "I take about a quarter of what I pay you and about a percent of any profit left over after all expenses come out. Sometimes it's good, sometimes it's not."

"Fine, I'll do that. Just hope my landlord is ok if rent is late."

"I think she'll understand. But honey, you got to understand, with this change over, you will be losing money. He's right we will take a hit, some of the regulars will walk, most will likely stay, but the walk-ins are going to take a nosedive, especially to start with."

"Bitch we did Ramen in college. You believe in this enough to risk your bank, I can do the same thing. I don't know much about cyber punk, but you do, and you believe in this, and I believe in you."

Tears formed in her eyes. "God, you... I still love you, you know that?"

"Yeah, but you needed dick bitch."

"I think breaking up with you was the biggest mistake I ever made."

I thought of my growing apprehension of her and Allen, and it hit me. He was the first real time a guy had lasted more than a few weeks. Was I jealous? I mean he just looked at her like she was his entire world. Sure he was a bit of a creep, but other than using a different version of her diminutive? What had I really seen? Him being naked the first time we met? So, he wasn't body shy, so what? Izzy didn't like him either, but she also let him into her game.

I felt a reluctance loosen inside me.

"Yeah, I miss you sometimes, the feel of you, your smell. I get it. But if we hadn't you wouldn't have Allen and well..." I looked over my shoulder out into the void of darkness where I knew Izzy was already hard at work with that mind of hers.

"Yeah, I know. Just sometimes you know?"

"Yeah hun, sometimes." If we had stayed together, I might not have met Izzy, then again I might have, but I certainly wouldn't have dated Shadow. I absently rubbed the scar on my forearm. Things had gotten bad. Beth was why I was still here. "Beth, we're still together, just different. I live with you, you literally just made me a partner in your business, not sure why, but you did. You've been here for me, and I will be there for you. Liz."

She pushed me hard, "God no. It sounds weird coming from you."

I grinned, "Hey, I'm trying. You deserve all the respect I can give you." This was getting awkward, to me at least. "So what's next?"

"Well, I've been looking over it, and given recent events? I think you need some time off."

"Excuse you?"

"Yeah, it's called a mental health scare. It's paid but only at ¾, its only two weeks but it's something."

"What? Why?"

"You were attacked at the store, on the clock. Call it covering my ass, call it being a good friend, call it the last thing I do as your boss, I don't care. It's usually meant for suicide attempts but I pay big bucks for the insurance you guys got and I'm damn well going to use it. Assault during a robbery attempt definitely qualifies."

I found myself shaking my head. "Ok, so let me get this right, you want me to take two weeks off, you will cover my shifts, and you want me to take care of Izzy, at the house, because you will be spending that time with Allen?"

"Hell no. I'm promoting Rita to your old job. As for the rest? I'm spending a few nights with him, but definitely not two weeks and sure Izzy can stay if it makes it easier, but I figure after a day or two you'll want time to you." She got up and hugged me. "You've been attacked twice in as many days. Take the time. Get to know Izzy."

"You know her from outside here, don't you?"

"Iz? Hell yeah. Remember that LARP I went to in college? She ran it."

I blinked at her, "That was ten years ago. Why didn't you introduce her to me?"

"I was trying to, but you didn't want to LARP, and that game where I was trying to get you to come play a rogue? Yeah, she was the one running it. Then you dated Shadow... and both of you kind of fell off the map. I knew where you were, but her? Until she started coming in here, I thought she moved."

Beth had been trying to set me up for years with this woman, I didn't do blind dates, so she tried to get me into a game with her.

"So, tell me about her." I settled into the chair, I needed to know.

"Well, she's sweet and well you've seen her dressed given the skirt she's still wearing. Back then she was a lot happier, had about as many bad relationships as you did."

"Hey at least one of them wasn't bad."

"Really? I heard that bitch was so dumb she dumped you." I snorted and she continued. "She was a top and had a thing for human fauna, cat girls, dog girls, and the like. She's the one who told me what a furry was. She's like hard core, religious is the wrong word, but yeah she's a believer in some weird stuff. I knew you two would hit it off when you got into that otherkin stuff. Outside of game? Don't know her that well. The only reason I know that much is that she once flipped on a guy that touched her alter, and a few of her exes bad mouthed her pretty badly."

"Like what?"

"You know the normal shit, failed this test or the other, pseudo top, won't take control, gets weird sometimes, then there's the bird."

"D'eun?"

"Met it already?"

"Yeah, she's like really sweet."

"That's a first. Everyone she dated hates that bird, called it a pscyho. But it's a wild animal that just adopted her so? Who's to say."

D'eun didn't like her old girlfriends. "Cool, so… has she ever dated guys?"

"When I was gaming with her? Only one and trust me he was a piece of work. She's sworn off men since then I think."

She's bi…

Beth grabbed my hand. "Hey now, don't be like that."

"Like what?"

"Your face got all pouty. She's pan, and? She's more loyal than a golden retriever. She's not going to cheat on you. Hell even when she was dating back then and poly, she never so much as looked at anyone without letting her partner know."

"Wait, she's poly?"

"Well, yeah. It's one of the reasons I wanted to introduce you, at the time you were thinking you were poly, you were into kink, you were a furry."

"Hey, I was otherkin, not a furry."

From behind me, "What's wrong with furries?"

I was suddenly 6 years old again with my mom walking in after me saying a bad word. My eyebrows shot up and I could feel the color draining out of my face. I turned and looked at her. She had acquired a few smudges, some dust, and was holding a dish rag she was wiping her hands with.

My mind went in multiple directions at once. I wanted to explain myself, I wanted to be upset she had come up and scared me, I wanted to hit my knees and beg for forgiveness.

Explaining won out. "Nothing!" That came out way quicker and in a much higher tone than I meant it to. "I just never saw myself as one of them. I mean." What did I mean? "Like I'm so not getting one of those suits, they look hot as hell."

A small smile formed on her lips. "Oh they are. But that's only one group of furries, they're called mascots. A lot of furries want a mascot costume, but not all, most want something to show off their fursona, but again not all. A lot of the otherkin crowd came over when the first blush of otherkin wore off."

"Oh." It was all I could think of to say. It wasn't the first time she woke those old feelings inside of me, but this was the first time I felt like she had challenged me, chastised me.

I shook it off. "So, you ready to go?"

"More or less. I got a few ideas, some decent design thoughts, took a look at what passes for a hub... gonna need a bigger boat. If you want to go all out I can do it, anything from a hub, to a dive, to someplace to meet a Johnson, to a place for console cowboys and jockeys to unwind." She looked at me. "Hopefully we even get a few razor girls."

"Oh god leave Molly out of this."

I looked at them both. "Well at least now I know how other people feel."

"Cowboys and Jockeys are the same thing, hackers who run data for profit, a razor girl is slang," She looked over at Izzy, "and not very nice slang, for street muscle, basically a female assassin who has implants. Molly is the main character and the muscle for the books." Beth got a faraway look on her face. "It was social commentary on corporate greed and the advancement of computer science in the 80s. Great stuff really."

"Too bad it's pretty much happening."

"Got everything but the implants."

Both of them seemed bummed out by that.

Chapter 20

I took Izzy back to her place and helped her get some things, then we drove over to mine. By the time we got there it was obvious the pain meds were wearing thin. She had gone from slightly jovial, though a bit maudlin, to quiet and sullen. Once I got her in, she went to the couch and laid down.

I quickly scoured the house for blankets and pillows, made her as comfortable as possible and got her a drink so she could take her pills. I thought everything was fine, until suddenly she sat up.

"I got to get out of these clothes, I need a shower." She struggled to stand but managed, it was like watching a marionette come to life on its own, arms and legs weren't coordinated, her left knee buckled while her right remained steady, yet other than a brief drop on that side she seemed unaffected. Watching her move towards the bathroom was an interesting mix of someone intoxicated and someone piloting a damaged mech. She was completely disconnected from her body.

"Izzy, do you think that's a good idea?" I started moving towards her to help.

She shrugged me off slightly. "Not going to be a burden." The words were a mutter, had I not been right up on her I wouldn't have caught them. She turned to me, "I'm covered in sweat, blood they didn't clean off at the hospital, my top is ruined, my shoulder hurts, I just want a shower. Hot water pelting against my skin," she closed her eyes, "connected to something besides pain and misery for a few moments so I don't dream of only blood and death."

The look in those eyes, eyes that still had contacts in I saw, was a plea I felt throughout my body. I nodded. "Come on, at least let me help you undress."

One corner of her mouth slowly rose up into the single most annoying smirk I have ever seen. "Not how I pictured you getting me naked."

Heat rushed to my cheeks, I felt myself panic as flustered words started to pour forth from my mouth. "That's not, I mean come on you need the help, I wasn't trying to..."

A single finger landed on my lips, I looked into those eyes again. They were soft, compassionate. At that moment I knew all of her was in her eyes. "It was a joke love. When I'm hurt, in pain, scared, I joke." She looked me over appraisingly, she started with my eyes, went up to my hair. Her gaze started to move down; small darts of those eyes let me know she actually looked at my ears. A single finger lifted my chin and I watched as she viewed my neck as if it was the single most sensual thing on earth. Then she looked at my shoulders. Her gaze held things, a hunger I too felt. But where mine was a trembling thing scared to move, hers was a beast just out of sight. Felt, heard, smelled, but not yet seen.

"Every last inch of you." She leaned in and smelled my neck starting at my shoulder and slowly inhaled as she made her way slowly up. As if she were savoring one of those scents that just demands attention; fresh baked bread, cookies, a well-made steak, a good bouquet of flowers. Her lips stopped, not quite touching my ear, in fact the only thing that had touched me was the tip of that finger on my chin. Softly she spoke, words not whispered, yet barely heard. Somehow what she said echoed deep inside me as if she had screamed it into my soul. "Every inch is something to savor, to taste, to touch, a feast of flesh, need, desire. But it's your heart, your mind, your soul I want to touch. You, not your body, should be reached, you should be wanted, not needed. You should be that thing everyone wants, that peace in passion."

Slowly she breathed me in again, as if I was the first scent of fresh air she had had in so long.

"I will never lie to you, I might not tell you everything, but I will never lie." Her voice said she honestly believed that, it was so earnest, yet her tone was still that darkness, the spell she had started weaving with her words. "So, know this, I will not take advantage of you, I won't force you, and I won't just take you. You will come to me, you will ask for what you want, and I will give."

She leaned back giving me a bit of room, it let me see her eyes again. The eyes of the beast shining in the darkened forest of my mind, shining from whatever moon rode high in such a deep and cold night.

"I will serve you, I will play your body like the instrument it is, I will love you, I will fight for you, defend you and teach you how to stand at my back, shield and sword at the ready. I will make you quiver at my words and cum on my command, and I will show you every ounce of the respect you should have always had, respect you not as a human, but a person, respect you for who you truly are, not who I want you to be. I will accept nothing but you, all of you, the real you that you hide for fear of being rejected." She took another step back. "And that is why you must come to me. If I chase you? I could have your body. Sorry," she finished her hungry appraisal of my form. "The package is beyond exquisite, but I don't settle for anything but a mind, especial not when I find someone worth it."

With that she took a step back and the spell was broken. She was no longer the dark temptress in the deepest of woods inviting me to embrace my own doom. She was once more just a scared, hurt woman who had pushed herself too hard. "So don't worry about me trying anything. I would rather just be friends than lovers. If we work, we will work, if not? I won't force it." Then her eyes flashed back up at me. "But I'm not giving up that laugh, nor our future friendship for something so fleeting as a botched liaison."

My heart beat itself against my chest, my legs were weak. I had seen the forest, felt the danger, felt everything. Her words were fingers on my skin, and the more she talked the deeper they went. Had she asked, I would have nodded, and trembling gone to whatever hell she had in store.

Then she had deliberately broken the spell she wove, desperately dragged me out of it, told me she wasn't... wasn't what? Just going to take advantage of me?

A chuckle came unbidden from me. She raised a single eyebrow, a gesture I was beginning to understand was a question. "It's just. I'm not that easy you know. We just met and you're talking about? What?"

"Collaring you, if that is what you wish." She turned and with one hand on the wall started walking. "It's what I want, it's what I am looking for. If I say anything else it is pretense, and to me that is a lie. I would much rather get it out in the open right off the bat, including..." She looked back over her shoulder at me and I realized I had just fallen into step with her. "Telling you that no is not only an answer, it is the answer till you say crystal clear and explicitly that it is a yes." She shrugged and started slowly and with great care, to make her way back to the bathroom. "As well as telling you that I would rather have you as a friend than risk losing you to some imagined sexcapades, no matter how clear, wonderful, or desirable that might be."

I snorted. "You find me sexy, compatible, want me, and you actually expect me to believe you'd be happy if we were just friends?"

"Yes." With that she pulled a string on her skirt, and it simply fell off.

Strangely her answer was so sincere I think she truly believed that.

Chapter 21

Under that skirt were a few more layers. A body shaper, panties, something called a gaff... which I soon learned what that was for. It wasn't as big a shock as I thought it would be. The thing was ugly, but kind of cute, sort of.

What I found most interesting was the scent. I knew men smelled different, so I had braced myself for it. That fear never came, she smelled pretty much like any other girl I had smelled. Not all women smell alike, not by far. Had that not been there I probably would have just chalked the difference up to a difference in biology.

As I helped her into the shower, I realized that was exactly what it was.

"I'm going to go and make myself something to eat before I head to bed, want something?"

"Sure, just a sandwich would be fine."

"Oh, go make you a sandwich huh?"

"God if I ever say that after, it will probably be just so I can watch you struggle to move. I am a sadist after all."

I walked out shaking my head. She was certainly quite comfortable with who and what she was and wanted. As I hit the kitchen a few things struck me. One I kind of liked the blunt. It was altogether different from what I was used to, to be sure. I mean I knew plenty of people who would be blunt. Yet she was blunt without saying things that made me feel like she was being mean.

Two, she gave off the same predatory vibe Allen did, but he, well he was male, and she wasn't. It was as simple as that. Yet somehow? It was more than that. Yeah, Allen looked at Beth the same way I looked at her... I mean like she looked at me, but calling her Liz? Wasn't he trying to make Beth what he wanted?

"Well we all do that don't we?"

The jar of mayo just looked at me. Well, no but it might as well have been.

"Look we all change for our partners in one way or another. I mean, I'm a lesbian, and yet, I'm willing to overlook her..." I couldn't make myself say it. If I said it out loud that thing would be real. "It's normal, we grow and change."

The butter knife didn't have an opinion.

As I pulled the meat out from its drawer, I looked at it. Did she like ham? "Don't look at me like that. She would still be my friend if I can't, she said so." Beth and I had pulled that off after all, if it came to that, that is.

"She's got good lines I'll give you that. Hell, she's even sincere about it, I can tell that."

She wasn't what I wanted.

Tops were supposed to take you. They were supposed to possess you, to have you. I wanted that. I wanted to be taken. How could she not see it?

Still, I liked her.

Friendship, yeah friendship was good. I needed someone who would push me, test me, break me, I needed someone to make me, me, not just sit there. "She's soft. I mean I can hear the steel."

Two sandwiches made, one with my bread, one with bread from her place. I sat down and picked mine up. "Maybe I can, I don't know, push her over. Get her to make the first move?" I looked over at the snack I'd made for her. "She wants me, just a matter of getting her riled up."

I slowed my chewing, stood, and put everything up. I couldn't take the accusing glares. I saw her as a woman, but I was still hesitant, and yet I wanted her and didn't and I was going to seduce her, and I just wanted to be friends.

I needed air.

Once outside I took another bite. "It's no big deal." I chewed more. "God, I don't know what I want."

"Sure, you do." I jumped and wheeled around only to be faced with D'eun. "You want to give me part of that."

I rolled my eyes and tore off a bit of bread. "How did you find us?"

She choked down the bread, "You kidding? Who drives bugs these days?" I caught myself laughing. "Sides I can feel her."

"Oh, you can?"

"Yep."

I nodded. "That's right you're her familiar."

"Servant actually. Bonded and all. We just say familiar because it's easier to understand. I mean it's true, but its jedi true."

"Jedi true?"

"True, from a certain point of view."

I let out a sigh. "Of course, that's what she meant when she said she'd never lie to me."

The bird let out a squawk. "What? She's already made that oath to you?" I turned back to her in time to see her feathers smooth back down. "Look, she didn't lie. By every way you can think of that word, it's true. I'm her familiar. I do all the same things, more actually." It hopped down from the tree it was on and landed on the railing next to me. "But it's like saying someone has a bike and you go outside and find a 10 speed. Nothing wrong with it, it's a good bike and gets you where you need to go, but it's no crotch rocket." The bird sighed. "I'm the 10 speed."

I thought about it and got it. "And some day she'll have that motorcycle, and still have you. The two will be similar, based on the same principal, but different."

"Zactly." She looked over. "She needs help."

Quickly, I went inside and down the hall. Through the closed door I could hear her muttering. "Stupid bitch, that's not how that works right now." When I opened the door she was standing there towel in hand.

When she got undressed, I was so focused on her thing, I missed how amazing her breasts were. Plush, round, a few stretch marks, they were still pert despite her age, since she hadn't had them as long, I guess, but gravity certainly knew about them. I could see the signs that they also weren't brand new. They were large, but that's not what struck me. Her areolas were magnificent, and her nipples were big. I have to admit I've always had a thing for breasts. I mean mine were mine, they weren't a big deal for me, but another woman's? Each was them and uniquely them. Size was important when I was younger, but as I dated more, I cared less and less about size. I wanted breasts that I could feel and that would feel me touching them. Next to her skin which was very white, blind the beach goers white, the areolas were this beautiful peach. Her nipples were thick, the size of my fingertips easily. I wondered what they would feel like in my mouth.

I shook my head to clear my vision of scenes not yet happening. "You, ok?"

She looked at me and held up her towel with her left hand. "This, isn't working."

I went over and took it from her and began to pat her down.

"You don't have to do it that way, I won't break."

I looked at her. "Hasn't anyone ever told you girls pat, not rub? It keeps the skin soft."

She laid her hand on mine. "Not a problem with me. Feel."

I reached out and touched her shoulder, it was velvet under my hand. I also saw her wound, red and angry. I realized something; I had been looking at her but not seeing her.

I took a step back to fix that.

She was a larger woman, not an ideal petite thing, she had lean muscle up top in her arms and shoulders, but it was a corded affair. Her tummy was large with its rolls, but it was still quite beautiful, stretch marks and all. Her breasts, I had seen them before in a dream. Her hips were wide and had natural hand holds. I never understood why some men didn't find that attractive. I certainly did. Her legs were ripped, thigh to calf. Had to make buying boots difficult. But no, I was still not seeing all of her, only parts. Her face was round with a cute chin and her nose was that of her Irish ancestry, a darling little pug. Still, those were pieces, not the whole. Her lips, plump and kissable. Then I looked into her eyes. With her contacts out I saw a grey abyss. They were this fathomless grey, not my brown, but the edges were dark blue, maybe green, with that same kind of band at the iris. I was drawn in. I couldn't remember what I was doing.

"Earth to Lydia, come in Lydia?" Her tone was a bit teasing.

"Sorry, got lost in your eyes."

She smiled and blushed. It was a warm comfortable thing, a vulnerable moment for her to be sure, but she raised no defenses. For a moment her face blossomed into a whole, a girl, early twenties maybe? Certainly older than a teen. That girl was sweet and kind, the kind of person who would sing to birds and have them come to her. Just as quickly it was gone, and I was looking at Izzy once more. A warm person in pain, dripping wet and with those dark curls cascading around her.

I started drying her off, not being rough, but abandoning the patting I had been taught so long ago.

Once we were done, she slipped off, and I heard her rummaging around. I didn't realize I had been just standing there holding the towel. I had it bad. I couldn't just be friends. I just couldn't. Why was I falling for a soft dominant?

Chapter 22

Out in the living room she had gotten herself into a long t-shirt. The kind of shirt that was old, worn and a bit ratty. It was once purple and came down to her knees, a night dress for more modern times what with its faded picture of a children's book character. It was the exact kind of shirt the girl I has seen moments before would have worn.

"You know, I would have helped."

"I know, but I didn't want to assume."

That struck me as odd. "Didn't want to assume?"

"Yes." She shrugged. The movement cost her. Pain washed over her face and her knees gave way.

I rushed over and helped her to the couch. "Well, you should have assumed. Damn it." The faded purple was starting to darken at her shoulder. I pulled the stretched-out collar to the side, the stitches were holding, but the wound was weeping and the area around it was an angry dark red. "Wait here."

Didn't want to assume. She assumed at the hospital, hadn't she. Just knew I would take care of her. She wasn't wrong, and now that she was here, she was being stubborn. She hadn't even rebandaged her injury. An injury she got defending me.

I stomped back into the living room, she knew she was in trouble, she could see it on my face and I could see she saw.

"First and foremost, you didn't rebandage it. Now I need to get that shirt off and get the blood out of it." I sat beside her, stripped off her shirt, and started to rebandage the area. "Of all the bullshit. I mean come on." I tried to let it go, then I realized if this was going to work, if this was ever going to work, I needed to follow the rules she laid out. So, the truth. "And what the hell do you mean you couldn't assume, you're here, I said I would take care of you, what's to assume?" I could feel myself shaking with building rage. "And you already assumed. You assumed I would take care of you at the hospital. I realize you were probably going to ask me when I walked in, but you had already told the doctor like it was a done deal, and yes it probably was. But by that same thought and you being right, I could have damned well helped you out with the fucking shirt, taken care of the bandages, and I wouldn't be needing to soak your shirt in damned sparkling water."

I got the last of the tape on and just looked at her.

She smiled warmly at me in gratitude. "Let D'eun in."

I was up and moving before my brain registered it was a command. She hadn't yelled, hadn't raised her voice, three simple soft-spoken words and I rushed to obey. Before I could even fully grasp what I was doing, the back door was open and the bird flew inside.

"What's up boss."

"I need your permission."

I turned and looked at the two of them. D'eun was all but glaring at her. "Don't think that's a good idea boss."

"What are you two talking about?"

D'eun looked over at me. "Hush you." The beak stayed pointing at me, but one eye was laser focused on Izzy. "You know what happened last time."

"I remember. But I think she's worth it."

The bird interrupted. "Thought she was worth it too."

"This time is different."

"Oh?" The croak was quick and harsh. "How?"

"You like her."

Feathers fluffed up. She hopped from foot to foot, looking at me, then her, then me again. "I do... egg help me I do." She squeaked this small sound. "But that's why I don't want to lose her."

"Trust me D'eun, trust her."

"Permission granted." The birds head hung with sorrow, she looked at me. "I'm sorry." With that she flew to the floor.

"Show her D'eun, show her who would have seen to me."

Shadows started to form around the bird, swirling darkness with purple lightning flickering within. That swirling cloud of shadow grew in height, then it was just gone. In the bird's place was a sullen teenager. She was maybe 13? 14? All goth with her black clothing, thigh high boots and corset ringed with raven feathers. Her hair was a mess of short mismatched black spikes, her eyes dark black pits. She cocked her head at me with a look of utter contempt and defiance as well as a look of hope, the kind of look only a teen can have.

"Caw, bitch." The bitch was an afterthought.

"D'eun?" The word was hesitant. I had seen things, plays of light and shadow, but this was no mere trick of sound, no word simply whispered in the right ear. This was magic.

"Still a ten speed." She turned away from me... a hurt girl ready for rejection, something I knew all too well. 15 years ago, I had been her.

"You're beautiful."

She wheeled on me. "Am not. I'm all pale and limbs and pink." She lacked feathers, yet sill I could see them ruffle.

I reached over and took her hand, each finger ended in a black talon. She wouldn't pass close scrutiny, you would know something was off even if you didn't have words for it, but if you just passed her in the street, just talked with her even if you were only a few feet away? She was just any other goth girl.

"You're beautiful D'eun, bird or girl. I can think of no more beautiful bird."

I watched with a heart melting as this girl blushed at my words. She quickly pulled her hand away and covered her face.

"She's who I meant when I told the doctor I had someone to look after me, not you. I don't like assuming like that. Assuming someone is mine to use."

From their conversation they had shared D'eun's secret before, and it hadn't gone well.

"I'm sorry."

"For what? Speaking your mind? Never fail to do that and we'll be fine. Thinking I was just going to invite myself? It's what every lesson in this life has taught you." She took my hand. "No, you made a mistake, that doesn't need an apology. Just, try not to make the same one again."

I smiled. "Thank you."

"Careful with that." I looked over to D'eun as she spoke. "She doesn't care but when you start meeting the smallers, they can take lots of offense to that."

Izzy glared at her. "Most of the modern ones don't care anymore than I do."

D'eun had picked up a small bit of crystal we kept for its look and was staring at it. "Yeah, right, you they don't care, you mean it. They don't know her yet, and you know how they get if they think you're giving them platitudes."

"Look, I have a lot to think about and you need to lay down. Give me the shirt." I laid her down and covered her up. "Get some rest."

She smiled but nodded. "Come on bird, let's get some food in you."

"Her first."

"Crap, your sandwich."

With that I ran off with the shirt and brought her back her snack.

I put the shirt in the sink and poured the seltzer on it, D'eun came up behind me to watch. "That works?"

"Does for my underwear."

"You said food?"

I looked back at the fridge and realized exactly how tired I was. "Sure, help yourself. I'm going to bed."

Chapter 23

The vastness of the wood was open before me, my legs were pumping away. Each foot fall was thunder in my ears, but maybe it was my heart. Both were going so fast it frightened me. That only added to my growing terror.

Something was behind me, and it knew the wood as well as I.

I could hear its ground eating lope, the way it crashed through the brush of undergrowth. I even imagined I could hear its growl, feel its hot breath on my neck.

All of that was nonsense of course. This was my wood, and nothing in my wood was faster than I. This was my wood, and nothing knew it better than I.

In fact, yes just what I needed. I broke left, and put my ears down, slipping past the hungry thorns of the brambles. Follow me now you fucker.

Behind me I heard just what I expected, my pursuer hit the thorns and howled. It set loose the terror that I had just barely held back, that sound wasn't human, it wasn't wolf, it wasn't hound... it was something else.

Blind panic was good, if I wanted to wind up in that thing's jaws. I was too small, needed more.

I stretched out my legs and felt the ground hit my feet. Chase me now bitch; I bite back. I put on more speed. I was less maneuverable like this, but I could last longer. I certainly didn't want to find out who my new friend was. The new colors around me flared to life, colors I could only see with my nose. It gave me an idea.

I looped back around; the thorns did slow it down even if they didn't stop it. If I could get the wind to bring its scent to me, I would have a better idea what I was dealing with.

The detritus gave way to my feet, it could be slippery if you stepped wrong, but I was made for this. I kept my head down and my body low and moved into position for the wind to be my eyes. It shifted just in time, and I got a nose full of my pursuer.

Panic flooded me anew, a deep part of me knew that scent, it meant capture, it meant an end to freedom, it was death and darkness and worse. I changed again and with my hair flowing in the wind stretched out my neck. I was fastest like this, but not as sure footed on the forest floor. I needed ground beneath me for this, not dead leaves.

That was my undoing, I swerved to avoid a tree and my feet went out from under me. All too quickly the shadow was over me, I could see it, darkness, eyes, thousands of them, all for me, then teeth from more than one mouth, all pointed, all coming in.

I felt a hand grab me and pull.

My senses cleared and I looked right into D'eun's eyes. "You were screaming chick. What's up?"

My heart was still pounding, I looked around my room, my room. Safe and sound in my bed and night had fallen outside. "Just a dream little one. Nothing big."

She snorted. "Sounded more like a nightmare."

"Yeah, well." I got up and looked at her. Now with a clear head I noticed her face was a complete mess. She had chocolate smeared around her mouth, I saw the yellow of mustard, a little red I hoped was ketchup, in other words she was a right mess. Yes, she had come to wake me up, but in her other hand she had the remains of a whole pack of ham. I know it was the whole pack because what was left was the nice, neat block of individual slices with most of it having been consumed around like it was a single wedge.

"D'eun, have you been eating this whole time?"

She blinked at me, looked at her prize. "You said 'help yourself'." Her voice was part whine, part pure defiance, and part fear I would be mad with her.

I took a deep breath. "Yes, yes I did. You eating isn't the problem, nor is how much you have eaten." I looked at the girl, bird, whatever she was dead in her eyes. "But if you have destroyed my kitchen..." That was as far as I got before she was out of the room like that thing in my dreams was after her.

I went to the bathroom first to give her a few moments, well that and biology wasn't being friendly. By the time I got out I was pleased to find her diligently working to clean up the place. To be fair it looked like it was a matter of her just leaving stuff where she dropped it after being done with it. It was a mess, but not 'I tried to make spaghetti and had no idea what I was doing' kind of a mess. In fact, I don't think she bothered with the stove at all.

What was still left was an empty ice cream container, a few of the packages that let me know there was no longer any cheese in the house, the ham container, strangely an empty pack of tortilla shells I know was full, and the remnants of a thing of spray cheese. The rest was already packed into the garbage.

"Geez kid, I didn't know you were that hungry."

She froze in her tracks, turned her head and looked at me. "Um, I'm not. I'm a scavenger." She gestured around. "Eat when you can, what you can." She shrugged.

"She doesn't feed you?"

"Sure, all the time. But it's not part of our deal." She went back to cleaning her mess. "And I hunt for myself, even down to actually hunting if I have to."

"I'm sorry, I forgot you were a wild bird."

"Na, it's all good." She looked around, leaned in and in a conspiratorial whisper, "But I owe you. If she woke up and saw this, I wouldn't get treats for a month." Then she went back to cleaning up her mess.

I don't know why, but it made feel better that she saw me as a co-conspirator. As I watched her flit from place to place picking up the mess she had made, it struck me how bird like she really was. Whatever she laid eyes on was what was next, and odder still her movements were both fluid and graceful one moment, then halting and jerky the next. She would suddenly stop with one leg still in the air, look around for her next target and pounce on it as if the trash would somehow get away from her.

"Do you spend a lot of time human?"

"Not really, no. It's too weird." She stopped and looked at me turning her head slightly to the side. "Not bad, just weird. Like, things move like they should, 'cept for my head." She leaned into another one of those whispers. "The eyes you see, they move, like, move a lot. I can even look at something without turning my head. Not being able to fly like this sucks, but it's the eye thing that gets me." She gave me a nod as if she had just shared great yet unspoken wisdom with me. "Took a while to get used to, that did."

She surveyed the area and seemed pleased when nothing else was out of place. "Course, it's got 'vantiges too." She suddenly held up both of her hands to me fingers splayed. "My feets up here and I don't got to walk on 'em." She leaned against the counter. "The whole lip thing is weird too. I mean I got to move 'em to talk and that took a bit. Had to learn from scratch I did. But I knew what the words should sound like, so it was a matter of getting lips, tongue, and squawk to all match up."

"Squawk?"

She looked at me and grinned, and I knew I had been had, I got it just before she opened her mouth and went "SKQUAAAAWK."

I looked at her in horror as she dissolved into a giggle fit. My head swung around to the couch to check for movement.

"Relax. She out. Takes her a bit to get to sleep sometimes, but when she's out, she's out. Nothing that's supposed to be will wake her up."

D'eun was right, there was no movement from the living room, and the sound of her breathing was steady. I turned and looked back at her.

"What do you mean nothing that's supposed to be?"

"If the sound is normal, you can be bout as loud as you like. Just don't be stupid with it." She rubbed her head, and I got the idea that was a lesson she learned the hard way. "But let a mouse fart in a room it ain't supposed to be in and she snaps awake."

"Caught you, has she?

She leaned back and nodded. "Every time."

"What's she like when she's not turning on the charm?"

"Ya seen it. I'd say she's got no charm, but I seen her turn it up. She ain't used it on you. That's just her. Sweet, kind, and eloquent one moment, bawdy the next, scary when it strikes her, and damn frightening when she needs to be. It's all her. If she's shining you, she don't like ya."

I thought about that, the bird didn't seem like a liar, well it didn't seem like she was lying. For all I knew she could be a hell of a liar. This time though? Why not take her at her word. "So, she really is a person who lives without pretext."

The noise that came out of the girl was this sound, half laugh half strangled choke. "Don't believe that for a second. You got her respect. She respects you," she jabbed a finger at me, "she respects you. Pretexts is disrespectful. But if you don't got it?"

"So, if she doesn't respect you she will lie to you."

The girl shook her head no again. "The lying things kind of big with her. She can mind you, but I only seen her do it a few times." She was frowning and thinking hard. "See, she's always going to be as truthful as things 'llow. But if she don't respect you, she is gonna hold things back or say things in such a way as to let you draw the wrong conclusion. Course she will also look you dead in the eye and tell you leaves ain't green."

"But leaves are green, well sometimes." I thought about it, sometimes they weren't green after all, and if you did a binary thought process sometimes not being green meant leaves weren't really green.

"Na, see leaves ain't ever green. The stuff in leaves. That's green, But not the leaf." She thought about it and nodded. "She won a bet with that one. See leaves ain't ever green, never gonna be green unless you paint them green."

I blinked, "A bet?"

"Long story. Guy was a jerk. Don't member all of it." She looked around. "You smell dead?"

I looked at her and raised my eyebrow at the odd question. "No, I don't smell dead, nor have I ever tried to smell the dead."

"No." She stomped her foot. "Something smells like dying." She looked annoyed with me.

Suddenly both of our heads turned to the same place and we both took off towards the couch.

Chapter 23

Izzy's breathing wasn't even, her naturally pale complexion was gaunt and slightly yellow, her curly dark brown hair was drenched in sweat. Worse she had kicked the covers off and I could see angry red lines creeping out from under the bandage, lines that hadn't been there before. D'eun took one look at her and started making this low chirping sound.

I reached over and touched her; her skin was burning hot. Carefully I removed the bandage, other than a whimper, Izzy didn't move. As I peeled up the bandage a scent like rotting meat greeted me, and around the wound itself the flesh had turned black.

"Go into the hall, you'll see a couple of doors, the one just past my room is a closet, on the top shelf you will see an orange box. Get it and bring it here, then get me a bowl of water from the kitchen as hot as you can stand it."

"But..."

"Don't argue, go."

She ran off to fetch the med kit Beth took with her to every SCA event she went to. I had taken a few first aid courses in college, but to be honest I didn't know what I thought I was going to do. I reached over and turned on the lamp to get more light. It wasn't enough. Then it hit me.

I got up and made my way to the other side of the room, past the kitchen and into the craft room. Stacks of every bit of Beth's nerd craft greeted me when I turned on the lights, but I wasn't looking for the sewing stuff. No, I needed my miniature painting lamp.

It was still where I had left it from the last time I actually sat down to paint, God it seemed like such a long time ago, back when I was more into gaming and stuff. The lamp is an armature with a magnifying glass set in the center of a light that was meant to illuminate whatever you were looking at through the lens.

I unscrewed it from the table and carried it into the living room. Once there I clipped it to the side table right next to her head at the arm of the couch, plugged it up to the strip and turned it on. Moving it into position I could see the stitching as if it was right in front of me. All of them were intact, but the seepage was discolored, kind of black and smelled foul.

"Here, I got a kettle on. The electric one, I don't use stoves."

I nodded. "When it clicks bring me it and a bowl." I took the case from her and opened it up. Beth keeps it well stocked, but her organizational skills aren't the best, either that or someone had pawed through it recently. I took out ointment, some alcohol pads, the bottle of alcohol, and fresh sterile bandages still in their wrapper.

As I worked I heard the click from the other room. It seemed quick but I think my sense of time was screwed up, because no sooner had it clicked than D'eun was beside me.

I took it, poured the water into the bowl and stopped myself just in time. I got up and rushed to the bathroom. "Come on, I'll show you how to do this." Together the two of us washed from fingers to elbows. Then we went back, opened a pair of gloves and I put them on. Sadly, with her claws D'eun ripped hers.

She was crest fallen. "Don't worry, just hand me things. Touch only the outside." It took a while, but with her help we got the area clean and I got a look at it. It was infected, but the lines looked like blood poisoning. That didn't seem right.

"You think he pissed on the shaft or something?" Or worse wiped it in human shit...

"Or something. If it was normal, I think the doctors would have cleaned it out."

I looked at her... "Like what?"

"Like something only she would react to. Something that would only affect a Fae."

"Shit, shit, SHIT!" I got up and started pacing. "How do we help her?"

"We can't, not unless we know what he used."

I started pacing. "What is she susceptible to?"

She stood up and looked at me. "I don't know. Lots of stuff, nothing, I never asked, oh hey boss, what do I use to kill you, now have I?"

"What the fuck are we going to do... it's not like we can just ask him what he used, we don't know who he is or where he is?"

She stopped and went dead still. "I know where he is."

I looked at her. "What? How?"

"I fly all over, I seen his house."

She knew where he was, I grabbed my keys.

***

A short time later, just long enough for her to realize I wasn't going to argue about if we should go, the two of us were in the car. D'eun didn't have anything useful like a street address, but she had a sense of direction like no other. I drove like a maniac all the while with her giving directions. We hit a few dead-end streets, took way too many wrong turns for both our likings, but she at least was so focused on giving me the lefts and rights and not that ways she began to really have fun with it.

By the time we got there I had a good idea of what the place would look like, and it was staggeringly normal. It was a house, hell it could have been any house on the street, and there were many of them. Small, ranch, basic white door, part brick part siding, basketball hoop in the driveway, and more importantly a truck in the drive. Plain old suburbia lost amongst the trees, any street USA.

I stopped the car and shut it off. In the passenger seat D'eun fidgeted. "Now what?"

"Now we knock." I opened the door and got out.

As if on strings she popped out the other side. "Are you crazy? He's a hunter!"

I shrugged. It didn't matter, I had to go.

We rang the doorbell and waited. I could hear someone moving inside, a light came on, the door sort of moved slightly, then nothing. As I was reaching up to ring the bell again it opened. Before me was the man, the hunter. Last night he was impossibly large, now he was big, but he seemed human. The look he gave me was of contempt but worry. He looked to me, then D'eun.

"Who's your friend?"

"Rain." The lie was out of my lips before I even thought it. I didn't want him to know who she was.

"Liar... but if you can still lie." The power seemed to go out of him. "Is she dead?"

D'eun lunged at him. "No, she's not dead." I put a hand on her chest and held her back.

"No, but she's sick."

"Thank god."

"Thank God? You sick bastard."

He looked at me and that anger returned. "Thank god she's still alive." The words were a snap. Then the anger fled out of him. "I'll go get my kit."

"What? Why?"

"To save her life." Then he looked at me. "My God, you're new at this." He seemed to regard me. "How long have you been at it?"

"I didn't know there was an 'it' till your son attacked me the other night."

"Are you even awakened?"

D'eun spoke up. "No."

He nodded. "I'll get my stuff and fulfill my oath." Then he looked at me. "I'll be right back."

With that he turned and went back inside. Guess we weren't getting an invite in.

Chapter 24

I didn't have much of a choice, I led the man that had tried to kill me just last night to my home. I wasn't happy, he wasn't happy, D'eun wasn't happy. D'eun was however in the car with me.

"This is stupid. It's a bad idea. He's going to kill us."

"Hush, if he was going to kill us, he could have." I tried to convince myself of that. "He could have just left her to die, ran us off, or worse shot us as trespassers."

"Trespassers, who would believe that."

"He attacked her and I at a restaurant, I don't think thinking it through is his strong suit."

"So maybe he's going to finish us all off together!" At this point she had worked herself into a panic.

"D'eun, hush." I took a deep breath. "It'll be ok."

"How do you know that?"

"I just do."

She leaned back against the seat and seemed to think about that, at least she did for enough time for us to get home. It was upsetting to me that Beth and I lived so close to the man who had tried to kill me.

I pulled into the driveway, and he pulled in behind me with his off-white pickup. I got out, went to the front door and opened it looking back for him. He and a mid-sized suitcase were right behind me.

I opened my mouth to be polite when he snapped.

"Don't you dare invite me in, don't give me that kind of power."

"What, are you a vampire?"

He pushed passed me, "Fuck you're green." He went over to the opening of the living room and looked in, I followed.

"Nice set up, where did you get the light?"

"Hobby store, I use it to pain miniatures."

He turned and looked at me funny. "Get outta town, they got stuff like that? Shit I'm going to have to go check that out. Be great for engraving prayers on bullets."

Wonderful I just helped a psycho.

He went around the couch. "Don't invite people, people like me, in. If you do you got to give them hospitality. For your kind breaking hospitality would have all your magic fail at once and leave you damn vulnerable."

I looked at him. "Why are you, you know, helping us?"

He looked at me. "Remember that deal she made while you held the knife?"

"Yeah, something about you quitting and leaving us alone."

He nodded. "There was a lot unsaid. Yeah, I had to quit, did too, that morning. Got my son thrown out too. After all he had us going after two humans."

"But she's not?"

"I told 'em you were. It will keep them off your back for a bit." He nodded. "Used the excuse the bell didn't work on you." He nodded again. "Well, here's the thing, see, if from that encounter, or from me being a hunter, you or she dies, then I broke the deal."

"And?"

He looked at me and frowned. "If I break the deal, either willfully or through inaction, my boy dies." He looked at her. "And with the state she's in, he dies slow, and painful."

I swallowed. "What? Someone is going to hunt you down? We didn't exactly tell anyone."

He was already making use of the surgical gloves. "Don't matter, your wyrd heard. It's your magic, you could both be dead and the wyrd wouldn't care, it would hold me to the deal cuz I entered it fair and square."

I didn't get it, but I made a noise that could be mistaken for anything or nothing at all. "So, I'm guessing the bolt was poisoned in case she got away?"

"Yep." He leaned in and squinted at the wound, slowly taking the bandage off. "You two might not be the worst, but some of the things I hunt are damn nasty. Both of you are basically human. Got a little blood in you from the beast, lets you do stuff, but you're still basically people. Being willing to deal fair like that, rather than her just sacrificing you and eating me let me know you weren't exactly what I was told." He took a knife out of his pocket and opened a pair of scissors off it. Then stopped and looked at me. "This is iron, you got any that are stainless, or better yet copper?"

"I got some titanium ones I uses for sprue cutting."

He gave me a funny look. "Sprue what? Never mind, go get 'em."

I went and got them, came back in and handed them to him. He nodded and started cutting the stiches.

"Hey now, what the hell?"

"Relax girl, got to let it bleed. Her body don't like whatever she's reacting to, got to let the bad out, got to bleed it."

"Want some leaches?"

"You got any?"

"No..."

"Then don't offer."

I watched in horror and mild fascination as he carefully opened the wound and got it to bleed. What flowed out was dark, oily, almost black, and the smell was disturbing. He kept at it, probing and poking, until a dark red began to more easily flow. He cleaned it up, then put pressure on the wound.

The entire time Izzy didn't move, didn't flinch, barely whimpered.

"Yeah, something on the shaft definitely had an effect."

"Something?"

"You lot can damn near look like anything and anyone. What harms you might boost her." He sighed. "It takes weeks of prep per bolt or arrow to make sure they will do the job." He took the bandage off and poured some of the alcohol right on the wound. "No reaction, it's not the wormwood."

"Can you narrow it down?"

"If I knew what she was sure. But you're so new to this I doubt you know what you are, let alone what your mistress is."

In a small voice from across the room, "She's Sidhe."

His face went pale. "That's not possible girl, she's human. Sidhe and human cross give you elves."

I looked over at D'eun, she wasn't answering him, she was gurgling.

She looked at me with absolute terror and pity on her face. Her hands were shaking and she was sinking slowly to her knees. "Cauaak." Forced its way past her lips. Then came the blood. It started flowing from her mouth as if her belly was full of the liquid and someone had squeezed her slowly. She looked at me pleading, begging.

I screamed and went over to her.

The hunters head snapped around. "Shit, she's a familiar." He looked at her, then me, then back at Izzy. "She broke oath, oh god, how is this possible. Sidhe can't be human." He opened his bag and started digging around. Finally he pulled out a bottle, its liquid was dark, the label was long gone, the shape was a simple round, but at its top stamped into the glass was a stag's head. He took it raised Izzy up and started pouring down her throat.

"Help me!" D'eun was convulsing in my arms, I know a seizure when I see one. Red foam kept pouring forth from her mouth, and her eyes had rolled back enough for me to see white.

"Nothing can be done, she broke oath with a Sidhe, she's as good as dead. If you value her, just kill her."

"No, there has to be a way."

He laid Izzy down and started pouring the liquid over the wound. It bubbled and orange sparks flew out. His next words were a whisper. "I see Brig owes you something girl, fight, I beg you, fight." Then he looked back over at me. "Shit. Earlier, when you lied about the girl's name, were you really lying?"

"Well I wasn't going to tell you her real name, now was I?"

"Answer the question, did you really lie about her name, or did you name her. Look at her, is that her name?"

"I don't..."

"Damn it, woman, stop thinking and think. Is it a name you would give her, you're a damn goth for Christ sakes, is it her name?"

A use name. A name from me to her. I looked down at D'eun. Was she a Rain? Yes, yes she was. "No, it's something I would have called her, something I wouldn't have looked at her funny for if she told me it was her name."

"Then call her by name girl, call her by name and call her back. I have your mistress."

I nodded, started petting that mess of black spikes gently. Her hair really was a crow's nest. "It's me Rain, I'm here. I have you. Come back to me sweetheart. I'm here. I have you. Please Rain, please come back to me."

Slowly, she stopped shaking, her body began to relax. Then the mist came and surrounded her, and I was holding a bird, a raven sat limp in my cupped hands. Tears streamed down my face.

A foot twitched. Then a ragged little breath sounded, and I could feel her breathing. One eye opened and looked at me and she gave the weakest, most pathetic little squawk I had ever heard, and it was music to my ears.

I looked back over at him in time to see him laying a polished silver cross on Izzy's chest. That cross had a ring around it, a Celtic cross. He leaned in and whispered. "Sorry, it's the best I got on short notice."

"How is she?"

"Poisons stopped, for now at least."

"For now?"

"Sidhe are immortal. They don't die, it's what they are." He gestured at Izzy as if it explained everything. "She shouldn't exist."

He looked ragged. "Want some coffee?"

He looked at me and blinked. "You really can't help yourself, can you?" He looked back at Izzy, and then to me. "Sure."

Chapter 25

As the pot brewed, he came in. "Look, I'm going to try to explain things. It's the least I could do with all the trouble I caused."

I tightened my hands on the counter, not quite ready to face him. "Why'd you come after us, after her."

"My son." He sighed. "He got a tip, went to follow the lead and found you."

"A tip?" I turned around and looked at him. "I've never done anything, hell until that night I'd never even seen anything."

He sighed. "A psychic maybe?" I raised an eyebrow. "Hey, you going to see what you saw tonight and question believing in Psychics?"

"No, just figured they'd be on your shit list."

"200 years ago? Probably." He took a deep breath. "Weren't a lot of distinction made back then. It was either human or not." He shook his head like he didn't agree with that. "But people can't help how they were born. Most ain't done any harm and some try to be helpful, in their own way."

I rolled my eyes so hard they hurt. "Right, and the rest of us are such monsters."

"Girl," He began, but I handed him the coffee.

"I'm not a girl, I'm a little past drinking age."

He took a deep breath, then let it out. "Yeah, but you don't know shit about what's going on out there. You're a damn babe in the wood."

"So tell me, educated me."

He took a sip and nodded. "Alright, like I said, I owe you that much." His eyes unfocused and whatever he was looking at wasn't here. "It's real, all of it. It's not what you been told. The movies, the stories, if they get something right it's an accident. Hell, most of the lore is just something someone made up cause they saw something and made the best of what they could understand."

"Take cold iron and you lot." He walked over to the kitchen table and sat down. "It affects you. Why? Who knows? But what exactly is cold iron?" He sat the cup down and looked at me. "When a smith takes iron and makes it, taking it from ore to metal, they get it as pure as they can. Then they take and pound it out into something. But to do that they got to heat it up. So is cold iron, iron that isn't forged?" He shook his head. "No, its steel that wasn't quenched. When you harden steel a layer of Austenite, or maybe its Cementite or some other such, but no if the blade is tempered one way it's not cold iron, in fact to be cold iron it has to have almost no tempering at all." He thought about it, seemed to consider then moved on. "Can't remember which is which. Don't much matter, my bolt heads are just cast, not cast-iron mind you, that's a different thing, but there you go. Most of the exact stuff's been lost to time as old technology made way for new stuff and no one remembered this iron had other uses." He sighed, "Anyway they also figured out that that same type of Iron screwed up a lot of different magics, so the lore tells us that the two are connected." He turned back to me. "They ain't."

He downed the rest of his coffee and without thinking I poured him another cup. "Thank ya. No, Vampires are real, they die by having their heads cut off or a stake through the heart but so do a damn lot of other things including you and me. No, it's actually severing the nerve that runs from the heart to the brain stem. You can accomplish both with either, though you can miss it if all you're doing is staking them. Werewolves are allergic to silver, cuts 'em up just fine, but a determined hunter can do it with just a knife or sword. Leads useless so better stick to silver bullets."

He reached up and rubbed his neck. "First time I saw a ghost it was like someone had taken a video of a person put it through an old VCR that needed its head cleaned. Most of them fight hard to be seen and those are the ones that want to tell you something or scare you off, or something. Leave 'em be and you're usually good to go. Poltergeists are another matter, they ain't people, they're something a person was feeling so strong it left an echo... and that echo is usually mad about something."

Then he gave me his full attention. "Then there's you lot. See a vampire used to be a person, and like any revenant, it still thinks like one. Yeah, it's got to drink blood, and it drives a lot of them mad, but they still think like they did when they were alive. So, some of them are right bastards, some ain't. Wolves? They're confused kids mostly. Comes on 'em early, and now they got to truck with a dog like thing in their head and most of them wouldn't know a wolf from a dog so they try to treat it like a dog, and it always bites them in the ass. Wolves ain't vicious but you got to treat 'em like wolves. If they survive to 'bout your age, they aren't usually a problem but again they're still people so it's a mixed bag."

He reached a hand over and put it on mine, it was a comforting gesture. His rough calloused hand on my soft one arose an odd feeling in me. "See you would be a changeling. You are a human with a Fae soul, you can live your entire life human, or you can let that soul grab you. If you do you will become a fae. I don't know your type and I don't feel like testing you since most of the test are unpleasant, but that's the thing, I ain't ever been convinced you guys know what you are until you decide. Fae come in three kinds, low, high, and wee. The Wee are little better than forest spirits. They're smart and cunning, but simple, and they're as natural to this world as anything else born here. The Low are, well you. Creatures part spirit, part real, part here, part there, part lots of things, part nothing but you. Each of you is an utterly unique thing in your own right, though depending on type you got traits in common. Of all of you, brownies I like the most. They are the ones in the shoemakers and the elves by the way. Helpful little guys one and all, who love to lend a hand. At least till they turn bad, then they're boggarts. They break shit, and yeah, they'll break an anvil somehow. Nothing is safe from them. All it takes to go from brownie to bogart is insulting them three times. I think they all started out as changelings like you, and well after a while it just changed them into the little things we think of nowadays. No one's ever figured it out one way or the other. All we know is a Changeling looks human, hell can be human until one day they aren't. Used to be people thought someone came in the night and replaced their sweet child with this odd one, one that might burn down the barn, or talk to birds, or make the crops grow better, or make them fail and it would all be the same to the kid." His other hand was steadily moving as he spoke, but the one on mine was squeezing reassuringly. "I'm not so sure about that one anymore, I think you're born with it and then one day make a choice."

"So, I will have to choose?"

"From everything I've seen? Yeah, you will." He let go of my hand and leaned back. "Now you guys, it ain't so simple as all that. Once you choose you won't be human anymore, your nature takes over, like with you offering me hospitality despite me being your enemy. It's just what you are, not who, what. Now, that isn't so bad if you are say a Brownie or a Grick, or any number of other things? But a Goblyn? A Hob? A Puka? A Troll? A Red Cap? Hell, there is all matter of nasty out there. Then you got the courts, and no I don't know enough about them to tell you who's who and what's what other than the Unseelie are the worst of the worst. See you guys have to feed on energy, just like vampires do on blood. Brownies feed off the gratitude of a job well done. I think it's why they hate to be paid or thanked personally, means the free lunch is over. You didn't used to be paid till the end of the job you see. Goblyns and filth, Hobs and mischief, Puka and terror. The list goes on. Puka are a fine example. They used to turn into horses, wait for someone to climb on and start off running. The good ones would run for days not letting the person off, feeding the whole time."

If that was the good ones... "And the bad?"

"They'd run for a bit, then hit a river or lake and drown the rider."

I turned away from him. "And Puka are horses?"

"Hell no, they're Fae, shape shifters of the wood, they're anything with hair. Dog, wolf, rabbit, horse, you name it."

I swallowed hard. "How would a rabbit be terrifying?"

"How? Girl... ma'am ain't you ever been hunting? You are hungry you see a rabbit, chase it, send the dogs after it, whatever, now you're in the deep wood, lost, don't know where you are and up to your ass in briars. Don't know what's what, hear a wolf howl in the distance and you're scared shitless, and all with a damn rabbit three feet from you calmly drinking it all in."

"I..." I needed to know. "I think I might be a puka. I've had dreams since I was a kid, being a rabbit, a dog, a horse, a deer, always running, always outsmarting something, someone, loving every second of it." I turned back to look at him. "Am, am I evil?"

He got up, walked over and gathered me into his arms. "I, I'm sorry, but no. It ain't that simple. You're not good, you're not evil, you're just you. You lead people on a chase and feed off the mayhem. You're dangerous, but not evil. No more than a mountain lion or bear killing and eating a hiker."

"Then why?"

"Why do I hunt you? For the same reason I would hunt a mountain lion or bear that attacked an ate a human."

I nodded, it made sense. "What about the high?"

He took a deep breath. "Now there we got ourselves a problem." He let go of me and backed up. "The high, well they all have names. Sidhe are just one set of the high. Now I want you to understand something. If you say yes to this." He waved his hand around. "You will watch everything you love and care about wither away. I don't mean your loved ones, I mean everything. You'll wake up one day and the United States will be as far from where you are then as Rome is to you now. You'll watch empires die, ideas, cultures and more. I don't think the old ones are actually allergic to or inept with technology, I think they are just like me. Too much newfangled shit to what is for them far too fast. You'll be in your wood, munching away on leaves and wonder why no one votes anymore, why no one does those vine things anymore."

I chuckled. "No one vines anymore now."

"Yeah well it will be much worse trust me, and no one is going to know what you're even talking about." His words were still gruff, but he was smiling. I don't know why that mattered to me. "But you can be killed. They can't."

I looked over to the living room, "But?"

"I know, like I said we got a problem." He picked up his coffee cup, brought it up to his mouth then looked at it to realize it had all leaked out the hole in the top already. He set it back down. "See, they are like angels, or demons, or devils. They aren't of this world to begin with, and death shouldn't have a hold on them at all. You don't destroy a rogue sidhe, you fight it, kill it and the body kind of goes funny but they just slip back to wherever home is for them and in a few years, a blink of an eye to them, they're back. They fight and 'kill' each other all the time, but they don't die so much as lose a name. Names have all kinds of power over them. As long as they have a name, they are alive. If they lose all of their names, they kind of fade into the woodwork until they wind up with a new name, usually something that sounds like one of their old ones, and they are right back. She shouldn't exist because she shouldn't have died to be reborn as a human, she is a sidhe changeling."

"So, you keep calling her she?"

"Not she, sidhe. Sounds the same, but big difference.

"So, what is one?"

"As far as you and I are concerned? Gods."

I choked. "What?"

He nodded gravely. "That's the thing, they are the ruling elite of the high. Their ruling elite are even more powerful. They carry names like the Tuatha, a group of them so powerful to even be considered able to join you have to be a master, and if they already have that kind of master, say a master fisher, a master healer, a master at arms? You still can't join. But that master fisher is who you prayed to for a good catch, that master healer to help you heal the sick."

Great, "I have a reincarnated goddess on my couch."

"Yeah..."

Chapter 27

The silence stretched between us, neither of us wanting to think about the implications of her being there, let alone her dying. Movement out of the corner of my eye alerted me and I looked up. There she was, naked from the waist up. For a brief moment I again saw her, all of her. Only it wasn't a girl, it was a warrior. All hard edges, hard lines, the set of her shoulders and the grim determination of death written on her face. She was leaned against the door frame holding herself up with her wounded arm, and in the other hand she clutched the cross. Her fist was clenched so tight around it her arm was shaking. Just as quick, the glimpse was gone, and Izzy was once again just Izzy, she was hurt, tired, confused and glaring daggers at our guest.

He turned and looked at her. Both of his hands went up away from his waist, palms out turned toward her. "Peace great one, I've not forgotten our bargain, only here to fulfill it. I mean you no harm and thank you and yours for your gracious hospitality."

"Can it asshole." She looked at me. "You ok?"

"Yeah, the wound was poisoned." I hesitated. "I didn't know what to do so I got him."

She nodded. "You did good. Did you tell him?"

"No, your bird did." At his words anguish came over her face, utter despair filled her eyes as well as resignation. "Worry not mighty one, your young one saved her."

"Remove your ass from my lips..." She stopped and regained focus around her pain. "Your lips from my ass before I sever them. I'm not your queen, I'm not higher than you, and if you bow to me,

I will have to kill you." He took a step back, confusion, not terror showed on his lined face. "You did good kid, how did you do it."

"When I went to see him, she had to take me, I figured giving him her name was a bad idea, so I said her name was Rain."

Her smile was a warm day breaking through the dark forest of my heart. "I like it. I'll have to make my deals with her again all over." She painfully made her way over to me, leaned in and kissed my forehead. "You did good, I thank you and am in your debt."

"You're not mad I brought him here?"

She looked at him. "He saved my life, took care of you, probably told you the naming trick. Offering hospitality to an enemy is how you make an ally." She turned back to me. "No, I'm quite proud of you." Then she whimpered. "Now if you will excuse me, I have to go piss."

Even limping out of the room, and no I have no idea why she was limping, she seemed graceful, if a little jerky in her movements. I knew a ballet dancer once, on stage she was amazing, in bed wasn't bad either. She, like Izzy, moved most of the time perfectly normally, but when she got sick, the stage took over. Her movements went back to being exaggerations, overly fluid.

I accused her of hamming for sympathy, now I wasn't so sure. Watching Izzy make her way down the hall, I think maybe they both just feel, or felt in Amber's case, to awful to bother trying to pretend to move normally. You don't accuse the girl who nearly died and really shouldn't be up of hamming it up.

Yeah, definitely owed Amber an apology.

I turned back to see our visitor was still in shock, "Earth to psycho hunter, come in psycho hunter."

Without moving, without blinking, "I've never met a high that didn't absolutely revel in making lower forms of life grovel."

I shrugged. "Well, now you have." I thought about it. "Met many, have you?"

"Two, both extremely unpleasant." He shook himself out of it and looked at me. "Everything is a game to them, a dance of words. Our old court systems were based on those games. Shooting the messenger is quite common when said messenger can't die."

"So, what's the big deal? You're not her court, and as such she doesn't want you sucking up."

He let out a sigh, "They don't see it as sucking up, they see it as the bare minimum respect."

The bathroom door opened, and Izzy came back out. "The bare minimum of respect is treating people like people, human or not. You already failed that." She made her way in, still bare chested, wound uncovered, and still looking pale. "But people learn, grow, become more than they were before." She sat down and looked at me. "I smelled coffee, any left?"

Smiling I turned and made her a cup, I knew how she liked it, it might be the first time she was in my home, but I'd been making her coffee for years.

"How are you human?"

Kind of curious about that, well about everything really, so I listened.

"How do we do anything? I made a deal."

His eyes opened wide. "But you're getting your you back."

I set the cup before her, and freshened his up.

She took a sip then looked at him. "Here's the deal. I like humans, always have. I fought for you, I lost. It's that simple. I still believe in you, still believe you are more than the rising ape, more even than the falling angel." She sat the cup down. "You have gifts that you don't even know about, powers and abilities you have been taught to curse, gifts you have been taught to ignore, and talents you have been told to bury despite being told literally by every god on this planet not to do that."

He snorted. "There's only one god."

"He seems to disagree with you but let's go with that. He point blank told you to not hide your talents, he point blank said the prodigal son was more welcomed than the good son, he point blank said go out, screw up and do better. Told you not to judge, told you to love everyone, told you to leave the eunuch alone be it by choice, accident, or birth, they became that. That whatever you do to the least, you do to him, and how have you treated the least? The frightened little thing that dares to experiment and risk screwing up? Hmmm? You kill them."

"The bible is quite clear." He began. That's as far as he got. A look from her let him know that he had strayed into territory that might have been just where she wanted him to go. He saw the trap coming, if not the depth and breadth of it.

"Yes it is, quite so. Paul, Moses, they made things very clear. Well one of them did, one of them you've never read and have been taught to ignore the people who still read and debate to this day what he meant and how it applies." She took a deep breath. "But let's make this simpler. You undoubtably claim to be a man of faith, and of the Christian faith do you not?"

He shifted uncomfortably in his seat. "Yes." His answer said he was wary of whatever trick she was about to use on him.

"As such you believe the being you commonly refer to as Christ was indeed God in the Flesh?"

A slight nod was his answer, then he added. "What of it?"

"And correct me if I am wrong, but that means you believe that said god came down twice, once on a mountain and once in the flesh, and gave a list of things, say 10 commandments?"

"Again yes, where are you going with this witch?"

A predatory smile spread across her face. "Just trying to see which it is, and apparently it's that you think god, your god, is a forgetful idiot that needs men to clean up his messes."

He flew to his feet, knife in hand and his blade stopped inches from her face. She never moved. "I will not be insulted by a slut in service to dark powers."

"Oh, I haven't insulted you, your belief is an insult to your god. I'm just pointing it out." She stood and looked at him. "Or would you like to call me a liar?"

Visibly shaking with rage, he spoke, "I shouldn't listen to you, you will twist the truth, it's what you do."

Her words were quiet, barest of whispers really, but they echoed everywhere. "Then break hospitality. After all our host would very much like to know the answer to this riddle. I think she, like most people spurned by the church, would like to know."

He shook himself out of it, saw the knife in his hand and I watched as it dropped from numb fingers. "I sit in the lion's den and know the rules to pass safely, yet I almost..." His words trailed off.

She reached over and put a hand on his arm. "I'll not call you on the threat. It's why I didn't defend myself. I will not call that a break of hospitality." She looked over at me. "And I beg you not to as well. Remember when I said they had been at this a while? They have so many so afraid to think they react instead of act, even when they know the danger of it."

"What are you talking about?"

I spoke up. "We were talking about it before you attacked. She used to fight for us, but she lost to people, her people, people who would have you limited, people who would have you acting certain ways without thinking." I looked at her. "Thinking, I take it is bad for them."

"All illusions fall apart with questions, no matter how good. One this large? You have to condition people to think its normal, natural, just the way things are, inevitable, in their best interest no matter how much it hurts, and to defend it with their very lives all before they will ever question it."

He slowly sat back down. "So, what's the answer to your riddle."

"It's the riddle itself. If your God is all powerful, all knowing, all present, all merciful, why has he been down twice, given out the same ten laws twice, added to ten good ideas, said treat even the most wretched as if they were him in disguise, why then did he need Paul to come back and clear up a whole list of people who were exceptions to that, be it the gays, or others? If your god is perfect and cared so much about people like us, why did he forget us twice? Why does man keep having to add us to the unworthy list?"

He blinked up at her, his mind working.

She shook her head. "Answer it in your own time. I don't care what god you serve or don't serve. That's your business. But the people who added that little caveat to your faith? They've done it to every faith out there for well over two millennia, nearly three. That's who I fight, who we fight, and oh yes, there are many more out there like me."

"Is that who sicked my son on you two?"

"Short answer? Yes. Long answer? Probably not. We're not talking a vast conspiracy here, there's no cabal of whatever sitting in a cavern over a caldron whispering dark words and dark secrets. That would have fallen apart long ago. No, there is only words whispered at the right time, a grand illusion crafted and self-sustaining, and ever growing. Every once in a while, people shake off enough of it for people to grow a bit. Then it reasserts itself and pretends that it was responsible for that growth."

"Surely there must be a name for it, I've been at this a while, I might have some idea, something I can do, some way of protecting myself if what you say is true." Even I could see it on his face, he wasn't convinced. He believed she believed it, she had said enough for him to question, now he was looking for a name so he could shake it off as the ravings of a mad woman.

"Certainly, you know the name well and have fought for it and its ideas your whole life. It's sacred to you and the deaths it's caused are all excused."

With a snort, "Let me guess, Christianity?"

"No, Civilization."

Chapter 28

"You're barking mad." It took me a moment to realize he wasn't the one who said that, I was.

They both turned to look at me, she had a little smile on her face, but one eyebrow was raised. He looked if anything, amused. "The girl" he looked at me again. "Sorry, young lady has a point."

"Really? Think on it a moment, what are we sold every single time? Gay rights? A threat to civilization. Socialism? Communism? Capitalism? Global Warming? Islam? Christianity? Pagans, wiccans, beatniks, Blacks, people of color, all of it. Most atrocities in history? We're just spreading civilization to the uncivilized."

I found myself just blinking at her in astonishment, "But civilization has given us everything."

"Really like what?"

I looked over to the guy, he nodded. "Um, vaccines for one, electricity, science, you know everything."

She looked at the hunter. "See. We will defend it without thinking." She turned back to me. "Through most of our history, civilization has been against science, even now it is. Sure, when it does something useful, they love it and claim that it's because of civilization we have it. The reality is a little different. Most of our largest leaps forward have either come from people on the fringes of civilization, be they inventions, medicines, or what not, or from times when civilization was on the brink of total collapse and it was let the thing out or die."

"But we ended slavery, we got rights as women, we've gone to the moon!"

"Civilization made slavery, told women they didn't matter, hell before civilization you would have never had to worry about coming out gay."

"No, I would have just been raped."

"No, you would have just killed the man trying to rape you and no one would have bothered to ask why or blame you. What you want, what we all want is community and mutual protection. That existed long before civilization, and they got plenty done with it. Civilization came along not in the first larger cities and nations, but later, they point blank said, we're civilized, and you aren't so why should we listen to you?"

The hunter just nodded, "It's not the coming together or working together or technology you have a problem with, it's the 'this is the way things are done and if you don't do it that way, you're lesser and beneath me' you have a problem with."

She nodded. "How much further would we be if we worked together no matter our differences?"

I looked at her pleadingly, "But you have to have a single voice, a direction?"

"Sure, absolutely, so why is that single voice the one that says this one group of people over here don't matter for anything and should be ignored?" She looked at him. "For you it's weird not human things, for others it's people of your faith, for others it's queers, and the list goes on."

He nodded, "Yeah but there are some good people in that... some bad ones too. How do you tell?"

"Every culture out there has a story where the odd person coming into town is really one of the gods in disguise, everyone has that 'be good to the stranger, the traveler, you never know when it's literally your god.' Your own faith tells you that whatever you do to the least? You do to him." She looked at us both. "So how do you recognize the bad apples from the good?"

I thought back to every single person who had ever yelled at me, treated me like dirt, some spit on me, some did worse. Why? I was just the girl pouring their coffee, I didn't have a real job, I was a nobody.

"How they treat their servers."

At the same time, "How you treat the least."

She nodded at us both. "There are dozens of small groups of bad people out there, but even then, most of them are just people. They have a list of people who it's ok to ignore." She turned and looked at him. "Just be good to yourself, then be good to others. Do this and we're good."

With that she got back up and left to lay down, the talk had drained her.

The hunter stood as well. "I think." He paused, "I think I need to get going as well."

I smiled at him, "Come on, I'll walk you out. "

"Thought that you might."

Once we were outside both of us spoke at once. "Look." He shook his head and chuckled, I could feel my face brighten.

"You first." He said.

"So how bad will it get? How long before I'm not me, just a bunch of urges I can't control."

He seemed to think about it, then answered. "Before her? I would say as soon as you made the choice, though you would never realize anything changed. Now?" He fidgeted uncomfortably as if he was a man 30 years younger trying to talk to a crush. "Now, she's thrown up everything I thought I knew and just shredded it like smoke."

"So, she's right?" I tried but failed to keep the surprise out of my voice.

"What?" He looked at me, "No, god no. Civilization ain't the problem. She's as mad as a hatter on that." Then he kind of deflated. "Her conclusions are crap, but her questions, they're just about damn spot on. If I had to guess?" He looked back over his shoulder as if he could still see her though the walls. "I'd say she was one of the mad, a kind of seer." He looked at me, "She let slip who she was?"

I shook my head. "D'eun, the bird, said Izzy didn't remember. The way she said it I'm guessing it doesn't matter."

"Damn odd that, names and titles are everything to them."

"So." I looked at him, "What makes you think differently now? Why are you, why…?" I trailed off. "I don't even know what to ask."

"Why ain't I as worried about you as I was before?"

The only response I could manage was a nod.

"Cuz, her name should matter to her, me being polite should matter to her, she should be as much if not more so enslaved to her nature as any of 'em. She ain't, and that's worrisome."

"Why?"

His voice got quiet, far away, small. "Cuz it means I might've killed good people."

I leaned forward and hugged him. He stiffened up. "What are you doing girl? I tried to kill you too, you know."

I didn't let go, I just talked. "I don't know anything about this new world, but I'm gay. My mom taught me one thing that helped me out more than anything else. 'Everyone has done and said homophobic things, everyone. It's how the world is. When someone tries to learn better you help them, when someone is hurting because they realize the damage they did, you hug them." I gave him another squeeze. "Of course, she added to that, and if you find them going back to it you knock their block off."

He chuckled. "I think I like your mom." His hand found my hair, petted down then rested on my back. "Kevin."

I leaned back breaking the hug and looked at him. "What?"

"My name, its Kevin. If you two need me, you call."

I nodded then looked at him. "I'm Lydia, come get coffee anytime."

He smiled as he gave me his number, then patted me on the shoulder as he walked off to his truck.

Getting back inside I went to check on my two houseguests. Izzy wasn't laying down, she was by the fireplace holding D'eun. She looked up at me while she cradled the bird in her arms. "See our guest off safe?"

"Yeah, he's gone."

"Thank you, I owe you more than you know."

I sat with her and put my hand on her shoulder. "She's my friend too."

"You fit right in, so fast. She likes you, I like you, in less than a day you save both our lives." She looked at me, tears streaming down her face. "I will forever be in your debt."

"So, how do we get her voice back?"

"First, she needs to heal. To do that we basically pamper the hell out of her." She let out a soft chuckle. "It's going to give her a bigger head than she already has." She stroked the bird's head with her thumb. "Then we use her new name to bring her back. Should be easier than last time, after all I don't have to go in small increments, she already understands what's happening."

I nodded. "I'm guessing she has to agree?"

"No, I could do it against her will, but that just seems cruel to me."

"So, what do we need?"

"Not much, all the items are fairly easy to come by, I'm betting you have them all here. It's the meaning and attachment that matters more. Getting a voice box is easy, getting the voice box from a beloved toy is a bit harder."

"Does it have to be a voice box?"

"God no, last time I used a speaker out of an alarm clock I had for 15 years."

"So, we get stuff like that, then what?"

"We put them all together and I teach you to do the ritual."

"Me?"

"You named her, she's yours now."

Chapter 29

The next few days were interesting. With her system no longer being poisoned, Izzy healed at a good rate, together the two of use started getting the items needed to bring Rain back to herself, and they were indeed laying around the house. A voice, a body, a mind, and so on. I wound up using a laptop I had from college, it was covered in stickers all of which meant something to me. That covered the mind and voice nicely.

The body was a bit more difficult, luckily, we had Rain to help us out. D'eun was, after a fashion, still in there. Izzy promised me she would still be D'eun, just more and once she could make up for the broken vow, then she could even reclaim her name as D'eun, but for now we needed to always refer to her as Rain. It was the second day when the bird started being up and about, and the first place it headed was the kitchen. To her credit she did manage to throw away the bag after stealing an entire bag of potato chips large enough for her to crawl into. Luckily it was half empty.

As for a body? I was a goth doll collector back in college, just one more geeky thing to do, and one more money sink, or so my depression told me. As such I had plenty to choose from. The only ones left were the ones I really liked and cared about, I had long since sold off most of my collection... after the break-up I needed the money. That was before Beth took me in.

For a few years now they just sat in a box.

I laid them all out before her and had hoped she'd pick the vampire one. It was from a series dealing with monsters, if they were in high school, and I loved them. It took a while for her to decide, and it was fun watching her pick through them, but eventually she went with the gargoyle one. By day three we were ready.

I was all excited for my first real spell, but all in all, it was kind of anti-climactic. We got all the stuff together, took it apart, sat it all at Rain's feet with her name written on everything, and I do mean everything, and I read what was on the paper.

"Rain, please come back, I miss you." I flipped the paper over expecting more. "What? That's it?"

T-shirt, ratty jeans and bare feet, Izzy just smiled at me. "Did you mean it?"

"Yes, of course I meant it."

"Then that's it."

"But nothing's happened?" The frustration was building. Rain, D'eun, whatever, was pecking at the stuff in front of her and seemed to be examining it. "Isn't there something else?"

"Like what?"

"Like a spell, a chant, a circle for gods sakes."

She put her hands on either shoulder and looked at me. "Yes, of course there is. And they are very precise. They are meant to do one thing and one thing only. They focus what you want, all of it into a point so clear it cuts through reality itself. I can give you those words and they can focus you. But they will only do what the spells say because that's what they will focus you on. But that's not what you want." She petted my face. "Say it, out loud, what do you want?"

"I want my friend back."

She smiled at me. "Then say that, say it again and again, call her by name and call her back. Focus yourself, your will, everything you have."

"Will it always work like that?"

She blinked. "Yes, always, though it won't always work."

"Why not?"

She thought for a moment. "Ever tried to hammer a nail with a screwdriver?"

With that she left me, and I knelt by the bird and just kept repeating it over and over again, "Rain, please come back, I miss you."

I said it repeatedly, I said it in different voices, with different tones, sometimes they were pleas, sometimes commands, sometimes they were just words. I fell asleep saying those words.

***

A noise woke me, someone was once again in my kitchen and they were banging around pots and pans. I got up and went to see. Once more I saw a naked ass, this time it was pointed out of the refrigerator so that the light off the pale flesh all but blinded me. This wasn't Izzy's white bottom, nor was it Beth's. I'd seen that. No, this ass was shapely, but pallid. It was as if someone had put light grey makeup all over their body.

Then things got weird.

Something raised itself up and it was connected to that butt, it was a wing, a hand wing, no feathers, just demonic flesh like a bat, but the same pale gray skin as the ass.

While my mind raced trying to figure out what it was seeing, my body either displayed a complete willingness to die, or more sense than the rest of me had, it turned on the light.

A woman, in her early 20's with pale grey skin, pink hair with grey stripes, beautiful huge grey eyes, stood up and looked at me. She was naked, and had a thing of string cheese in her mouth.

"Hey Lyds." She mumbled around the snack. "Didn't want to wake you, you looked so cute sleepin'."

I stood looking at her dumbfounded. The voice was more or less the same, but the body was completely different. What's more is she sported two huge bat wings.

"D'eun?"

The girl in front of me hissed at me. "Shhhhhhh." I watched as this woman crawled over the table to get to me. "Don't use that name, it's not me anymore. Not right now anyway."

I closed my eyes and counted to ten. "Rain, get off my table." I kept them closed till I heard feet on the floor.

Over the next few hours, we figured out she could now cook, had a huge selection of songs and movies she knew by heart, way too many of them anime, spoke fluent Japanese as well as German, and, if she concentrated, could make those wings go away. For the record, there was well over 25 foot of wing to that girl. We also found out they came back when she went to sleep.

Izzy thought it was funny as hell, Rain didn't understand the joke, and I was just glad to have her back. After the first night, due to the wing problem, she reverted to bird when she went to bed.

As for Izzy? Well, I found out she was ambidextrous, like for real. She could write two different things one with each hand. She spent most of her time drawing out the shop and coming up with ideas. Her method seemed to be start at nothing, complain to herself, get up, go outside, smoke, come back in and draw simple sketches and then repeat.

When she wasn't obsessing over that she was planning her game, and at that she became quite engrossed. She would message both Beth and Allen, as well as two other guys she knew, all trying to get an idea of what they wanted to play. As she said. "I can craft a world out of nothing, I just need to know who is inhabiting it."

On the more personal level? We watched movies, talked about everything, anything, philosophy, politics, religion, she was interested in all of it. I got to dust off some of my rarely used psych education with her. She made me laugh a lot. She was a great cuddler, didn't put her hands in places that made me uncomfortable, listened to me and what I said. By Friday night she was insisting on getting up and cooking for me.

Her chili was something I never thought I would have, good chili. I like chili, it's ok don't get me wrong, but I've never had good chili. It's either eh chili, or its too hot or its not hot at all and kind of just there.

Hers? It was amazing. First off, I got nervous as hell when I saw how much cayenne she was putting in it, then she used red kidney beans and well, I always had pinto. When she was done what I got was a chili that burnt the lips only slightly, danced on my tongue, and set my throat on fire. She swore she had more recipes like that. Called it her inner short order cook.

When Beth came in about nine, I hadn't realized how much time had passed. It surprised us both when the door opened.

"Hmmm something smells good."

From the other room, I heard Rain hit the floor. She'd been obsessing over my computer all day.

Beth looked that way. I jumped up. "I got it, it's probably just the bird." I said it loud enough I hoped she would get the picture. I made it to my room in time to see Rain dissolve into that black mist smoke stuff and scooped her up. I quickly set some of my books down on the floor and looked around for what made the noise.

Nothing was visible, so I looked at the bird and whispered. "What the hell was that?"

In a soft voice she croaked, "I was looking up C++ and trying to learn it, I must have dozed off cuz next thing I know, my side was on the floor. And I bent one of those new stupid wings."

"You're the one that picked the only doll I had with wings." I hissed at her. Quickly I tucked her under my arm and walked out.

The two of them were already going over the details and talking about where to get things and so forth. "The easy part is going to be the decor. Old, grungy, gritty, etc.. Most of it can be salvaged for nothing or next to nothing, then I can turn it into something that looks like something. The hardware is going to be the money sink."

Beth practically chirped. "No, I love your idea of the Blu tooth radio hub thing taking over for the piped in music. It lets people tune into stuff they want to hear by pairing."

"Exactly, they pair from a menu while they wait for their coffee." She grinned. "Wall to wall geeks bobbing their heads to music only they can hear as they're jacked into your local mainframe."

"Any idea on how much?"

"Are you kidding? Not much, you could have 20 or 30 base devices slaved to things like a streaming service. They bring their own devices, but we use software to keep them from hitting forward and such, or better yet it will kick their headsets to the next paired device. Writing the code is the only real hurdle then, well that and the hub that controls them, but most base computers should handle it."

While they kept at it, I put the bird on the table, got more chili and went to the living room. All in all, things seemed to be ok.

Well, almost everything.

Chapter 30

That night after Beth went to bed, Izzy and I sat watching an old favorite from my anime collection. Once through with the disk we'd spent the last two hours going through, I got up to change it and I stopped.

I looked back at her and just smiled. Tomorrow was Saturday, it had been a week since I fell into this and I had to admit, I liked her. She was kind, funny, irreverent, but she was also serious when need arose, independent as hell but also willing to let herself be taken care of with only a little fuss. Yeah, I could do a lot worse.

"I know you like directness, so..." I took a deep breath. "I want it, I want to date you. I want to see where this goes." Her face lit up just like I knew it would. It did my heart good to see it. No rejection, just an acceptance of the fact I wanted to try. "You may not make a good top for me, but I couldn't ask for a better girlfriend."

Her face fell a little at that, but her smile was still all for me. "I'll take it, goddess knows you're worth it." She got off the couch, her arm was still bothering her but nothing her meds couldn't handle. She came over and petted my face. "But I got to ask, what's with the caveat. I mean, if you're not into it, you're not. I want you, not what I want to make you. But..." She made an off-hand gesture.

I had been thinking about it all week, I knew exactly what I wanted to say. "I gave up on that a long time before I met you. While it would be great, and I certainly wouldn't object to some interesting play if it comes up? Dynamic wise, you're not my type. You are in everything else, and that's what matters to me."

We were close, so close I could feel her. She wasn't holding what I said against me and that was worth more than she would ever know.

"I thought I got a good read on what you wanted in that, I'm sorry I was wrong. Care to correct me or should we just." Her hand brushed my shoulder, "Drop it."

I leaned in and kissed that hand. "You're too sweet, to soft. God I've always wanted that in a girlfriend, but in a top? I need hard. I need someone who can take me."

She stopped moving. "Say yes."

She was so still it stopped me too. "What?"

"You have to say yes. I'm more than willing to abide by your decision, it is your body, your life, your call. But you've never given me permission to show you that side." A tremble was starting in her hand. "If you want to see that side of me you have to do two things, you must tell me a safe word, and you must say yes. Otherwise, anything I do, no matter how it might seem, to me will be abuse. Abuse of power, abuse of trust." She looked me in my eyes. "Your read on me might be achingly accurate." Then she smiled. "I might be small time for what you want. But I don't do either one of us any favors if I don't at least offer. I'm equally important in this. I need to know." She gazed into my eyes. "Not that I'll mind sharing you with a Domme if we find one you like better. I think I know who's bed you'd be snuggling your sore butt into."

God, she meant it. This wasn't ego, she just wanted a shot. "Ok, so what safe words do you use?"

"I always go for the stop lights." She started moving herself slightly to the left and right, it might have been a quiet wiggle if I had eyes for anything but her and her smile. "Yellow means slow down; I need a second to adjust. Somethings off don't stop just give me a sec." She took and kissed my fingertips. "Red means, bitch get off me oh god, no, what the hell was that. Stop right now, don't pass go, no cash for you."

I couldn't help it, I laughed. She might not be a good top for me, but she certainly knew how to turn a phrase and make serious talk fun. "And green?"

Her head kind of just fell to the side in this half-cocked position as she side eyed me. "Either bitch please is this the best you got, step on the gas my ass is falling asleep, and I'm bored enough to notice." Oh god I had been there. "Or." Her face softened again. "All systems go I'm loving this." She leaned in and almost kissed me. "Granted if that was the case, I would be expecting moans and whimpers not intelligent conversation."

I closed my eyes and shook my head. Leaning forward I put my forehead against her. "Can't you take anything seriously?"

Her voice was just a whisper as she moved her face a little closer to mine. "I take everything about you seriously." Her tongue darted out and touched my lips briefly. "I just don't see why we can't have fun while we do so."

"Yes."

"You mean it?"

"Yes."

Without seeming to move, her hand was around my throat. Breathing became harder and my world got fuzzy. Fear flooded me as I realized how strong she was. I sucked air in and found I still could. I was restricted, her hand was there but it wasn't cutting me off, it was... hard to think.

"Mine." The word was a growl, something deep and feral. Her hand, the one not holding me up, roamed over my body, shoulder, stomach, arm. "Mine?" This time it was a whisper, an invitation, a question.

"Yours." I answered.

Her free hand explored more, my arms both of which had gone to my side, where her hand touched my skin, electricity flew from her and made things jerk. Her other hand kept up its cruel game on my throat, letting me breath yet somehow stealing the breath from me. Her free hand made it to my stomach then to the outside of my hips. I could feel where her hand was, both at the moment and where it had been. My world slowed and she was somehow touching every place she had touched.

A whimper escaped me. "Please."

"Please?"

"More."

She let go of my throat and pushed me against the wall, her lips brushed where her hand had been, her lips were molten steel against my already hot skin. She took her hands and pulled up my shirt and laid both of them on my bare stomach. My world turned into those hands and only those hands. As she kissed me, seared me with her lips, her hands were as cool as water all over my abdomen, caressing my ribs, but they never went further north, nor south.

"More, please?" The words were a whimper, a breath, nothing more. Yet she heard them. Her knee forced my legs apart and she brought her upper thigh up and ground it into me. She caught me just right to feel all of it, the power of her was as a wave washing over the shore, my shore.

"Cum for me." She whispered against my throat. It wasn't a request, but a command. I felt myself give way, come close, then go over. As I did she bit my throat. I felt her conform to my body as she rode it, rode me and my orgasm to the ground.

Then without seeming to move, I could still feel her teeth on my throat, I felt her lips by my ear and her breath was hot as she whispered, "Enough."

It was the last thing I knew as I drifted off.

***

To say I woke up would be to say I fell asleep, but it didn't feel like I had. I was on the couch, being held in her arms.

I sat up and looked around. A cover was over me, the show was queued up but not playing, and as I reoriented myself, she handed me a glass of water.

"Thank you."

"No problem."

I looked myself over. Except for my shirt still being untucked, I couldn't tell anything had happened.

She took a deep breath. "Sorry about that, I'm afraid I got a bit carried away."

Confusion swirled around me. "What?"

She pointed at me, "Your neck. I..." She hesitated and looked uncomfortable. "I sort of marked you?"

Given everything I had seen this last week, images ran through my mind. "Marked me? How?"

Her face showed her chagrin, but like she wasn't going to let that stop her. "I kind of left teeth marks on your throat."

I blinked, got up and went to the bathroom. Turning on the light I looked in the mirror. It wasn't a hickey. What it was, was a near perfect set of teeth marks right over my windpipe, and I hadn't even felt her do it. Well, I did. I felt her bite me. I knew she was biting me. I just didn't care, and I certainly didn't realize it was this bad.

I jumped out of my skin when Beth spoke. "You know, a little makeup will cover that right up."

"God, scare the hell out of me why don't you." I turned back to the mirror and stared at the near perfect circle on my throat. "It's just weird, that's all. I didn't realize it at the time."

"Sounded like you had fun."

I thought back, the last time I had a good scene was years ago. Whips, chains, a gag... I got to let go, just not be me for a moment, just float. "Lex was the last time I felt that."

"You dumped Lex."

I started laughing, I couldn't help myself. "She got too possessive. Started…" I stopped myself. Lex had started doing the things a good top does. Hell, she did everything I wanted. "Lex just felt wrong."

"Izzy has a reputation."

I stopped and looked at her. All tops have a reputation, but when said like that it's not usually a good thing. "You're just telling me this now?"

She came in and closed the door. "A couple of her exes accused her of some things, some pretty bad things. Devil worship being chief amongst them. But also, rape and abuse."

I grabbed her arm and through gritted teeth, "Jesus Beth, and you set me up with this woman?"

"Calm down Lydia." She smiled at me. "I'm not going to let a monster near you." If she only knew. "She's a freak, like we are. Of the couple of girls she's dated, two have said this crap. One you know, Rylie."

I rolled my eyes. Rylie calling her a devil worshiper and rapist made sense. She was a fanatic who hated being gay, always went after women, then always broke up with them and spread rumors about them. "God, she dated that bitch? Why?"

"She's a sucker for red hair."

I thought about it. "Interesting. And the other."

"A girl named Pam that Allen knows. He says she had a rough time, but is better now. Most of her other girlfriends seem to say the same thing. She was the best thing to happen to them, she's loyal beyond measure or expectation, she snores, she forgets things, and they all wind up calling her Mamma."

I raised an eyebrow. "Like a kink thing?"

"Only for one of them."

Interesting. "So? Like, why is she single?" If these women liked her so much, why wasn't she with them?

"Remember Sarah from Introduction to Economics?"

"Crap, that was Sophomore year. Wait, wasn't she dating someone she said was too super special and great, then dropped out?"

"Yeah, she had a breakdown due to her dad. She was dating Izzy at the time. Izzy was devastated, she didn't know what had happened to her for years. According to Sarah, that's pretty common for Izzy, she gets ghosted a lot. Sooner or later they come back, but they've moved on with their lives in the meantime. They still love her, and most ran to an extent because Izzy can be a bit intense, but I'm guessing you figured that out."

"Yeah." That was one word for it. Scary as hell was another. "So, you really going through with this Cyber Cafe thing?"

Her eyes lit up. "Oh yeah, I loved her ideas, I don't know if they will work, but I love them, I can't wait to see what all we can come up with."

We took it out of the bathroom and to the kitchen table, I made coffee and soon Izzy joined us, she had been outside enjoying a coffin nail. I sat and listened to them till three a.m. and I have to say, even I was getting excited.

"Of course, you can wear anything you want, like anything. Dust off all your goth stuff, trust me it will fit in."

"Like, my club wear and stuff?"

"Sure, why not." Beth's grin was as wide as I had ever seen it. "Remember that purple and blue industrial outfit you put together one time?"

"Oh god don't remind me, that outfit was ridiculous."

"It looked good on you."

"Yeah, well, some people didn't like it."

"Screw them. You wear whatever you want, you're the co-owner, I expect you to set a good example."

I started laughing, "We'll start a riot."

"Good."

All the while Izzy just sat back and watched, enjoying Beth and I being friends, talking of the future, and it was amazing. It was so odd, it was like I was back in college, hanging out with friends.

Chapter 31

Despite the late night, Beth was up and ready to go for work, she even sang in the shower. While I was definitely happy for her, I really needed to get her a bucket so she could carry a tune. Sleeping in wasn't really an option, I could hear her talking in the other room so I knew Izzy was up too.

I couldn't run from last night, I had to face it.

Grabbing pants, a tee, and my new bird, I scooted out. Izzy, it seemed, liked to cook more than I thought, she had made omelets. When she saw me, she smiled, nodded, and got out two more eggs.

Beth reached over and poked me, "Didn't expect you up sleepy head."

My stomach knotted up. All last night I had dreamed, they weren't good. That thing was still after me, and while I managed to duck it all through, it still didn't make for restful sleep. To tell the truth, Beth's caterwauling was a welcome break.

"I know that look, rough night?"

"Stupid forest chase dream again."

She reached over and hugged me. "Thought you stopped having that one years ago."

"Yeah, lucky me." I looked around. "So, what's up with you two?"

"Oh, I'm taking her in so she can get her car."

I looked over at Izzy. "What?"

"Yeah, need to do some stuff at home, get some of my gear to run tomorrow." She gave a shrug with her good shoulder. Took her a week, but she finally learned not to shrug her right. "Give you some time, let you sleep."

"You weren't even going to say goodbye."

She put her hand to her chest. "Me? Never. Too much of a Wham! fan to leave you hanging on like a yoyo."

Beth nearly spit out her coffee. "You like Wham!?"

"My mom did. Grew up listening to a lot of that music."

I looked at her, "You always make sneaky song references pertinent to the conversation?"

"Always." She leaned over and kissed me on the forehead. "Letting you know you're dating a weirdo out the gate, not going to spring it on you later." She set the eggs down in front of me and went to pour me coffee.

Should I let her ride in with Beth? I mean it would mean postponing the talk for a bit longer. Of course, that would also mean I got up for nothing. When she set a cup of coffee down in front of me, it made the call for me.

"You know, usually the sub fixes the top coffee."

Beth looked over at her, then me. "You know, she has a point."

"Perhaps, but one, you haven't said yes. You said yes to me showing you that side of me last night. Then you skedaddled during aftercare when I said I left a mark, which, fair. But we haven't exactly discussed it since."

Fair point. She was being a caring girlfriend and I was still picking at the whole thing. Wait, she said one. "And two?"

"Two? Two is simple. How I decide to treat my sub or slave or bottom or whatever is up to me. If I decide I want to let them know they are special to me by bringing them coffee, so be it. You say thank you Mistress and understand you are mine to do with as I please in any way I please... within the guidelines of whatever we discussed or agreed to."

Beth looked over. "Not to nitpick, but slaves do what they're told when they're told, they don't get limits, or safe words."

The look on Izzy's face let me know Beth had just hit a sore spot, maybe even a trigger. "Really? I disagree."

"Disagree all you want, it's what slave means."

"No, slave means I own you. Think of it like a car. I can lease a car, a sub, they still own themselves; parts, labor, and things are taken care of by the dealer, etc. A slave would be owning the car. I am responsible for everything, I own it. It's probably a bad idea for me to do things like not take care of it, it's a worse idea for me to do things outside of the owner's manual, like throw it into reverse while driving down the highway. A slave still has the ability to safe word, to set limits, it is a top's, their owners, job to respect those limits. No other possession seems to be as maligned as a slave. We're not going to stick our cellphone in the sink or run our laptop through the dishwasher. Yet we seem to think it's a good idea to ignore what a scene slave wants and do whatever we wish with them just because we own them." She stood up and looked at Beth. "That's not use, that's abuse. You certainly wouldn't just kick your dog just because you could, now would you?"

She didn't wait for an answer, she went to the living room, rummaged in her purse and walked outside to the back deck.

Beth mumbled under her breath, "Yeah, but my dog didn't sign up for being a slave with the express knowledge that anything and everything I wanted done to me and more would be done even if I said no either." Then she sighed and looked at me. "She's got a point, but she misses the point you know?" She deflated. "Some of us just want to give up control." I reached over and patted her hand. "Think she's mad with me?"

"I doubt it. I think you hit a trigger."

"Oh fuck." She ran a hand over her face. "She's... a lot of her exes came out of bad relationships. She's probably dealt with some shit."

"Or been through some, she is a trans woman after all."

"Fuck, I don't know if she ever bottomed. She just like showed up one day on campus and was just kind of there. I have no idea what she's been through. Geez, I'm an asshole."

"No you're not, but maybe I should take her in. Give her time too cool off."

"Yeah. God." Beth got up and looked to the back porch. "Just, just tell her I'm sorry. Ok?"

"I will."

She went to walk off, then looked back at me. "Maybe she's too soft to be a good top for you, not because she's soft but because her past will keep her from pulling the trigger."

As Beth walked off to finish getting ready, I took my coffee and went outside. She had a point, if Izzy was too damaged to give me what I needed... but after last night I owed her a chance.

Izzy was leaned against the railing, looking out to the small clump of trees in the back yard. She looked steady as a rock, but she wasn't using her gothic holder, just bare filter touched her lips as she inhaled.

"When I was a girl, god, six, seven maybe? My image of myself started to form in my head. Katharine Hepburn and Audrey, Hedy Lamarr, Julie Newmar, Carolyn Jones," she turned and looked at me. "Natasha Fatale." She continued. "You know, the basics."

"I would have figured you for a Morticia Addams."

"That's Carolyn Jones."

"I thought it was Anjelica Huston."

"She was, in the movies. Did a hell of a job. Hell, she updated that picture in my head."

"I would have figured you for a Lilly Munster."

"Yvonne De Carlo." She just smiled. "No, she was my monster mom."

"No, I get it, a lot of strong women, smart, kind of dangerous, femme fatale." I looked at her, "That's why the holder?"

"Yeah well, I got a kink, what can I say."

"Not a popular kink."

"Guess not."

"Beth says she's sorry." The timing couldn't have been worse, the words were barely out of my mouth when we both heard Beth's car start up. The look on Izzy's face said it all. "Look, she figured, hell I figured you might want some time to calm down." I took a deep breath. "Besides, I wanted to talk with you."

"It's cool." She looked off into the distance. "So, what you want to talk about."

I closed my eyes. "First off, did you mean what you said in there?"

"About slaves? Fuck yeah."

"Well, that and the coffee thing."

She reached over and cupped my face in her hand. "You deserve someone that actually works to show you that you are worth it. I can have you fetch, carry, crawl, grovel, beg, whimper, whatever we decide on, and still bring you coffee in the morning to watch your eyes light up because you know someone cares."

I smiled at her, "You're just one big goofy romantic, aren't you?"

In answer she reached out again and cupped my face.

"Yeah, so I want to try, you know. You're a top, maybe an odd one, but still. I want to try." I kissed her fingertips. "So, what now?"

"Well now, you get homework, I want you to think about..." the back door swung open.

Beth poked her head though, "Izzy, you ditz, am I taking you or what?"

I blinked, "I thought you left, I was going to take her."

Izzy just chuckled. "I'll be back." She leaned in and kissed me, a brush of sensation on my lips. "Just figure out what you want, write it down." She turned and started walking towards Beth. "Medical stuff I need to know, hard limits, soft limits, safe words, kinks, dos and don'ts, I want an owner's manual." She stopped and winked at me. "Because I intend to truly enjoy my new toy." With that she was gone. Back in the house and off for a while, giving me time alone to think, to process, to plan.

I liked that toy line.

Chapter 32

As I opened the door to go back in, Rain flew out with a squawked "Be back" trailing after her. I went inside shaking my head and reminding myself she was a wild bird. Undoubtably, she had bird things to do.

I quickly went to get paper and a pen and sat down on the couch.

There I sat, staring at the blank sheet, remembering from my writing classes that what stood before me was the white bull of legend. I could feel it staring me down, peering into my soul as if to ask, "What now?"

"Right, what now?" Setting it aside I got up and went to the kitchen, as per usual when Beth left first the morning dishes were still on the table. I found myself smiling as I took and started to clean up, right down to my uneaten omelet. It smelled ok, the grilled innards were onions and mushrooms with cheese gluing it together and congealed quite firmly in place.

Ugh, if I was thinking of food in such a way, no way was I eating it. Still, I'd been too hungry during college to just throw it away. It might not look good now, but ramen never did, and I distinctly remember it tasting fairly awesome.

I secured the leftovers and went back to cleaning. To be honest, it wasn't just when Beth left early, if I left first, I came home to dishes. Yeah, doing dishes, nice and normal.

Normal. What was normal?

The refrigerator kicked on cutting the silence like a knife and I dropped the dish I had been holding. Its crash let me know without looking that I needed to get a broom, yet I stood there leaning against the sink. I felt the first tear roll down my face, it was hot, wet and soon it wasn't alone.

Turning I walked over, got the broom and dustpan and started to pick up the larger pieces. As I did, I realized it was my cup, my favorite coffee cup, I hadn't even realized I had taken it off the table. Now here it was, two pieces on the floor one in my hand, and small fragments, scattered like the dust they had become.

My cup, gone.

My life, gone.

As a kid, I ran around the woods, sometimes as a bunny, sometimes as a horse, sometimes as a wolf loping along on a hunt. It was a game. In college, I found a girlfriend who took me to my first furry meet up, all those anthros. I thought I had found my people. Still, something was off, and I wound up with some otherkin from the group, people who thought they were animal souls trapped in human bodies.

It was fun.

For a while.

I joined a coven, that lasted a month. They were fine people, but it was always so hollow. It didn't help that this jerk of a jock once barged in and demanded we do some magic for him. One of his buddies dragged him out. I think he wound up baking cookies for them as an apology. I'm not sure, it was my last meeting. I too wanted magic.

Now I had found it.

"Careful what you wish for." I turned the broken thing over in my hand. "I'm sorry, I don't know how to put you back together." I realized I meant it. Sure, there was glue, maybe epoxy, but it wouldn't be the same. Neither of us would be.

My mom was raised Baptist, after I came out... we didn't go to church a lot after that. I tried looking for something there but got tired of being told I was going to hell if I didn't lie about who I was.

"And now apparently what I am."

I gathered up the three main parts and put them on the counter, then swept the floor.

"I want to date her, you know? I really do." I said to the broken cup. "And the, whatever the hell that was." It wasn't a scene. It was just, just...

"A few moments of intensity like I've never had before, that what it was." I wheeled back around to the broken cup. "Like how the fuck did she make me cum in my pants? I mean, how the hell?" My cup didn't have an answer. "Now I want her to collar me? To top me?" Yeah, that seemed healthy. "Co-dependent, that's what that is."

I sat the broom down and went to turn off the water. Sitting down at the table didn't help, my coffee cup with its broken body just kept staring at me. "Now I'm supposed to decide if I want to be a Puka? What the fuck is a Puka?"

In the silence that descended, I actually expected something, someone to answer me. I even looked around. A ghost, an angel, a demon, a god only knows what.

"Figures, find out the supernatural is real and of course I'm not important enough to have my own ghost or guardian spirt or whatever." I tapped my finger on the table. "I wonder if I can get one?"

Life is strange. I had always believed that. But this? Strange was staring at it from down the hall, ducked behind the far corner waiting for the next thing to blow up. For Christ's sake I had saved a raven's life by renaming it. Don't get me wrong, I loved D'eun, I loved Rain, they were definitely the same bird, and I was happy to have her back. Sure, she had picked up a few quirks from my laptop.

My laptop, my old laptop, I gave a bird a body, voice, and mind with my old college laptop and a doll. Now I had a familiar of my own and had to make sure she didn't raid the fridge or bogart the last hotdog.

"I now have a wild bird that can turn into a 22-year-old college student who uses my fridge as a base of operations."

Saying it out loud really didn't help.

"And now you've said both that you want to date her... which is true, and bottom for her, which is also true." It was, it honestly was.

It had been years, don't get me wrong, unlike the dolls, he sat right beside my bed. He didn't have a name to start with, he was just bear. Then when I was about six he lost an eye, and my mom put an eyepatch on him. Yeah, he may not have a name, not like that, but he was my Patches. It had been years, but now I was sitting on the couch with my arms wrapped firmly around that ratty old teddy.

My ratty old teddy.

I glared over at my broken coffee cup. "Patches gets it. Don't you Patches?" With those words it hit me how childish I was being. I wrinkled my nose and went to put the bear down, only to realize, I had been an 'adult' these last few years... and was deeply unhappy.

"What makes someone an adult anyway?"

It was a damn good question. Paying bills? I did that and would keep doing that. Looking after myself? Did that. Cleaning? Yeah, my room was a mess, but it was a clean mess. I looked around at the rest of the house. I cleaned, Hell I kept this place clean, I even cleaned when I was angry or upset.

What even is being childish?

Every Karen, both male and female, ran through my head at once. The only word I could think to call them would be childish, and they were also definitely adults according to everything I had ever been taught. Everywhere I looked there was adult after adult who were beyond miserable, but my mom? Hell no, she had a ball.

What did my mom do that was so different?

"She long ago gave up on trying to be an adult and just was one. If she wants to play, she plays, if she needs to work she works." Visions from my childhood of her dancing to CCR, Coven, Sabbath,

Hendrix, Joplin, and many more flashed in my head. Money was tight, and still she danced. I went goth, she introduced me to both Ozzy, and Bauhaus. Through her I found Bad Seeds, Sisters of Mercy, and so many more. As my tastes grew, she grew with me. She's the one who found Shakespeare's Sister about the same time I was finding Rasputina. She's the one that taught me not to care, if I liked the music and it spoke to me, then rock on.

I decided to do something I hadn't done since I was a kid. I sat Patches in the chair, went over got the broken cup and sat it in the other chair. I looked between the two of them and ran back off to my room. I took the clothes and put them up as I went. Not the neatest thing in the world, but I wasn't just going to throw them on the floor. Books went back on shelves and I kept going until I found what I was looking for. To most it was a crappy ceramic mask, but to me? I made Chester in high school, half white, half black, it was a prop for my first real character, a thief from back in the day who had a serious religious streak.

I ran back into the living room and set it up on the couch so it could look at me. "Ok guys, here's the deal." I took a deep breath. "I know I haven't done this, in like, forever, but I need your help." I felt silly, I felt foolish, but this also felt right.

"I like her; like, like her like her." I nodded and started pacing. "And I really want to date her." I turned back to my little council. "And I absolutely will." Good, I was on good solid ground. "And I kind of like being tied up?"

I shot Patches an apologetic look, only to relax as I almost heard him say 'duh'. "I know, I stopped covering you when I was 19." Suddenly I felt very embarrassed. "You've seen things."

Patches just sat there, no judgment.

"Anyway. I really want this, but it's also way too soon. I mean the dating thing; I can do the dating thing." I thought about it, "Maybe a little slap and tickle." Yeah, like that described what I was into.

"And I know, mom said don't do it if you're ashamed of it, and I'm not." That last part sounded so fucking defensive. "It's just after... her... I feel like a fool for doing that again." Images of those three weeks, three weeks tied up, beaten, ran though my head.

If it wasn't for Beth.

"It's not the same, it's not even remotely the same." I looked at them all. "She honestly seems to care about me." No making me chase her around, not overly clingy if I was paying attention to anything else, not cutting me off from my friends. "She's a little too perfect." A thought sprang into my mind unbidden. "Well except the, well you know."

"It's so strange looking, its uncanny." I had toys, quite a few. They just weren't realistic. "That was not what I was expecting." What exactly had I been expecting? Not that, that's for sure. It was so small, underwhelming, it looked like some sad shriveled up old alien from some low budget sci-fi movie.

I sat down on the coffee table. "I wonder if it works still?" Did I want it to? Images of it turning into my more interesting toys sprung into my mind. Then a pink rabbit popped out the top. I snorted. "I mean, I really liked having a strap-on used on me."

God was I bi?

I tried to think of me with a guy... it didn't work. I mean, I had a whole list of male geek icons I thought were hot as hell, I just wasn't sexually attracted to any of them. I am a lesbian, not dead.

"Izzy's different guys, I know she is." I think that might have been part of the problem, I did know it. For as unreal as this last week was, I think things might have just got a little too real.

Chapter 33

I heard the rattle of an old pickup pulling into my driveway, looking outside, I didn't recognize it. Old, rusted, collared with a white top, it wasn't dirty, and seemed to be well taken care of, but it was, well old, older than the 80s, but it didn't have the rounded look of the fifties. Undeniably a classic just not one I was familiar with. The sound of it was distinctive, you could hear the personality of the thing, it practically bragged about being a pickup, a work truck. Not someone's vanity, but a modern-day mule who didn't give a damn what you thought.

Inside was Izzy, but not like I had ever seen her. TV movies make country girls that look like her and yet never seem to get it quite right. Those curls were up in a messy ponytail, there wasn't a lot of makeup on her face, but definitely some, the red flannel over the white t-shirt was well worn, and when she stepped out she even had the faded blue jeans that had once been something she undoubtably had to be poured into and now had just conformed to her body. Her boots gave her away, they were black work boots, scuffed and real leather, with cute little silver skull and crossbones charms riveted into the sides. As she came to me, I saw more telltale signs, the belt, the earrings, her lipstick was a little too dark, yet none of it ruined the image of the cowgirl getting out of her pickup. She was a walking country song, but one by the man in black, or one of the old bad boys of what was once outlaw country. Definitely more Copperhead Road or The Night the Lights Went out in Georgia, than Red Solo Cup. She suddenly reminded me of my childhood, but in all the right ways.

"What's the look for?" She asked as she came up and petted my face.

"You're a country girl."

She gave a snort, "Grew up a farm girl, lived way out in the woods." She looked over at the truck. "Had her since I was 15. My dad had to fix her up once I flipped her. Took a while to find all the parts." Then she ran her thumb over my bottom lip. "I'm just me, Goth through and through. Country, City, it doesn't matter, dressed up or down, I'm me. I just am."

Chuckling I took her hand and brought her inside. "It explains why you went for a car reference earlier."

"Don't get used to it, I pretty much used everything I knew then. Not a car girl."

"Really?"

"Nope, I can change a tire, my oil, and check the fluids. That's it."

"Something tells me you're a bit more handy than that."

"Sure, if you want your cabinets fixed, or your deck. Give me a hammer and I'm great, give me a ratchet not so much."

"A carpenter huh? How did you get into computers?"

She went and sat down, or would have, my mask was in the way. She adjusted and sat beside it, not messing it up.

"It's just building stuff, wood or circuits." She shrugged one shoulder. "So, what's up?"

That didn't take long. "I think we need to talk."

"I'm all ears."

"I don't want you to collar me." I said it as fast as I could, I needed to get it out. Opening my eyes, I looked over at her. She wasn't mad, didn't look shocked, just had one eyebrow raised. "At least, not yet."

"Go on."

I took a moment and gathered my thoughts. "It's like this. I like this, I want this. Hell, you seem to keep hitting all my buttons." Her walking up the walkway ran through my head again. "Even ones I didn't know I had." I mumbled to myself. "And it's great, I want that, I want you, I want to be with you. It's just..." I trailed off.

"It's been a week, you only knew me as the girl who got coffee from you, you've been dragged into the deep end." She looked at me. "And you're acting like I'm going to be upset you want to take things slow?" She pulled back a little, her warm exterior cooling considerably. "Who hurt you?"

"What?"

"Lydia, I don't know what you're used to, but you don't just jump into these things. I like you, hell I'm pretty fucking sure I love you. But I barely know you."

I blinked at her. "But..." I was so confused. "But last night you, well you." Her putting me against the wall ran though my head.

"Yeah, I did. I needed to know, just like you did, if we were compatible. Sure, it feels like it, that doesn't mean we are."

"But, the..." I was confused. This was happening so fast and yet, it wasn't.

She reached over and took my hand. "Yeah, this is a whirlwind romance, and we should dance in that wind. It might last a day, a year, or a lifetime. I want to grab every second of time I can with you, to show you how I think you should be treated. If you asked my honest opinion right now, I would gladly tell you that I would be honored to own you for the rest of our lives, to marry you and be with you as my wife and my sub and slave and whatever else we decide." She squeezed my hand. "But that's my opinion, not reality. The reality is there are two of us in this, me and you. Your views, your wants, your needs are just as damn important as mine."

She reached up and cupped my face, then gently picked my chin up. "Hey, look at me. It's ok. You could feel the exact same way I do and still want to take it slow and it would be perfectly ok. I know I do."

"You want to take it slow?"

She did this kind of nod thing with her head, it was cute. "Yeah. I mean, slow for us. Like if we feel like doing things, we do them, if we feel like trying things, we try them." She took a deep breath. "What we have should be a journey, not a destination." She offered her hand. "Walk with me, for as long as the road is under our feet."

I lunged forward and hugged her. "Thank you."

She petted my hair with one hand and rubbed my back with the other as she rocked me. "You're not a prize, not a trophy, not a game to win. I want a partner. One that lets me take care of them and serves me as I do them, sure, but a partner."

"You mean it?"

"You're a person. I don't care if you tell me you are an end table who needs to be waxed every day, or an uber slut who needs dirty things, human, nonhuman, whatever you want to be no matter how humiliating and degrading or not, you're still a person. You should be respected for it, and always my partner so I can give you whatever you need."

"You have the oddest view on the lifestyle I've ever heard."

"Yeah, well which is more dominant? The person who takes someone like you and breaks them, makes them think it was their idea, who never questions what is done to them, and doesn't have the ability to think anymore? Or the person who wants someone who willingly gets up every day and makes the choice over and over again to serve knowing what's going to happen to them and looking forward to every last bit of it?"

That stopped me cold. I had always thought that training was to, to... to what? "Wait I thought training was to make sure I obeyed and crap like that."

"Training should be to get you used to what you want as some of it might embarrass you, or make you upset, it's to get your body used to what you want, it's to make sure you know how a dominant wants to be addressed and what you should do. Same as it would be for say, you training your coffee house employees."

"But..."

"But?" She pulled me in. "But nothing, anyone who tells you, you must be that, that you must do this, that submitting is this over here, they are making it so you won't leave, won't even think to leave."

"But contracts."

"Yes, and we'll have one. They aren't a 'you can't leave my dear'. They are the guidelines we both agreed to. A road map. Hell, the page of a coloring book that is your body as well as the crayons I use. I get to color however I wish, use whatever colors I wish, that's true, but I have to stay within the lines and I have to use the colors set out. I can do anything I want to you, at any time, within that framework." She kissed my forehead. "Right down to there being times that I can't color at all. Anything else is abuse dear. It's the only way I can slap you across a room or shove my entire hand inside your body. We both agreed to it. End of story. Anyone who tells you different is wrong, or worse an abuser."

I held on to her for dear life and broke down crying.

Chapter 34

Three years ago...

"Aren't you the one who came to me, told me you wanted this, begged me to do this to you, slut?" The whip came down across my back again, but I was too numb to feel it.

I was too numb to feel anything, and I had been for weeks. "Yes mistress." The words were automatic, rote, as meaningless as saying my times tables. It had been days since I had showered, even longer since I had eaten anything that wasn't on my prescribed diet, but that at least I had asked for. She'd offered to help me lose weight. She was right, I had asked for all of this.

My choice.

I felt my body respond to what she was doing again, it cut though the numbness. More proof I liked what was going on, that this was where I belonged. Well, except the shower thing. The shower thing bugged me.

I was either tied to the bed, or up like I was now. Exercise time. Sure, I was tied down so I would lose some muscle mass, and the diet so I could lose weight... but why couldn't I get a shower?

Her and I had been dating for about a year. It was fun. I really liked the stuff we did together.

Someone is knocking at the door, great. If I could have just taken twenty more lashes, I could get a fucking shower. Now someone's gone and screwed it up.

Crap... is that Beth?

Shit, I can't let Beth see me like this.

***

Now

"Of course, I couldn't move. She came in, it was horrible. The cops were there, they got me down." I was sobbing, I couldn't stop. "I spent about three weeks in the hospital. She..." I couldn't name her. "The bitch, she, she told everyone we broke up and that she hadn't seen me. I'd been in her house about a month, but Beth never gave up. Hell, my mom came up here to help look for me." She hugged me tight. "Beth never believed her. Started stalking her, saw me through a window and called the cops."

I looked up at Izzy, "You didn't know any of this?"

She shook her head no. "Three years ago? No. I was, going through my own thing then. I knew you weren't at the shop, but when I asked, Beth just said you were sick."

"May I ask?"

"When I saw you with the young lady, and let go of the possibility of dating you, I went and... it wasn't as bad as what you went through." She nodded to herself. "Was that her?"

"Yeah."

"All I knew is you were sick, gone for a few months, and when you got back you weren't, well... you didn't dress anymore." She sighed. "I figured you had put it all away."

"I put everything away." I had, I had stopped gaming, going out, doing anything other than the bare minimum. "I thought I was growing up, moving on with my life."

She sighed, "Her name was Bunny."

"Bunny? Really?"

"What? She was cute. Red hair, liked to laugh. I needed a roommate and she moved in. It was all quite nice to start with."

"What happened?"

"The short?" She went still. "She asked for things, I gave them to her, she would break down, I would take care of her. Give her time to process, she would accuse me of not being interested. I would adjust, she would have fun, then... break down accuse me of being a monster and the cycle would start all over again."

"Wait, what?" I looked at her. "She would ask you to do things for her, to her, then blame you when you did?"

"She would have these huge fits, call herself worthless for liking what was happening. I would do my best... then she would calm down and things would be fine for a few days. Then it was 'you only want me for x' I would do what I could to show her otherwise, then it was you don't do x to me anymore are you losing interest' and on and on." She had set her hands in her lap and was now staring at them.

"Jesus Izzy, how long?"

She took a deep breath. "Let's see, I met Bunny about three months after I realized you were taken, we split up last year? I think?"

"You think?"

"Well, it was Christmas time. So yes."

"Fuck, Izzy, that was four years. I was only with Shadow for two." It took me a second. "When is your lease up?" She turned away. "Crap, you've been paying for a lease you can't afford for a year by yourself?"

"No," She still wasn't looking at me. "I was ok, I had savings."

"No wonder you were thinking of moving away." She'd missed me not being at the shop for months, because in her own way she too was tied to a bed. "I'm going to tell you the same thing my therapist told me, it wasn't your fault."

She turned back to me, a sad smile on her face. "That's the rub, isn't it? I know what a narcissist is, I've pulled more than a few women out of that situation, a couple of men too. But me? I just sit there smiling and eating shit."

I took her hands, I squeezed them, "How about we meet in the middle and work together on this, all of this. You don't be Shadow, and I won't be Bunny."

She smiled at me. "That would be the point love." She rolled her eyes a bit, "Well that and a shit load of communication."

That sounded just perfect. "Deal."

Chapter 35

The next week was blissfully boring, at least compared to the first. Izzy started spending a lot of time at the house, both with me and with Beth. They started drafting up what everything would and should look like and Izzy started building some of the stuff. Rain split her time between us, coming to me, checking on Izzy, begging for scraps out the back door, any door, either at home or the shop.

The days wound around going from the agony of dead times to the hectic madness of the rushes. It was home, and it was mine. Before it was a place I worked, but now? Being part owner made me look at it in a new way, belonging felt good. Oingo Boingo showed up and were happy to see me back, everyone seemed happy. Rita actually hugged me when I got back. She was making a hell of a manager. Mom and Doc both missed me, but it was Walt that surprised the hell out of me the most after I had been back for a few months.

"Here." I looked up and there he was, he'd just sat a huge box down on the counter. "It's not much, but I don't like you not being here. So, I thought I would get you something. You know, to welcome you back."

The box wasn't wrapped, just a hunk of cardboard about three foot cubed. Hesitantly I opened it up. Inside, on a white towel was a patch of utter darkness staring up at me with gold eyes.

"She's had all her shots. I found her last week, one of my neighbor's dogs was trying to play with her, but she wasn't having it. I asked around, no one knows who she belongs to, and since you started dressing witchy again." His voice trailed off. "I missed seeing you dress like that. It suits you."

Years, Walt had been coming in and being a pain in the ass for years. "Walt, are you autistic?"

He shrugged but didn't look at me. "It's no big deal if you don't want her. I just thought, you know, since you're finally starting to be yourself again."

"Walt, is it ok if I hug you?"

He looked at me and blinked and his mister asshole mask came sliding right back into place. "Yeah, sure. I'm not going to turn down being hugged by a hot chick. I'm not gay, you are. Shit yeah, I'll take a hug."

"Walt?"

"Yeah?"

"Just don't talk."

"Ok."

I went around the counter and hugged him, and he hugged me, no he didn't do anything creepy. I took my new little mew machine back into the office and made her as comfortable as possible.

Closing time saw Rita and I locking up when Beth and Izzy came in. Izzy had a carpenter's tape and soon the two of them were going over sketches and taking measurements of everything.

Rita eyed them both suspiciously, "So we actually doing it?"

"Doing what?"

"You know," She hesitated. "The thing?"

I looked over at the two of them deep into the sketch book. "Hey Beth, are we really doing it?" Rita reached over and slapped my shoulder.

"Doing what?"

"You know, the thing!" I said, surviving Rita's death glare.

Beth stopped and looked around grinning as she saw the world she wanted unfurling before her mind's eye. "Yeah, yeah we're doing it."

Rita and I could both hear the joy in her voice as she spoke.

"Good Chica, cuz I got some outfits I can't wait to wear here. I'm going to rock this place."

I looked over at her from over the cash register, "Really? You're into cyber punk?"

"Me? Never heard of it." Then she grinned. "Until I found out what a lot of my industrial friend were into."

"You're Industrial?"

"Hell yeah, love me a thumping base." She started dancing, swinging her hips from side to side. She looked over at me, "You gonna gatekeep me white girl?"

"Hell no, I'm just a goth. Couldn't gatekeep you if I wanted. Besides, never been into that crap. Like what you like."

"Hell yeah, that's what I'm talking about. Knew I loved you girls."

Beth laughed, "Hey Rita, once you two get finished, come over and let's pick your brain, I want your opinion on all of this."

Once the front was taken care of, I took the drawers back to do the counting and get ready for the deposit. Furious meows greeted me as soon as the door was open.

Beth had got her some wet food before she left earlier, and I took and emptied the rest of it into her makeshift bowl. She was black, but I thought I could see darker black stripes amongst her fur. She really was beautiful with her gold eyes and scraggly kitten fur sticking up all over the place. Watching her eat was funny as she pawed it with claws out, growled and hissed at it despite her mouth being full of food at the time, and genuinely gave the impression that she was a fierce beast devouring her prey. Poor thing must have been starving when Walt found her.

"Kitty, how do you like Kitty?" On she nommed. "Star? You like Star? You have beautiful golden eyes, two stars in your blackness." I reached down and pet her, not that she noticed, food had her complete attention. I thought for a moment. "Miss Howl? No, you don't look much like a Howl." She seemed completely oblivious to my presence, instead choosing to eviscerate her prey. "Darkness, you like Darkness?"

She stopped moving, slowly looked up at me, blinked those gold eyes, "Mreawwow" and quickly returned to her food.

"Darkness it is."

Cash was perfect, orders got done, paperwork signed, trash out, machines cleaned and ready for tomorrow, and stock looked good. I went out and joined the three of them.

"Let me get this straight." Rita said looking at Beth, "Both the lesbians drive stick?"

Izzy snorted around her drink. "Hey now, I may drive stick, but that's because my classic pickup is stick." She smiled at me as I came up to join them. "Besides, I'm pan, stick, automatic, I'll drive it all."

Conversations to walk in on, oh boy. "I like the control, gets better handling if you ask me."

All three of them burst out laughing.

I shook my head. "How did we get here?"

Rita looked over. "Well, it started out on the millennials vs boomers, and tool use."

"To which Izzy pointed out Xers get left out altogether making them truly generation nothing." Beth added.

Izzy spoke up, "Which led Rita to talk about stick shifts and this idea that only men could drive stick."

"And of course it's because they got so much practice wrapping their hand around something long and hard to get themselves where they need to go." Rita was snickering at the image, and I was starting to. "To which I got to wondering, does that make gay guys the best drivers in the world?" She finished.

I couldn't help it, the images in my head just weren't decent. "So how did I come up?"

"Well," Izzy began. "I pointed out lesbians did just fine with stick, as long as it actually functioned as advertised and didn't try to control everything. You just had to handle them right."

"Right," Rita chimed in again, "Then you said both you and Lydia knew how to drive manual." She looked at me, "That's when you came up."

I sighed, "Where do people get this idea that women can't drive stick? Is there someplace you got to put your dick into a manual to get it to turn on? If so I've never had an issue. Besides, I'd just shove a dido in if it did."

Silence descended over the table as all three of them looked at me, then burst out laughing.

"God, I missed that snark." Beth looked over at Izzy. "Thank you, I like having my girl back."

"Oh no, don't blame me." Her eyes danced as she looked at me. "She's always been there, just healing. Just because I showed up as she was loosening up? No." She smiled. "She didn't need me to bring it out, she just needed to know it was ok to."

Beth looked over at her. "God you are just so much cheese."

"Thank you."

For a moment everything got quiet, then Rita asked. "So, I hate to ask, but... How do I put this? Any of you girls ever left the bedroom," she stopped and considered for a moment. "Less that satisfied?"

The three of us burst out laughing.

I looked over at her. "Men don't have a monopoly on being selfish lovers."

She looked disappointed. "I thought since, you know..."

Izzy looked over at her. "That since they all had one, they knew how to play with one? Girl, I've had women that didn't know what a g-spot was before I showed them. I got lucky and my first girlfriend let me sit on the floor and just play around inside and see what everything was and where it was."

Beth looked at her, "Seriously?"

"Hell yeah, a lot of women are actively discouraged from exploring themselves. Sure, most find the clit, but I can remember being told that clitoral orgasm was childish. Women, even me, grew up hearing all kinds of bullshit, and since it was their moms or aunts or whoever that told them that they believe it."

I nodded. "I know my mom tried, but it wasn't until I got to college that I found out yeah, a woman can get pregnant on her period. I grew up thinking you couldn't because my mom had been told that, so she told it to me."

"Not that you lot got to worry about that."

Izzy got a far off look on her face. "Yeah..."

Beth looked over, "While technically true, I know I want one at some point."

Rita got embarrassed. "Sorry Chica, forgot you went both ways."

"Yes, I do, but that doesn't mean much. A lesbian that wants to be a mom still has the right to be one, we do have turkey basters after all."

The cis het girl turned bright red. "I thought that was just a stereotype."

I looked over and smiled at Beth, winking at her, "More like an urban legend. We all know some woman who had a friend who knew someone who did it. Give me invitro."

"Oh you want to be a mom?" She asked.

"I've thought about it."

"What about you, creepy chick? You want to be a mom?"

Izzy sat uncomfortably and Beth and I looked at each other. I hadn't realized Rita didn't know, and I wasn't going to out her.

Finally, our goth looked up, "Oh in a heartbeat." She said solemnly. Then she got a wicked grin on her face. "But lacking the plumbing? Not going to happen."

Rita's face softened. "Oh Hun, I'm sorry. My mamma had to get a hysterectomy right after she had me. In a catholic family? One kid and it a girl to boot?" She nodded. "I feel for you Chica."

For Rita the discomfort was past, how she missed the few times Izzy had come in with a little stubble was beyond me. For everyone else? I traded another glance at Beth. Izzy could have left it there, part of me hoped she did. Not for her sake, but for Rita's.

Izzy didn't do a lot of backing down. She calmly picked up her coffee, "Actually, more like born without it. Though I did carry a respectable six inches that was as big around as an energy drink." She took a sip, seemingly not caring about the fall out. I knew that defense mechanism all too well.

For her part Rita's eyes got wide and her face got red. She processed all the girl talk we had been having with Izzy right there, the reality of it hit her. Then she just blinked.

"Oh, you like my Uncle Carlos." She shook her head. "He gets so pissed every damn month. I get to listen to him bitch about 'can't these estúpida pañales come in a scent other than pedo flores?'"

I stared at her and realized so was everyone else.

"What? I'm Catholic not a bigot." She chuckled.

The laughter was a good palate cleanser, and let us move on, or so I thought.

"So Chica, I get it, you're a woman. Your heart and soul aren't your body. Got to ask though." She looked Izzy dead in the eye. "Could you like show my next boyfriend what to do? I mean, the last one was a complete wreck. I took that pendejo by the hand and he still couldn't get the job done." Then she looked her up and down. "Hell, will you be my next, well not boyfriend, cuz it sounds like you get the job done a lot better than he did."

Beth snorted. "You'd have to ask Lydia. Izzy's poly, she might take you up on it."

I shrugged, "I don't mind, I always thought you were hot."

That was it, Rita face was on fire. "Me rindo." She shook her head. "I know when I'm beat."

I thought about it for a moment. "Rita, you never realized Izzy was trans?"

"What?" She looked at Izzy. "Her? Oh hell no. Maybe a little butch, defiantly a bruja. But I never saw her as anything but girl. Hell, till you guys told me, I thought she was like 18 or something." The she looked at Izzy, "And now I know you a Bruja." She nodded, "But I like you anyway."

"Thanks, I think."

Rita nodded again. "Anyway, this cyberpunk stuff, why you think it didn't happen?"

Izzy leaned in, "It did, we're living on the verge of it right now. It just doesn't look how they thought it would. Then the template for it was all 80s stuff. Bio or wet wear is at the bleeding edge of medicine, cybernetics is catching up, we went apple for the look instead of the dirty dystopian. But with the state of things right now? We have multinational mega corps that have more to say in our laws and politics than the average voter, the mega cities are growing, New York, LA, Dallas, Hong Kong, Tokyo, Kyoto, hell even Seattle is trying to stake its claim to being a free city by actually paying attention to the needs of the workers. So, the aesthetic is a bit off, the reality isn't that far away."

Rita nodded, "And you guys are going to be using that aesthetic?"

Beth nodded, "Mostly, with a few updates. A little more apple than I would like, but a dirty apple. Just so long as we don't do Billy Idol's version."

Izzy groaned. "Oh god that was so terrible, and so dated. I don't mind a little cheese but I swear to the gods that man scooped up Wisconsin for that album and those horrid videos."

I looked at them both, "Um, I kind of liked it." They turned and stared at me. "What? I looked it up online and well, since I liked Rebel Yell, Dancing With Myself and White Wedding... I thought, well..." Their looks were getting uncomfortable.

Izzy stepped in. "There's nothing wrong with liking it, don't ever let anyone gatekeep you. But if you want the sound? Go Industrial Metal and Industrial Goth, both have more to do with the feel than Billy's synth pop attempt. But yeah, it wasn't all bad. He did try to at least give it a sound even if, well one, there wasn't one, Cyber Punk wasn't a genre of music, and two? He kind of missed the mark."

Izzy isn't a fan of gate keepers, but I had heard that too many times only to be met by them. It was nice that a noobie like me wasn't being left out.

"Any suggestions on what I should read then?"

The two of them looked at each other. "Neuromancer."

Chapter 36

We broke it up, gathered up everything, I grabbed my new kitty, and we all headed out. Over the last few months, I had gotten used to Izzy walking me out. She held my hand and leaned in for a kiss. I eagerly greeted her. She cupped my face and I swear she breathed me in.

I kept waiting for the love bombs, that or for the honeymoon to end. Yet she seemed to get more intense with each passing day, not less. She always left me time for myself, and her random acts of romance were small things, not large. I still waited for her to pressure me, or get bored with me, but neither happened. She always seemed genuinely excited to see me, and I had to admit, I was excited to see her.

"Want to come back to my place?" I asked. "After that talk, I'm interested in seeing exactly what you can do."

Her face lit up, and that smile was worth it. "Really? Are you sure?"

I thought about it, the decision took me no time to reach. "Yes, I want a session, a full scene." I took a deep breath, "Nothing too heavy mind you, um." Spur of the moment negotiations, what did I want? "Some bondage, maybe? Um..." Crap, what did I tell her, this was my idea. Then I realized what I wanted. "Keep it light, but I want to feel. I want to give you that control."

I nodded to myself, feeling her fingertips still on my face and neck. "No visible marks, I still have work tomorrow, but you've earned my trust." I looked into those eyes of hers. "I want to let go."

She traced my jaw line with one claw point. "As you wish." She stepped back and it caught me off guard. Just like that, just that little bit of letting myself feel, trust, and already her absence hurt. I stumbled forward and she steadied me.

"I'll see you shortly." She breathed into the night air as she walked towards her truck.

Still trembling slightly, I got into my bug, cranked it, and turned on the heat. A meoarw greeted me as my little car surged to life. I looked over at Darkness's head peeking out of the box. The scraggly kitten fuzz made a halo in the yellow sulfur lights of the parking lot. The little thing was blackness, eyes, and that glow, at least till she spoke up again and showed off her white fangs.

"Meerow!" She insisted.

"I know, it's cold, we'll be home soon."

"Reaerrw." She said with a little less enthusiasm. She turned her head looking around, then stuck her nose on the frost covered window.

"I know, it snowed, the windows are iced over. Just let me warm up." I looked in the glove box and got my hand scraper. The big one was in the trunk, but it really wasn't bad enough to need it. Over the past few weeks I had gotten used to Izzy being unaffected by the cold. It made me wonder if that was just her being an ice mutant, god knows they were always around, or some bit of magic? If the former, I looked forward to her ice-cold ass on me as we cuddled. I realized I really was looking forward to that, to cuddling with her, cold butt and all. If the latter?

"If the latter I hope she teaches me."

"Raow." Darkness it seemed, agreed.

I got out and scraped, shoved, chipped and slowly freed my ride from its icy tomb. Every scrape of plastic against glass with its grind-slop noise greeting me gave the doubts in my mind voice.

Grind- "Are you going to be able to handle her being, different?"

Slop- "Penis, say penis, she has a penis."

Grind- "That taste was intense, terrifying, exhilarating, terrifying."

Slop- "Dick, she's got a dick, a great, big, fat, dick that a straight woman was impressed by the size of it."

Grind- "I want this, she's been nothing but sweet, and kind and excited to see me, and sweet."

Slopt!- "She's going to try to stick that thing in you."

Grindsloitgrindslitgrindsliscccchschrechscresh!

Ice flew everywhere from my sudden burst of frustrated scrapping. My little bug didn't seem to care too much as its engine puttered away. Inside I could see that the frantic scraping had amused Darkness and that she, somehow, had made it to the dash. Little gold eyes looked out at me as clawed paws whiled the inside of the windshield.

Getting back in, I scooped her off the dash and put her back in her box, dropping the ice scraper on the passenger side floor.

The ride home was, if possible more frustrating than the chore of scraping the windows, for much the same reason. I only managed to stop my brain from obsessing when my tires encountered the edge of the road and that sound jolted me out of my thoughts. Visions of impending penetration by 'flesh swords' were replaced by visions of slippery, icy roads, and twisted broken blood covered steel and glass.

Once safely in my own driveway, I closed my eyes and turned the engine off. I took a few deep breaths, opened my eyes, and looked over to the right. Darkness was peeking out at me as if her little life had flashed before her eyes, and she found it far too short.

That thought struck me.

"Me too kid, me too." I reached over and pet her.

I could wait. Izzy would understand, and if she didn't then she wasn't the one. She had waited all this time, and would do so again probably not even being upset by it.

Waiting wouldn't do anything though. She'd still have a dick, today, tomorrow, next week, next month, next year.

Either I could do this, or I couldn't.

I liked her, hell... I was falling in love with her. She made my heart race, my palms sweat, everything I had heard and thought so odd. More importantly the thought of being without her made my chest ache. If I couldn't do it, fine, then we'd burn that bridge when we came to it.

If I could?

I mean straight women did 'it' all the time. Izzy was worth trying it.

Chapter 37

Beth opened the door for me as I got to it, her keys in hand. "Hi hun." She kissed me on the cheek. "Back tomorrow night." She swung past me, barley aware of anything.

Why should she be? Her and Allen were getting on well, she was spending more than half her nights over at his place. How was she to know I had decided to jump off a cliff? There was a time that she could sense what was going on with me even when I couldn't.

Now?

Now she was young and in love, spending as much time with her partner as she could. It made me smile.

I wanted a Shower before Izzy got here, I reeked of coffee, the days sweat, and my own nervousness. Izzy had a key, true, she even had a few things she had left over here. I knew my girl, she was going to try to make tonight special in her own way.

I picked up my phone and shot her a quick text.

Foxbutt987:: Hopping in the shower, let yourself in::

I went and peeled myself out of the days clothing, taking the bra off was as wonderful as only removing a bra after a long day could be. I stood for a moment just enjoying not having it on.

I'm not small, not huge either for that matter. I'm large enough that not having a bra sucked worse than having one, but no matter how much of a relief taking one off was, bopping around all day hustling coffee without one was far worse.

::Pin-ting::

I knew it was coming, I knew she would message me back. Hell, I was looking forward to it. Her I wasn't annoyed at, but that sound had interrupted the rapture of freedom. I couldn't help but look at the traitorous device with all the energy that, at the moment, I just didn't have.

Feeling that look on my face let me know just how exhausted I was. My mind once more raised objections to my midnight plans. Not that it was midnight, that was still a few hours away.

I glanced at the clock. 10:32.

I felt my face fall, I felt all of the day rushing back. I hadn't realized we had spent so much time in the shop after I finished closing. Did I really have the energy for what was coming?

Picking up the phone, I opened the message.

Thigh high patent leather black boots, a corset of black satin, black leather pants someone poured her into covered what the boots left visible of her thighs, black gloves peeked out of the sleeves of her black trench coat as she held it open to show me what lay underneath. She had on goth makeup in black, whites, and reds with silver highlights around her smoky and intense eyes. A hat sat on her head, it was a black biker's cap and looked to be as highly shined as those boots.

I heard myself react to what I saw. I had, in a way, waited for a woman like this for my entire life, right down to her ruining the 'I'm a Dominatrix, do as I SAY' look she had cultivated to show me, by the shit eating grin of a kid who had been told they could play with their favorite toy. She was every ounce the sweet loving person I had wanted and had shown me, although be it only once, that she could be as forceful as I craved. She was quick with a joke, some bad, some good, some that went over my head because they involved concepts I hadn't ever cared about. I could forgive the math and computer jokes. She never talked down to me either.

"What the fuck is wrong with me?"

"Mroww?"

I shook my head. "Wasn't talking to you kid." I scooped her up and out of the box and settled her onto the bed. "Just wondering why I have to make this so complicated."

I looked at the picture again and realized I had missed the message that came with it.

EraNocta:: Hope you like, not that you will see it for long::

I realized she had been holding a blindfold in her other hand. To be fair it was as black has her glove.

Foxbutt987:: It's a good look, I think it suits you::

Foxbutt987:: Hitting the shower now see you soon! ;P::

I sat the phone down. "No turning back now."

***

The shower felt amazing. The water cascading over me, beating into sore muscles, reviving me. I used it to wake myself up. I wanted this. Was I scared? Yes. Home alone, no back up... but I trusted her.

When the front door opened, I knew she had arrived, still she called out "It's just me hun." That did a lot to calm my nerves. As the water did its work of removing the sweat of the day and removing a weariness I had only discovered once the bra came off, I heard her go in and out several times. Something was bouncing around out there, and I knew she was 'setting up'.

Another unwanted thought hit me. "You better not be setting up camara equipment out there."

I heard her laugh and realized I was already too far gone to object if she did. That laugh was far too warm, at least to me, to say no to.

"Maybe another time, if you're into it. I certainly wouldn't mind having photos of you."

That made me stop and think. Was I into it? It had never really come up. I had done a few pics for past girlfriends, but when some of them wound up online? It was why I worried.

Turning the water off, I followed the stream of it down letting the last trickle bounce off my head. I let the motion bring my forehead to the cool of the tile. I had left the door open so I could hear when she came in, and as such didn't realize she had come into the bathroom until I moved the curtain aside.

There she was.

Gone was that cheesecake grin, and what stood before me was a goddess. I had caught glimpses of her, young, old, powerful, and now this, masterful. She was majestic, in command. No need to say our session had started, it was obvious just in the way she stood. I had worried about that, had wondered what it would be, and here it was catching me off guard completely.

A wicked smile, predatory and yet loving, spread across her face. One side of her mouth crooked up further than the other in a cocky, slightly lopsided grin. Her head inclined slightly toward me as she slowly moved closer, taking a towel off the rack. To my surprise, she didn't just throw it at me, but instead started drying me.

"The rules for the night are simple. You are mine until I am done with you. You can speak as you wish, and since I read eyes you may look at me in the face as much as you wish. I will answer all questions you have, but you will obey."

She gently rubbed the towel over me and handed me a second I didn't see her grab so I could wipe my face.

"Safe words and the rules you laid out earlier are my road maps, the lines I won't cross. I have a preference for safe words but will use which ever you wish."

I hesitated. "Sa-Safe word." I closed my eyes as images came unbidden to me. "I had a safe word..." I turned my head. I couldn't do this. "It didn't work."

"Pain." Her voice was soft. "But not the kind I want." Her tone dismissed it, not my pain, that's not how it felt, but dismissed, something, something else I couldn't define. It made my chest lighten. "We'll come back to your old word. For tonight, we'll use mine."

She put a finger under my chin and brought my eyes to hers gently.

"Tonight, we will use words your mind has already been gauged for." She brushed a wet strand of hair out of my face and a smile came to her lips. "It's called the stop light method, red, yellow, green."

The stop light? I felt myself chuckle. "Really?" Wait hadn't she told me that already?

"Of course. Each color is easy enough to remember. Yellow for slow down, give me a moment. Red for stop right now or I'll take your fucking head off." I laughed. "Green for, come on you stupid bitch," her grin split into a real smile, "Go already, hit the gas, it's the long skinny peddle on the right, god."

My mind jumped back to us in my car, me driving and just being myself. Just like that, I was back in my house, safe, warm... well cold, I was still wet, but with someone who was there for me.

I leaned into her and she wrapped her arms around me. "God I'm sorry, I'm so messed up." She simply petted my hair. "I'm ruining it, and your just holding me."

"You're not ruining anything." Her voice, it still held all the heat, all the warmth it had. More it was still the voice of my dominant. "You haven't said red."

I hadn't. We were still going; she was comforting me but hadn't stopped anything. I nodded into her chest. This close I could feel her breasts, could tell she had actually used some type of perfume, it was like wind and trees and earth and safe. She just held me.

Finally, I pulled back. "Thank you."

"For?"

"Not..." I trailed off. What was I thanking her for? "For not being... for being here for me. For not getting upset."

"You were hurt, that wound runs deep. I see it as clearly as if it were carved into you, because for me it is."

I looked at her oddly.

"I see you."

"And..." I took a deep breath. "You still want me?" Those words hurt to get out.

"Of course."

She led me, now mostly dry, by the hand and out to the living room.

Chapter 38

In the living room, the blinds were already all closed, candles were situated around giving the place a softly lit quality. The coffee table had been moved and a scaffolding and harness had been set up. A cube of black tubing with a sex swing and all its restraints and stirrups stood proudly in the middle of the living room floor.

She ditched the gloves and led me over, and gently helped me into the set up. Soon my body, neck, head, and my back were supported, then my legs just behind the knee. I watched as she attached cuffs to my ankles and wrists, these too were attached to straps coming off the cube. It wasn't a quick thing, set ups like this aren't. It took time and both of us working together to get me into it. The entire time she spoke in that smooth commanding voice. By the time the last click of metal on metal happened I was not only floating, but kind of giddy. Now that I had decided to do this, now that I had worked for it, I was getting excited.

She held up the blindfold and looked at me. "I'm not gagging you. One, I love all those little sounds I coax from throats, and two I want you to be as loud or as quite as you need to be." As she said these words, she trailed the tips of her nails of the hand that wasn't holding up the mask down my throat just as she said that word. "I had intended to blindfold you, to keep you at the edge, let my claws and teeth be what you felt with little to no warning." She got a far off look on her face as she spoke, considering dark desires of her own. "But... I will let you veto the thing if you wish." She locked eyes with me. "The terror of anticipation I will see there will be as sweet."

She was giving me an out, letting me keep some control because she knew I had already been set off once. Do not misunderstand. I wholeheartedly believed she would indeed watch my eyes as she worked me over, and I believed she would enjoy every last bit of it.

I closed my eyes deliberately and shook my head no.

"Then say it, speak. You have a tongue do you not?"

"No, I'm fine."

"Fine?" Still she stood there, holding the black satin cloth. She looked me over. "I quite agree, you are most fine. But that's not what I asked." Her voice was light, but the tone switch let me know she would only play this game so long.

"Please Mistress." Please? Please what? She didn't say that, she didn't have to. It came unbidden to my mind. "Please blindfold me, I want to lose myself tonight." I took a breath, eyes closed once more. "Please." An unintended whimper came to my voice with that last word. My need, my need to feel, to let go had put it there.

The click of her heels on the hardwood of the living room floor and with a whisper soft touch, the dark cloth slid over my eyes. I lifted my head up as she secured it. Darkness became my world.

"Now." I felt her straighten, her heat so close a moment before was now absent. "Remember, this, all of this, it is what you want. If ever it is not, you can stop it at any time. Scream no, as loud as you want, if you wish. Beg, plead... I am sure you will." She moved; the click of her heels let me know she was maneuvering down my body. "Oh, you will, but nothing stops until you say RED." Then I felt her hands grip my inner thighs, her nails, no, claws were prominent, painfully but not unbearably so, digging into me as she squeezed. "But I swear, if you are so much as having a minor cramp, or scared, or uncomfortable and I find out you didn't stop, that you didn't safe word, that you suffered through because you thought it was what I wanted." Her words already dark turned into a hiss. "I will do the worst thing I can to you, I will never hurt you again."

The pressure on my thighs eased and those claws traced lines as she withdrew her hands. The worst part of her threat? I believed her.

"Worse thing you can do to a masochist is promise not to beat us, am I right?"

The tips of her nails landed lightly just above my stomach. "No," She said as the tips of those things started making their way down my stomach. Just the tips, barley touching. I found myself trying to arch into them, but they were just out of reach. I would feel what she wanted me to feel.

"No, I can think of worse things." Her words were breathy, and I could feel them on the skin of my stomach, she must have been mere inches from me. "In this case." Something soft and moist touched me just above my belly button. The sound of a kiss reached my ears and those soft lips were gone. "What I want to do to you, how I want you to scream." She was still close; I could still feel her breath with her words. "That requires trust, on both our parts."

I got it. She was always saying how she wanted me to just be me. "You need to be," My breath caught as I felt her teeth on my thigh, her hands grasping me. "You need to know you're not," She bit. It was hard and a gasp escaped me.

"I need to know you want this, want me, even if you're screaming stop." Those last words were my only warning, her breath had hit the difference between my two legs.

The first lick was quick, a dart of the tongue, the second was longer, more probing. I tried to pull back.

"I'm not shaved." I wasn't, it had been days since the last time.

"If it was a problem, I would shave you myself." She growled, hands holding me still, keeping me from escaping. "I will shave you if I wish, dress you up if I wish. You are mine. Mine to take care of, to love, to" she licked again. "Enjoy."

I was no stranger to what she was doing, not by a long shot, but this was different. She tried to take me into her mouth, I felt her teeth, her bottom teeth lightly scrape me as she gathered up my lips in her mouth, sucking me in. Her tongue hit my opening, then my clit. Once she found it, thing got fuzzy fast.

She was sucking it, licking it, nipping it, but I didn't mind. Right at that moment she could have drawn blood and I doubt I would have noticed.

I squirmed, but she held me fast. She seemed to be trying to get all of me at once, to lick it. I whimpered; I know I did, I could hear it. I could feel my back arching but couldn't quite remember why.

The heat of her was gone. I hadn't heard her move. Panting, I tried to figure out where she was.

"Izzy?"

"Shhhh love." I felt her touch me, but something was blocking some of the heat from her skin, something smooth. "I'm ready to have a little fun." I felt her finger trace my opening, maddeningly not doing more than that. I didn't feel her claw tip. Not that I cared at that moment. Claws, no claws.

Slowly she sank her fingers into me and I could feel the glove over her hand inside. I was grateful. I mean, right now I didn't care, but come morning I certainly would.

For now, though? The slow buildup of pressure was more than enough.

I have no idea how many she was using, but it was enough. It was a slow, steady rhythm I could definitely get used to. She was pushing in and I could feel when the rest of her hand got close to me, but she didn't touch me, didn't grind into me.

"Geen..." I breathed out. Then I tried again. "Green." This was more of a pant. I'm not sure what I wanted, what I thought was going to happen, but I wasn't expecting the reality.

"As the lady wishes."

I felt her readjust as she brushed my leg as she did so. Then she slid them out almost all the way, changed angles and slid them back in... and up. When her fingertips hit that spot, when she pressed it into my pelvic bone, when her thumb came down on my clit, and she lifted, my world exploded.

Sensations ran though my body and my world contracted to just what she was doing at the moment. Pressure, warmth, friction, the sliding, the rhythm, her finger on my clit. I tried to close my legs, not because I wanted to but because, it... my mind... it was... my legs wouldn't close.

Why wouldn't my legs close?

I tried to pull away, but she was there her hand was inside me, all of it, everything. She was in me. My hips lifted; she was pushing but so was I. I tried to open my eyes, but everything was black.

Then it hit and I fell. Colors, lights, sounds, smells, the forest, my feet were pounding soil, litter, grass.

The second one hit and I came crashing back to reality. My entire body was roaring?

No, I was, I was.

She was still in me, still playing me. My body was responding to her commands.

And commands? She only had one command.

"Cum for me, cum for me my little one. Cum, I want to feel you. Cum for me." She was stretching me, penetrating me, pushing deep in me, and still she was hitting that spot. I will never know how men can't find it. It's right there.

Every time she hit it, she would lift me by it and I would cum, I was almost cumming every time she said to.

"Yel..lll."

The weight that was me lowered down, slowly. The intensity, whatever that was, pulled back. Petting, I was being pet.

"Are you all right love?"

Breathe, I was breathing. It felt like she pulled something out, out of my body. "GIv," I tried again, "give me a damn minute."

"Take your time, take all the time you need. I'm right here, I'm not going anywhere."

I hadn't said stop. She hadn't stopped. She had slowed down. She was listening to me. While I recovered... I actually began to truly believe she would stop if I said to.

"What. The Hell. Was. That?"

For a moment there wasn't an answer, then. "I made sure you were wet, open, and pliable, then worked over your g-spot while playing with your clit."

"Bullshit. I've had my g-spot played with before."

Again, there was silence for a heartbeat. "Each one I've ever touched feels a little bit different. They have ridges, bumps, just different textures. I like playing with them."

She liked... playing with them. "What was with the lifting me up?"

"Tilting you really. When I got your clit under my thumb and my fingers on your g-spot... well the pubic bone is right there, I use it to give me leverage and control your hips."

I leaned back and just thought about it. It all seemed so simple. "How the hell have I never heard of this?"

"Women aren't encouraged to talk about their bodes or experiment?" Her voice even went up at the end. It was really the best answer she had. She honestly probably knew less than I did overall.

"You had an early girlfriend that just let you play."

"Well, yeah."

I had been a college girl, I had dated women like myself. Hell I was most girls first time, some of them I was their only time. Izzy was the first older woman I have ever dated. I never had a lesbian mentor, or dated an older one. No one had taught me, no one talked about... I mean, that was intense.

"What the hell else have I missed?"

"If it makes you feel better, I've dated women who never even had an orgasm until me... let alone knew where their g-spot was."

No, it didn't make me feel better.

"Ok, new rule." God how did I put this? "You can play with me, however the fuck you want, but you have to show me what to do."

"Deal."

Chapter 39

After that, she just started playing with my skin.

"The skin, all of it, has nerves. Thousands of them." As she softly spoke, she started lightly running her hands over my body. "Each nerve feels, that's what they do. What they feel is exceptionally basic." Her hands and their warmth were a feathers touch of movement just barely kissing the surface of me. "They feel pressure, and temperature, no more, no less. It's why even with gloves on, if they are thin enough, you still feel the wet of water as if it had touched your fingertips."

She was on my arms now, that touch, so light, so fleeting. "What about rough, smooth?"

"A trick of your mind. You feel rough when different nerves pick up a difference in the pressure your skin is feeling. Rough things have a lot of different pressures, while smooth things are more uniform."

"Soft?"

"Soft and hard come down to how much the substance yields to that pressure. A lot of yield, like a pillow, is soft." She switched and her hand had new textures. "For the amount of pressure there is, if it is not causing much pressure, then it too is soft. A feather can be soft against your skin because as it's pressed down it flexes. Yet you can get the same soft from something like steel, if not a lot of pressure is used."

"Ok." What did that have to do with what was happening? I still felt her hands, even in places I knew they weren't.

"All the sensation you feel other than temperature or pressure is made up by your brain, right down to pleasure and pain." That feather touch finally ran over my breast, but not the top, not the nipples, but the underside. "To make up for the time it takes your nerves to communicate with your brain what is going on, it anticipates."

I could feel that too, my skin was already reacting to where her fingers were going to be next.

"This anticipation can cause a skin reaction," she chuckled, "Like goose bumps, before." She slowed the rate of movement of her hands. "I ever touch the area."

It was slow, torturous even, but her fingers played against my skin.

"I sit and I read your skin, how it reacts, where it tightens, or loosens, where it goose bumps, and I adjust," Those nail tips were suddenly against my skin, tracing out lines on me. Still feather light but now with more bite. "Accordingly."

"What about sharp? I feel sharp, the sharpness..." I inhaled as she finally brought one of those claw tips to the outside of my areola and traced around it. "I definitely feel sharp."

"No, just more pressure in a small area."

She was reading my skin as if it was her own personal road map, a road map to me. "So this is just practice?"

"Of a kind. Each person, and each skin is different. I'm practiced at reading skin, among other things, but each person is a brand-new playground. What works on one, may not work on another, and I love a new playground." She still had yet to do more than brush against the outside of my areola and I was already panting.

"So, once you learn me, you will move on?" It was a fear. She was poly, I knew that. It made me wonder if she would tire of me.

"Oh no. You see," She began as I finally felt one of those sharp tips on my nipple. I had expected pain, but that's not what I got. This was, different. "Tonight, my playground is frightened but brave, she is inquisitive, she is determined. Tomorrow when I play again, whenever that might be, the playground will be different." She quickly cupped my breasts. "Sure, there will still be hills to climb." She ran her finger down my body, down my stomach and finally down my slit. "A slide to play with." She ran it back up and over my stomach once more, her second hand joining the first, then each spreading out. As she did so the pressure of her touch increased, they slid over my breasts and they gave to her touch. She squeezed them firmly, then ran her hands up to my shoulders, then down my arms. "And plenty of fields to run on. But the weather will be different. Sometimes I won't want to play with the hills, sometimes I will want the slide, sometimes I won't want either." She leaned up and whispered into my ear. "I could spend a lifetime learning your body, your moods, the ripples in you, your energy, your soul and never fully master everything. A new toy every week is great for some, and more power to them. But me?" I could hear the smile in her voice. "I want an instrument I can pick up and play everything on, from a symphony to classic rock, to death metal and everything in between. And that takes." Her hand slid around my throat, I tensed immediately as she began to squeeze, but it was like she said just pressure. She didn't cut off my air and it wasn't hard. It was simply her fingertips, there was a tremble in them, a flutter, and I grew lightheaded. I could breathe so the panic started to slow. With everything else she had done, now that I realized she wasn't trying to kill me, and yes for a second that did cross my mind, I relaxed into it. "Time, energy, trust, practice, understanding and respect."

She kissed my lips and I found myself wanting more, but it was not to be.

"Now cum for me."

Four words, and my world was undone as I arched. My mind just let go and my body came as a wave of pleasure washed over me. It was not big. She had given me bigger this very night. It was the fact that I came on command, while not being played with.

As soon as the heat of it was done washing over me, I came crashing down back to earth hard, shattering my newfound wings on impact.

Chapter 40

"God, you're such a little fuck slut aren't you?" Cursed words filled my ears. "You always were one to throw it at everyone around you. This is where a slut like you belongs. Right here right now, you will never be anything but mine and you will never be free of me. You should thank me, it's not like anyone else would ever want you. Well... not anyone normal."

I tried to put my hands to my ears. I couldn't, I was trapped. I was in the cage, I was trapped. I was trapped. Oh god I was trapped, I was in the cage, I never left, I was trapped.

The sound of steel clearing leather made its way through my world. I heard it and flinched. She was finally going to kill me.

Then my hands were free. I cradled my head, tried to roll away from the knife, the pain, the pain I knew was coming. I heard the blade whistle through the air, once, twice, more and I fell, I fell to the floor and arms were around me.

A new voice, an old voice, it reached in. "I got you, I got you. It's ok. It's not your fault. You're safe. You're safe. I got you." Arms, strong arms were around me. I was drawn in tightly, I was warm. I was held. Then darkness came, it wrapped around me too. I was being rocked, cooed at, talked to.

I don't know how long I was in Izzy's arms. I don't know how long I cried.

But I did. It was ugly. All of it, all of it came pouring out and I couldn't stop it. Even the things I didn't want to think about, that I had buried, right down to me orgasming while she did... things to me. I won't call it coming. Coming feels good. This was just shame and pain.

When I came to, she was still holding me. The blindfold was off, I was free, we were on the ground and huge black feathered wings were wrapped around me. Her wings. As I cleared my eyes, wiped my face, I watched as they faded from sight. I could still feel them but after a moment, I couldn't see them.

I looked up, looked her dead in the eyes. I was going to ask, ask about everything. She had shown she was willing to teach me, to explain things to me. She had just shown she could be trusted. I was going to ask damn it.

"I..." My voice was a little shaky. "Really need to pee." FUCK! Oh god I really did.

Chapter 41

I sat on the toilet, and... sat.

I still had the cuffs on, hell what was left of the tethers were still attached to them. Each one was sliced clean through. She had cut me out of the harness. They were leather, and she didn't hesitate. I went nuts and she just cut me down. Looking at them I would like to say I sat and just thought, ran all of it through my mind.

Nevertheless, I just sat.

"God, I need therapy." I had seen a therapist for a while. Money dried up, it wasn't helping anyway, so I quit. Here's the thing with therapy. If you want it to work, you have to put the work into it. I didn't. I wanted to forget.

"Forgetting isn't an option." I hadn't forgotten anything. I was going to need to deal with this.

Getting off the toilet, I walked out and turned and went into my room. I needed clothes, I needed not to be naked. Pants, shirt, underwear, hell I even grabbed a bra. The ratty one, my comfy 'I'm just popping down to the store' bra, but a bra none the less.

I looked at my wrists, they were still cuffed even if not to anything. I frowned for a moment. That was going to make matters interesting. I didn't want to take them off. Not because I thought she would be mad, I knew she wouldn't. I just didn't want to take them off. If I took them off... if I took them off I... I shook my head. If I took them off she would win. She would have taken something else from me. I didn't put them on, I wasn't going to take them off.

Halfway into my pants I remembered I could take them off and put them back on.

Stubbornness wouldn't let me stop.

I would get this damn it. I would do this!

Darkness thought it was funny and pounced on the straps. Not a true pounce but one of those hop step hop things kittens her age love to do. It made me feel better.

Shoes thankfully were easy, once I had on everything else.

It was time to go face Izzy. She had offered to come with me to the bathroom, but I needed a few. I walked out to the living room and spotted her through the back glass on the patio deck. She was still in her outfit but had put her gloves and coat back on. As she leaned against the railing, a gray haze drifted up from her hand and I realized she was having a smoke.

"Got tired of waiting on me?" I said as I stepped outside.

She turned and greeted me with a smile. Her makeup was ruined, not from crying but other things. I was probably wearing most of it and just didn't realize it.

"I'll wait on you forever." She looked me up and down. "I'm just not going to stand around like a prop while I do."

I nodded. "Fair enough."

She walked over to me, her heels tapping out their beat on the cold frosty deck. She got close and stuck the thing between her lips and in one movement had the coat off and around me. I hadn't grabbed one.

It was still warm from her body heat and hung around me like a mantle as it settled on my shoulders. I realized I was cold and pulled it in tight.

"Thanks."

"How are you?" Her voice held concern, but not tension. She would let me talk about it or not as I saw fit.

"I'm, good." I said after a minute. "Can, can I ask you a question?"

She looked at me, confused. "Of course."

"I, I could have sworn I saw wings earlier, are you an angel?"

Her face flamed bright red. "Um, yeah." She looked away, then turned and walked off. "Look, to be honest... I know I'm fae." She turned back to me. "I was born human, I am human. I've..." She took a deep breath. "I've never lied to you, and yes it seems like I'm some kind of high, thing or whatever. As I started exploring myself, I just kind of started falling into place." She gave a shrug.

"But everything you told me?"

"It's true. At least, it's what I have been able to piece together. I'm not an angel, I've never grown wings before, not like that. Huge black shadows? Sure. Black feathers?" She shook her head. "At one time in the past, I was someone, someone before I was born this." She gestured at herself. "She was someone powerful, even feared. Most of us run from me."

She put out the one she was smoking and lit another. She did, on average, about 7 a day. She most certainly didn't smoke back-to-back like this.

"When I first heard Sidhe and me, mentioned in the same breath? I knew I had found, something, but a Sidhe doesn't have wings, not like that, not that I've found." She took a long inhale. "Until tonight, I was 100% sure what I was."

"The Hunter, his stuff worked on you."

"Did it? The bell should have left me flat for days, unable to touch magic by some stories." She shook slightly. I couldn't tell if it was from the cold, or something else. She was after all half naked. All she was wearing from the top up were leather opera gloves and a corset.

"So, you're Sidhe, and maybe something else?"

She shrugged. "It's why I can't say no to your question. I don't believe it, I wouldn't even begin to know how it happened. It would certainly be the oddest thing I had ever heard of... but I can't rule it out."

I thought about it for a moment. I had been doing some research. "Mab can turn into a crow."

She looked back at me. "Raven, and she'd have your head for calling her a crow."

"You know Mab?"

She went and leaned over on the railing again. Took a long pull and tapped her head. "In here. In dreams. In my past." She looked at me. "Yeah. I knew her."

"But not now." I walked over and put my hand on her shoulder.

"No. I've run into maybe a hand full like us, 20 tops."

"That's quite a handful."

She looked at me, then at herself, then smiled. "I got big hands."

"Ok, those are those like us. What about...?" I trailed off.

"The real deal?"

"Yeah."

She smiled. "They're all around us." She took my hand and pointed out to the woods. "Look out there."

I turned and looked out into the wood behind my home. The snow was still light, lighter than it should have been for this time of year. Trees were bare except for the one or two evergreens. The air twinkled with the cold, as if small shards of ice danced in the wind.

"No," she whispered into my ear. "Look again, look as you did when you were a child."

Amused more than annoyed, I looked again. Trees, limbs, shadows, snow, small animals, ice dancing in the air, the evergreens.

Ice... dancing in the air. I looked again, really looked.

Suddenly the air was filled with the glitter and flutter of gossamer wings, wings that looked to be made out of ice crystals. They were quick, too quick. I could barely see them. They blended in perfectly with the night, easy to miss. Easier to dismiss. They, whatever they were, didn't have a care in the world, or I should say didn't have a care for me and my world. I soon realized they were zipping around not at random but with purpose.

"There's a nest near here. I watch them from time to time when I'm out smoking. I think it's one of the reasons I never really gave it up despite really never smoking inside."

I had to know. "How did you start?"

"I would like to say the same way every kid did, to look cool, or feel like an adult, or my friends made me." She shook her head. "But I was never that kid. All the women I identified with growing up did. So, I guess it was sort of to look cool, but not really. I fell for the femme fatales and the like. The bad guys, or the bad girls. The ones queer coded to hell and back."

"So, you started young and never really stopped?"

She looked at me. "Hell no. I picked it up at 19. I was out of the house and I was going to be me. Lipstick on the filter, bad ass walk, high heels clicking away." She shrugged. "By the late 90s it became a fetish for me, part of who I was, something not his."

"His?"

She looked me in the eyes. "His."

With that I got it. His, him, the boy from before. Yeah, not going to ask her to stop. Maybe get her over to vaping.

Chapter 42

We found bed a bit after 4 am, the only good news was I wasn't opening, Rita was. I hope she got some sleep.

The alarm hit far too early, and received its customary smacking around. By the second one, I actually opened my eyes for it. 1:15, I should have been there at one.

In a blind panic I grabbed my phone and hit the store's number.

"E'llo, this is The Coffee Bar, soon to be Razor's Edge Cyber Café. This is Rita how my I help you?"

"Shit, I know I'm late, I'm sorry. I didn't reset my alarm time."

"Chica, no big. I thought you were just caught in traffic."

"I am so sorry." I was already up and stripping off the cuffs. Izzy and I had cuddled till we fell asleep and I had forgotten to take them off.

Laughter came from the phone. "Sounds like you had a good night. No big, get here when you get here." She stopped. "And pick me up a burger to make it up to me, I want a gut buster, a real grease bomb. I'm going on break as soon as I can and I am starving."

"Want any fries with that?" I couldn't help but smile. I loved her but she could eat anything and not put an ounce on that tiny body. Not that she was small mind you. She was a good-sized girl. She didn't do the diet thing to try to get smaller, and despite what she ate she never got bigger.

"Hell no. You gonna pick me up one of those big ones. I'm not gonna have room for fries."

"You got it." I hung up and got ready.

Izzy for her part laid and watched me, a dreamy look on her face.

"What?"

"You're beautiful and I love you."

She said it, she meant it. It's how she was. A smile crossed my lips. "Yeah, well you're biased."

"As hell." She got up and wrapped arms around me. "I'm also right." She kissed my forehead and let me get back to it.

As I scrambled to become presentable, she slid on jeans and a tee-shirt, one of mine, and tennis shoes she had in her bag. Smart girl, if you're going to wear heels, always have back up shoes. I wondered, did someone tell her? Or did she learn the hard way like I did? I had once thought platforms were the exception, live, learn.

As I got outside, new snow had accumulated and we were finally getting something that could be called a blanket of snow. I skidded to a halt and nearly hit my ass as I saw my car.

"No, no, nonono." The front passenger side was lower than the right. "Please please, please." I made my way around, and sure enough, I had a flat. Crouching down I inspected it to find a rusted nail had slid into one of the treads point first. I closed my eyes as I remembered nearly going off the road last night.

A groan escaped me, showing itself in the cold. "Shit... shit." I looked up at the heavens and wondered if this was my punishment for having fun last night. Frustration at myself, the thought, the situation, all of it welled up within me. "FUCK!" I kicked the tire.

Let me say this again, I kicked the frozen piece of rubber attached to the cold, hard metal of my wheel.

This was not a smart move. I hit the ground and felt the last of my dignity go sailing away.

Izzy was there in a moment. "What's wrong?"

I helplessly gestured, at the tire, my foot, me being on my ass, the sky, all of it.

As she helped me up. "What am I going to do, I'm late, I promised Rita a burger, I needed to be there nearly an hour ago."

She turned me by my shoulders to look at her. "You're either going to borrow my truck, or I'm going to drive you."

I looked at her truck. I couldn't drive her truck. I mean, I could, it was easy enough. With the day I was already having? Visions of twisted metal ran through my head. That truck was about all she really owned, especially if you considered her tools were in there.

I looked up at her, my white knight... no my own personal black knight. "Would you? I mean. Right now, I'd flip it, or..." A kiss cut me off. It was brief but there.

"No problem, I need to get a few more measurements anyway." She smiled at me. "Let me grab my keys."

As she dashed inside, I looked at my poor bug. "I'll change you as soon as I can, and no more wool gathering while I drive."

She was out in moments, and we were away, house locked up tight and burger stop on the way.

The drive with Izzy was nice, she had made me feel better by the time we got to the drive thru... only for me to realized I forgot my wallet. She took it in stride and paid, even had me smiling again by the time we got me to work.

As I was going in, I double checked to make sure I had my keys, thankfully I did. Once in, things calmed down. Only the regulars were in, Rita was happy to see me despite me being an hour and fifteen late, and sliding behind the counter felt like coming home.

So, I was hopping and the morning was fading away.

The day from hell had other ideas.

::pin-ding::

I checked my phone.

RougeRogue13:: WTAF Lydia? Where are you, your car is outside. Get in here NOW we need to talk::

I looked at it. Read it again, then read it again.

Foxbutt987:: Um... at work. You make the schedule.::

Foxbutt987:: What's the problem?::

I watched and watched the three little dots go. Oh boy, this was going to be a doozy.

RougeRogue13:: What's the problem? Allen stepped in a pile of cat shit from your cat you didn't even discuss with me about bringing into the house. Did you know Allen is allergic to cats? Then there's a fucking sex swing, a fucking sex swing!!! Set up in the living room. It smells like piss in here!1! The coffee table's been moved, there are scratches on the hardwood. The picture of my mother is missing. GOD MY MOTHER!! What if she walked in here and saw this????::

I blinked. "What the fuck?"

Rita came over and looked at my phone. "Sex swing, nice." She looked at me. "Her Momma really have a problem with this?"

"Not to my knowledge."

Foxbutt987:: I'm at work, I have a flat, Izzy drove me in, we didn't have time to clean up because I was late for work::

The response was almost immediate. Far too soon for what was written.

RougeRogue13:: Look, if you can't show me some basic respect and clean up after yourselves I don't want you fucking here and certainly not in the living room. And what do you mean you were late? Is a little dick all it takes to make you completely irresponsible?::

By now Izzy had come over. "What's wrong?"

I wiped my face. What was wrong? All of it. I have one good night, one! And this was the price? "Nothing."

"Boss Ladies going off on her because you two left the sex swing in the living room." Rita added.

"What?" Her face showed a little shock. "She said she was going to be gone for a few days. Just clean up when we were done."

I raised an eyebrow. "I didn't tell you she was out?"

"No, she did. Called me while I was on the way over last night." She thought about it. "Look, let her know I'm on my way. I'll take care of it."

"Get the kitten a shit box too." Rita chimed in.

She nodded and walked out.

Foxbutt987:: Iz is on the way, she'll take care of it.::

RougeRogue13:: She better::

Bitch, I thought to myself as I put the phone down.

Rita shook her head. "It's that boyfriend of hers. She snapped at me a few times while you were out." I looked at her horrified. "Don't worry girl, I don't put up with that shit. Besides, it's only when she's around him." She leaned in close to me. "Get your bruja to work some magic and get rid of him."

I snorted. The laugh felt good. "Don't tempt me."

She was right. Beth had been different since she started dating Allen, but only when she actually spent time with him. The rest of the time, she was her sweet old self... mostly.

Chapter 43

Rita took her break, and her burger about 30 minutes after that, and I took mine just before she left at four. As the night wound down things were more or less calm. Less because there is always that one customer who doesn't like the service, the coffee, the music, the temperature: of the coffee or the room, more or less normal retail hell. More because after about 6, it was just down to me, Walt, the Twins, and Doc with randos wandering in for their caffeine fix.

I was on automatic until his voice shattered my world.

"Hey doll. Let me get a tall or grand or whatever the hell a small coffee is. You do serve just regular coffee, right? Or does it have to be some highbrow grandiose bullshit?"

My heart froze in my chest. I couldn't be right, yet when I looked over, there he was. The man who had tried to stab me, who him and his dad had tried to ruin my first date with Iz.

"You all right honey?" He said leering at me. Guess he was still a creep if not a hunter.

"Fine, and yes. We have coffee. How strong do you want it?"

"Strong enough to put hair on my chest sugar." He winked at me and I suddenly needed a shower.

He wanted strong, I automatically went to ring him up a blond, but remembered he didn't want nothing fancy, and just went with a medium dark. Looking at him and that oil slick smile he was giving me turned my stomach. Kevin was an ok guy. Hell, after what happened, I liked him. His kid? His kid was a jerk.

"What's the name?"

"Excuse me?" He seemed surprised.

"Your name, for the cup?"

He shook his head. "Call me Jacob."

My blood ran cold, Jacob was what Izzy had called his dad when it looked like she was about to eat his face.

Numbly I walked over and let the muscle memory make his coffee. He said black so I didn't bother with leaving room for cream and sugar, something told me he would think that unmanly.

He was the only customer at the counter, and he was leaning and waiting for his drink. They sit down, they normally sit down. He wanted to talk.

I watched him, deal or not, I didn't trust him.

When it was ready I brought it over to him, his grin split his face. "Thanks doll." He took a sip. We were done, he had his coffee, I could slip away, yet I stayed. "Side's all healed up you know."

I blinked at him. I had stabbed him last time we met. I'm glad it was healed, but why tell me? He shouldn't even know who I was.

His face turned dark. "That's right little lady, I remember." His voice went quite. "You and that bitch did a number on me, my dad made me quit... but I got other friends. Powerful friends."

My blood ran cold, I looked towards the door.

"Oh sure, make a scene you fae bitch. Call the cops. I'm sure they'd like to know you got that wet back workin' here."

My blood went up. All the fear he had caused evaporated. I leaned in. "She was born here you son of a bitch."

He just smiled at me, it was as sick as he was. "I know that, you know that. But I bet our boys in blue will want to check that now won't they. They'll call immigration and I.C.E., and she'll be sitting in a cage well before they ever figure out she's nice and legal. Hell, if we're lucky they'll just deport her before they figure it out."

My jaw was clenched so tight my teeth popped.

"Now ya getting it. We already got things going." He winked at me. "I just couldn't resist letting you know how fucked you and that whore are." He leaned in. "He told me I get you, and I can't wait to break you in."

Rage filled me. I was so mad I didn't register someone walking up behind him until I caught the movement out of the corner of my eye.

"I think maybe, you aren't as quiet as you think you are." A cold voice said.

"Buzz off, this don't concern you." He didn't even look up. That was his mistake.

Walt is a lot of things, soft spoken mostly, a raging asshole, kind of doughy around the middle. He's also huge. One hand went to the 'Jacob's' belt, the other to the back of his head and before I realized what had happened, he picked the bastard up by his pants and slammed his face into the counter. After the impact Walt just let go of him.

His hot 'real man' coffee tipped over in the exchange, and was now pouring over him. It was enough that if what Walt had done had knocked him senseless, it woke him up.

He was on his feet in moments. "What the hell was that for faggot?" He screamed. The look on his face was rage, a rage that quickly gave way to something even more primal, terror.

Walt, little hunched over Walt, was standing up straight. He was easily over six feet. Behind him stood Doc, and both Oingo Boingo's. None of them looked pleased.

"I think you owe the lady an apology." Was all Walt said.

"It's a free country, I ain't got to apologize for shit."

Doc stepped closer. "Actually, you were treating an employee of this establishment with harassment, even threatened to file a false police report. That's a felony."

"What do you know about it suck ass?"

"Suck ass? Do you get all your insults from old movies?" Jacob sneered at him. "As for what I know about it. See," Doc shuffled a foot. "Here's the thing, I'm a lawyer, and you? You're an idiot. Your whisper was a little loud there friend." His smile and aw-shucks attitude faded. "I suggest you get the hell out of here and don't even think about coming back. Or I will see you prosecuted for trespassing. And if anything does happen to Miss Sánchez, I will see you in jail for filing a false police report, and when you get out, I personally will sue you for everything you have got." Doc leaned in. "And just in case you're judgement proof, I will take every last penny from your paycheck that the law allows until you have paid my clients' grand kids to go to college. I'm thinking Yale." He smiled. "Clients, plural."

Jacob rounded his shoulders and stood his ground. "I know my rights, it's a free country, I can go anywhere I want, even a queer hole like this. Besides, it's your word against mine. And that's hearsay."

A flash went off, Oingo held up her phone, Boingo's had been pointing at him the entire time.

Doc looked back and smiled. "That's, not actually how it works, besides we have video and photographic evidence. And you're right, you are free to go anywhere you like. But this place is free to ban you from coming here except in cases of discrimination, and asshole is not a protective class. I assume this fine upstanding gentleman is banned Lydia?"

"Oh yeah, big time."

"Good." He looked at Jacob and smiled. "By Monday morning Lydia here will have a restraining order against you, if you come so much as with in line of sight, I'll make sure you spend at least one night in jail." He glanced over at me. "Pro Bono of course."

"Run little Jacob." I said. "Run away very fast." Something in me was beating against my chest. I wanted him to run, and I wanted to run after him.

Sadly, he didn't run, he straightened himself and pushed past everyone. The twins were eyeing him as he went. "This ain't over."

He said with a shaky voice. "You still gonna pay. He's gonna make you pay." With that he was out the door.

After it closed and he was gone the four of them turned towards me, Walt spoke first. "Nobody messes with my friends."

I smiled at him. My big, dumb, asshole. "Walt, you could have got yourself hurt."

He just shrugged. "Nobody messes with my friends." Then he looked at me. "I don't got many."

Doc put a hand on his shoulder. "You got a few more. But seriously dude, we have to work on your people skills." Then he looked at me. "You know calling the cops won't do anything, and a restraining order is just a piece of paper. Do you have a gun, and do you know how to use it?"

Before I could answer, Walt, who was looking at him as if he grew a second head, spoke. "I thought you lefto commies hated guns."

Doc looked at him. "Us lefto commies hate people being irresponsible with guns. Some think if that many people are going to be children about it they should lose them, yes, but most of us want more people to have them, people like her." He looked at me. "We just want you trained and registered. Minorities should definitely have firearms. The world's not safe, not for you."

I shook my head. "I know how to use one, but I don't own any."

Walt looked at me. "Hell, I'll get you mine."

Doc shook his head. "Don't. If you do, anything that happens with that firearm is your fault and you are legally liable for it."

"She isn't going to do anything wrong with it."

"No, she's not. But she's rusty, and if he gets it and shoots her with it, legally it's your fault."

"Man that's fucked up."

"No, that's so a felon can't get a gun by getting his buddy to buy it for him." Doc looked at me. "Go to a gun shop, one with a range, and buy a gun."

"Yeah." Walt snorted. "And wait 15 days. She needs one now."

"And if she had one now it still wouldn't do her any good because she is out of practice and doesn't know how to use it properly." Doc countered. "A firearm isn't a magic wand that makes all your problems disappear in a puff of smoke. It's a tool. And if you don't know how to use it," He looked at me. "All you're going to do is hit your thumb with the hammer."

"Yeah, right. All she has to do is not put her thumb between it and the firing pin." But then he stopped. "Oh, you meant like, if someone picked up a hammer and just tried to drive in a nail... yeah no." Walt looked at me. "Don't hit your thumb."

Doc smiled. "Chances are he won't try anything else tonight."

"Don't be so sure." Said Boingo from over by the door. God, I need to remember their actual names. Did I know their names? Right, Nissa and Lissa. Now which was which? "We got a truck that keeps driving by real slow."

"Three of them." Said Oingo from the window on the other side of the store.

One of the only other non-regulars in the café said, "Should we call the cops?"

Internally I felt myself laugh. "For what? Cars driving by?"

"Well, I couldn't hear it." She came closer. "But you're friends seem to think that nice young man was threating you, and we can't have a man threating a young lady." She was one of those women, white, older but not middle aged, hair in the swoop they all seem to have, bleached blonde, makeup that tried so hard for 'I'm not wearing any' but ended in a line around her face that made it look like a mask or a bad spray on tan. Maybe both.

She had been closer to the side of the counter where the encounter happened, closer than any of the others were. How did she not hear him when they did.

In her best let me speak to your manager voice, "We pay their salaries and for their fancy tanks, the least they could do was actually protect us."

I was white, and I knew that wasn't how it worked. The twins were white, hell they were see through, and I could tell they knew that wasn't how it worked. Hell, from the look on his face I knew Walt knew that wasn't how it worked. A room full of white people and somehow we knew more than this woman about reality. I knew it because I'm gay.

How the fuck did Walt know it?

Doc smiled. "Under statute, Lydia has done what is legally permissible and while a police report would help, ultimately they will say there is simply nothing they can do about a few vehicles driving around where a vehicle is supposed to be driving around."

This woman, commonly known to every retail worker in the world as a Karen, just nodded. "Then make them get off their doughnut munching asses, put down their tinker toys, and do their jobs."

Walt laughed. "I like her."

"You would." Said Oingo. "David, we don't have time for this. You heard what he called her, you know who he's got to be with." She walked over to him. "Your lie of being a lawyer won't work forever."

'Karen' looked at him as if she had been betrayed. "You're not a lawyer?"

He rolled his eyes and just took a long look at Oingo. Pretty sure she was Nissa. I think. "No ma'am, just in law school." That was new, but hey for a moment I forgot he was a nurse.

"Then young man, you just don't know what you are talking about."

Walt looked over. "Anna isn't going to like this."

Ok, now I was lost. What the hell does Mom have to do with anything?

"Karen!" Snaped Boingo.

"How dare you, I'll have you know that is a racist, sexist slur against whi..." That was as far as she got.

Boingo's eyes turned black. "You will go home, the coffee and service were great, you will leave a good online review and encourage your friends to come to the place when it is back up and running." Lissa, yes, she was definitely Lissa.

With that her eyes bled back to normal. The woman just smiled, went and picked up her purse and coffee and walked out with a huge self-satisfied smile.

"Oh Anna is going to so kill you for that." From Walt.

I just stood in shock. "Wait, you're all fae?"

The four of them looked at each other, then burst out laughing. The twins went back to opposite doors with their drinks and kept an eye out. Walt picked up his phone and started dialing numbers. Doc came towards me.

Doc came up. "God no." He looked at me. "Not in the least." He pointed over at the fireplace. "But that is the oldest hearth left in this area. As such, some of us, from," He looked around, "Different communities and backgrounds," He turned back to me, "Use it as a safe place. We call ourselves the outsiders." He thought about it for a moment. "Mostly because all of us are outcasts."

Our place, our little hole in the wall was a safe place for outsiders. It's what I was always looking for, it's what Beth wanted to keep it. Beth! "Does Beth know?"

"Her uncle did. He left it to her. I think because she is one of us, even if she isn't, you know, one of us." He smiled. "There isn't a roster, we don't know who each other all are. We just learn of this place through word of mouth. It's safe." He smiled. "We had no idea you were, well, you."

"I did." From Walt.

"You did not." From Oingo. "You though she was a witch."

"Well why not." He countered. "Witch seems to be sooo popular with college girls these days, so trendy, and besides her new girlfriend is a witch."

Both the twins laughed in unison.

"What?" Walt countered.

Doc looked over. "Did you call her?"

"Of course."

"Call who?" I asked.

"Anna. She's the den mother. This is her baby."

Mom, always quick to help, always looking after everyone, even Walt. Mom, who practically lived here. Mom, who I hadn't seen in days.

"Oh god, where has she been, is she alright?"

Walt shrugged. "She been trying to figure out how that idiot attacked you. He shouldn't have been able to."

I leaned against the counter. I knew how he had done it. "Izzy cast a spell in here. She was lonely, looking for a mate, and..." I trailed off, this was all my fault.

They all turned to look at me, all of them. Finally, Boingo said. "Hun, we all cast spells in here all the time. What's the point of a safe place to be ourselves if we have to hide who we are?"

So we sat and waited, or rather they sat, I kept working. It was three hours till closing and I was getting more nervous and upset with each tick of the clock. Outside, according to the twins, the trucks kept driving around, circling, waiting. For what I didn't know.

It started small at first. Two Black men came in and ordered coffee. Then two more. Three were next and they wanted to try our house special. Then four men and two women, both women were part of the local college, and the men, three white and one Black, were in a heated discussion with these two women of color on feminist theory.

"So you're telling me, this patriarchy is the root of all of my problems even though I'm white and a man? I thought I was supposed to be the bad guy?"

"That's what they want you to think, so we look like the bad guys." Said one. "See," she got up to the counter. "I'll have a triple shot, and whatever these morons want."

"Morons?" Said the Black guy. "I look white to you?"

"No." said the other professor. "But you look like a man who uses white man's points on why women should be home makers."

I got their orders and over the next 20 minutes I had one hell of a rush. All of them for dine in, all of them seemed to be deep in one conversation or another, and all of them were people of color, or with people of color. It wasn't just African Americans; Latinos, Hispanics, Pacific Islanders, and more came in. A weeknight now looked like the height of shopping season.

I was by myself, at least for the start of it.

"Why you no call me?" Rita slid in beside me.

"For what? A rush?" I looked at her. "I'm happy to have you but I couldn't exactly get away."

She bapped my arm. "Not the rush." She leaned in close. "That red neck coming back and bringing his buddies."

"I'll have a half caf full pump of vanilla." Came a familiar voice.

I turned and looked at her. She was at the registers, smiling away at me.

Rita slapped my arm again. "She called me. You get her coffee and I'll handle the rest."

Numbly I nodded and rote made Mom's coffee.

Chapter 44

When it was done, I came from behind the counter and took it to the very back of the room, where Anna sat waiting on me.

Looking around in amazement as our little shop had been turned into a liberal paradise. Christians, Jews, Muslims, more. I even watched as about ten lily white red necks came in, one of them clapped Walt on the arm, ordered, then went and sat at a table of black academics and started talking like they knew each other.

I looked at Anna. "Did you do all this?"

She shrugged. "I made some calls. Then they made some calls and here we are."

I shook my head in amazement. "So, like are you a witch, or a..."

"Let me stop you right there girl." She leaned in close. "This ain't no 70s TV show or movie, it's not some half ass book. I'm not no magic negro, I don't have any old time slave wisdom to pass on." She looked at me, then her face softened. "I'm just an organizer and activist."

I was confused. "But how?" I looked around. "Doc said you were responsible for this place."

She let out a sigh, one I knew too well. Time to explain things to the straight, with my queer ass standing in for the straight.

"I missed marching with Doctor King. I was too young. Then he was gone. Well I thought, let me go up to Chicago, then they killed Fred Hampton." She shook her head. "I went to college in the 70s, I was going to continue the good work, only the good work seemed to have stalled. Nixon had undone what little progress had been made,

Kent State happened, the war on drugs since Nixon couldn't make it illegal to be Black or a hippy..." She sort of smiled.

I did what I wanted every straight person I ever talked to, to do, I sat, nodded and listened, actually listened.

Taking a long drink of her coffee, she continued. "By the 80s? I was already feeling it. Run down, ignored, like it didn't matter. A new feminist push had begun with Roe V Wade and a new push back had come with it, and the plight of Black people?" She shrugged, "I just wasn't media relevant."

Leaning back in she looked at me. "And I did what a lot of people like me did, and do to this day, I thought, what the hell is the point? White people don't care, they oppress their own all the time. They oppress anyone and everyone and if you give one of those oppressed white people a chance? They will oppress you. I got mad. I started to change how I looked at everything." She nodded. "Then I turned on the TV. There, in living color was the President of the United States talking about protests. A chant from those people rang out and it hit me. 'Medical care is a human right'."

She sat for a moment drinking her coffee and was silent. I waited. I didn't want to interrupt. I knew that look, something hard for her to say was about to come up.

"You know, all my life, I hadn't given the queers another thought. I knew queer Black people, mostly women mind you. I knew who was credited with throwing the first brick at Stone Wall, but all that? That was queer issues. If a bunch of queers wanted to be nasty, that was their bag." She looked at me. "I heard what good white people were saying about those poor homosexuals, how their hearts went out to them, but if they had only behaved." She nodded. "Different beat, same words, same song." Nodded again. "And I had believed it, right up until that moment. I just knew they and I wasn't fighting different fights."

I nodded. "Intersectionality."

"Just so. But I swear if some of them damn white feminists don't learn it I am going be smacking me some highlights off some heads."

I chuckled. "So, how did we get from there to here."

"After that revelation, I started working with anyone who would let me, organized marches, sit ins, walk outs, whatever I thought would get things done. It waxed and waned. Then the Satanic Panic really took off, I thought it was just a smoke screen to start with, so I went to look for pagans to recruit, witches and such." She shuddered a bit. "I went and did all my fancy research, found what I thought was the most marginalized group I could, and walked my happy ass right into a nest."

"Nest?"

She nodded. "You'll find out sooner or later, a nest is a group of more than one family."

I blinked at her.

"Vampires girl."

I closed my eyes. Kevin had said they were real, but part of me hoped that like with a lot of things, he was just full of shit.

"If it wasn't for the twins I don't know if I would still be here, or if I was, if I would still have a pulse."

I looked over at the two of them, each sitting sentry at the doors. Oingo and Boingo? Vampires? I tried to imagine it. I amazed myself with how easy that thought solidified with me.

"So, what happened?"

"I found out they had their own version of the bullshit we deal with. When they spoke up for me they said just hear me out, so I made the same lame pitch to them I had originally intended to. The first of it was in this shaky oh god I'm going to die kind of way, but before I was even halfway through I was fired up and spit all kinds of hell and told them they could kill me or join me but I wouldn't back down."

I shook my head and could easily see it in my mind. "So, then you all ended up here."

"Hell no. This wasn't some magical overnight thing. It took years, damn near a decade for me to get this kind of neutral safe haven recognized. It was supposed to just be a meeting spot, but then the outcasts from the different groups started claiming it, and well here we are." She looked at me. "This place is exactly what you and Beth want to turn it into, a safe place for the 'other', for queers, for whomever." She leaned back and looked at me. "It's the ultimate punk, gay bar, night club, meet up, whatever."

I nodded. "So, when they said you were looking into how I could be attacked here?"

"There's no magic pill here girl. But everyone is supposed to leave it alone, and I don't just mean the bump in the night brigade. You just being attacked? That was bad enough. You and that girl Izzy being attacked again? Someone was after you."

I knew that to be true, Kevin said they were sicced on the two of us. "Any idea who?"

"Sorry, no."

Chapter 45

Some people in my position might be sitting around feeling sorry for themselves in that moment. I mean, come on. The creep who assaulted me, who ruined my date, who I gutted, who wasn't supposed to remember any of it, by the way, was not only back, but right now him and his redneck friends were cruising up and down the road that made up our little parking lot. That would be weird enough. But oh no, the Coffee Shop my best friend had inherited from her uncle is a safe haven for the outcasts of the outcasts. Two of my regulars were honest to God vampires.

Coffee.

Drinking.

Vampires.

I obviously had no idea how anything worked.

Me, I was actually kind of hyped. Not about the being hunted part. That totally sucked. The rest? Beth's place, our place, was the hub of a community like no other. I looked around in wonder at all the people who had come in and filled the place up; liberals, leftists, academics, red necks, small government conservatives, activists one and all. All called in by Mom.

"Are like all of these people?" I gestured around. "Other?"

She gave me a great big laugh. "No hun. Well…" She looked around, "I'd say a little over half of them were some flavor of odd on that side of things. But everyone here has one thing in common. Someone at some point tried telling them they didn't count as people."

I raised an eyebrow, "Even the red necks?"

"Child, Redneck was the term for the striking miners at the Battle of Blair Mountain. They were the laborers that dug the coal but got paid in vouchers living in a company town and couldn't escape because of it. They tried to unionize and the government came in to shut them down. Now all their grandkids' grandkids remember is that they have a strong disdain for the government." She shrugged, "Throw in a little Ayn Rand and cold war propaganda and they don't realize most of their ideas are socialist as hell." She shook her head. "That's where small government conservatism came from."

"Wait, is everyone going to be ok while we do the renovations?"

Mom gave a chuckle, "And that's why I know you two are the right ones to oversee this place. We'll be fine. Before Beth's uncle took over the place it was a barbeque pit. Before that it was an honest to god standalone building way before the rest of these shops were here. As long as that fireplace stays the hearth magic stays. We could all meet up in the parking lot and wag tongue. We've done it before, and we'll do it again." Then she shook her head. "Our problem now is what do we do about your stalker?"

With a sigh I said, "I don't know? Wait him out?" It wasn't a bad idea, after closing he wouldn't have a reason to... wait no. Some of the shops were opened later than we were. "Get a police escort home? I mean, he did try to rob the place before as far as they know." That could work... Unless of course I got the runaround. Which I likely would. They would do it tonight, maybe tomorrow... but they'd tell me to get a restraining order, order of protection, or some such. I had one of those, against Shadow. Not that I needed it any time soon. She, at least, was safely in jail. "I guess I could call his dad."

"Wait, you know who that boy's daddy is?"

"Yeah, he was the other hunter that attacked us that night."

"You seem way to chipper about that, you trust him?"

"Yeah, he saved Izzy's life. Of course..." That's when it hit me. "God that creep is so lucky he didn't actually hurt me?"

"Why is that hun?"

"Well, that night, after he pushed me down and was on top of me, I kind of gutted him with his own knife. Izzy made a deal with his dad and let them go so he could see to his son's wounds in exchange for our continued life and safety. Kevin definitely believes that if Iz or I die due to something he or his son does, if we're further harmed..."

She looked at me with amazement, "You took that boy's hunting knife from him?"

"Well, yeah, it was still on his hip." It was... Why was it still sheathed? I mean, the water attack, then that bell, then he was on top of me. I should have been done for at that point. But he had been too busy watching his dad, watching Izzy. He was there the night Izzy cast the spell. He attacked us on our date.

"God he's not after me, he's after Izzy."

"Miss Dorcha?" She nodded, "That girl is one of life's great mysteries. Everyone who knows, knows she's fae, but no one quite knows what kind. She's so all over the place most people just leave her be." She let out a sigh. "Honestly it makes her extremely lonely, I'm glad you two found each other." She cocked her head, "But what makes you think he was after her? One, no one in the community and their right mind wants to tangle with her, all of them say there's something creepy about her." So extremely true. "And two, you were the first one he attacked."

"I was, but he was surprised to see me. He asked me if I was one of them and said 'you saw it too didn't you' or something like that." I racked my brain to try and remember his exact words, only to have it tell me those were the right words.

"Wait, that spell she did that night?" I nodded. "He shouldn't have been able to see it at all."

'You saw it feed didn't you.'

"He saw her feed on the emotions."

"No way hun. You need fairy magic to see that."

Izzy had said it, she said it that night. "Humans can use fairy magic."

Mom blinked and looked at the hearth. "Well I'll be damned, of course they can. We've been using it for years." She shook her head. "You know, I never thought about it." She gave a slow smile, 'I guess there is some magic here protecting us after all, not just the agreement."

Agreements were the one thing I was sure about in my new life. Agreements were binding.

"That little shit has got to have made an agreement with someone." That made sense, I think. How else did Hitler use that magic without a deal. Dear god, someone out there was willing to make a deal with Hitler? Too weird. "I've got to call Izzy and warn her, I need to call Kevin to come get his son too before the little shit gets himself killed."

I tried Izzy's phone first.

No answer, it rang then went to voice mail.

"You really care what happens to that boy?" Mom asked.

I tried Izzy again. "No, yes. Look. If he dies and I didn't try, that's like my fault. If I try and he dies, it's his own dumb ass fault." Same thing. "Damn she's not picking up."

I called a number I never expected to call.

Ring

Ring

"Hello?" His tone was inquisitive. No doubt because he didn't know who it was.

"Kevin? It's Lydia."

"What's wrong?" The concern in his voice was deep. He knew if I was calling, it wasn't good. "She alright?"

How to answer that? "I don't know, I can't get ahold of her. Look, it's about your dumb ass kid. Him and some of his buddies are up here, riding around in pickup trucks, and Kevin, he remembers, he threatened me."

A mumble from the other end sounded like cursing, the normal human kind, involving female dogs and parentage. "He ain't hurt you has he?"

"Made me uncomfortable, threatened one of my employees, tried to resist getting thrown out, but no, he hasn't hurt me yet."

"What in the Sam hill does that damn boy think he's doing?" Then as an afterthought, "And how the hell can he remember what happened?"

"Kevin, there's more. He saw Izzy eating glamour. Mom says he shouldn't be able to do that. I think he made a deal with a different fae, and I think it was Izzy he's been after this whole time."

"Shit, fuck. Damn it all to hell. Dumb ass. Look, is he still there?"

I looked up, Oingo was still on the door. "Is he still out there?"

"His friends are."

Back to the phone, "His friends certainly are."

"Damn it, you stay right there. I'll be down in a minute, already headed out the door." I heard his truck crank. "I got him. Maybe I can talk some damn senses into him." His tone was completely exhausted. "He ain't been the same, not since his mother died," his voice was fading, I knew he was closing his ancient flip phone. One last thing came though before it cut off, and that filled me with dread. "And especially not since he started hanging out with that damn Ferris boy."

Eyes wide, heart racing, hand shaking, I redialed Izzy.

Straight to voice mail, no ringing whatsoever.

I turned cold, panic gripped me, and just like that, I ran.

Chapter 46

Phone, keys, purse, out the back door and I stopped dead in my tracks. My bug was at home with a flat tire. Panic surged though me as images of unnamed dangers ran through my mind. No way out, every fiber of my being froze.

"Lydia what the hell is wrong and why you out here where them idiots can see you?"

I don't remember moving but I was suddenly facing her. "Rita I need to borrow your car."

She blinked at me, "Ok, why?"

"I hate to ask you this, but could you close up for me? I think Izzy's in trouble. I want to be overreacting, I want to be wrong. I want..." That was as far as I got.

"You know what?" She handed me the keys. "That boy's here for you anyway, take my car, go, check on your Bruja, and stay gone till this is over." She hugged me. "I'll cover for you, say you doing paperwork or calling the police. Don't worry, I got this."

I gave her a quick hug. "Thank you Rita."

She gave me a huge smile, "Abuela's got you girl."

I did a quick look around "Um, so which one's yours?" She pointed to a white Hyundai and I took off as she closed the door yelling at me. "Girl you just stay back here and do that paperwork, hell, start calling a lawyer and see what can be done." Pause. "No, I got the counter, damn it. You stay." With that the back door was closed and I was in her car.

The inside was neat as a pin and a medal of some sort was handing from the rear view. Shoving the keys in I gave her a crank and heard the strange machine purr to life. My left foot automatically patted and my hand went to the center for the gear shift that wasn't there. Confusion gripped me until I realized it was an automatic. Of course it was, it started without the clutch being depressed.

Putting it in gear I peeled out of the back parking lot and made my way to the road. Part of my mind was screaming get out, get away, run, go far, go home, go to mom, go to safe.

A different part wasn't screaming at all. It was running alright, running flat out, but it was on the hunt, and when it got my jaws on whatever was keeping Izzy from me, it was going to rip them apart.

Suddenly I really, really liked that part of my mind.

Visions of ripping flesh with teeth I didn't have sprang unbidden into my mind. "Soon, we don't know what's going on yet, soon." Soon it agreed, soon we would rip them all, tear them all. The interstate was packed with traffic, it was moving, but slowly. Magically, I kept finding openings I could fit the car into and out of, barely having to slow down. My exit was upon me before I realized it and the traffic flow forced me down its throat. All the while my left foot patted the floor with ever shift of that automatic transmission. Still, I had to come to an almost halt at the turn, then it was off to home. Street, street, street, subdivision, turn right, left, left, right...

All of a sudden a huge black shape coming from the direction of home, flew right at the windshield. I hit the brakes and Rain flew up just in time to not be a red splatter on the glass... or in the front seat the hard way. Momentum carried me forward hard with me barely managing not to crack my skull on the steering wheel. With the sound of the screeching rubber still in my ears from the hard breaking, a new sound penetrated my mind. The sound of someone furiously beating at my window.

Rain was frantically beating her very human hands on the glass and screaming. "They got her, they got her they got her."

With my worst fears confirmed I jabbed my finger at the passage side door. Thankfully she didn't waste any time. Still, I was already in motion before she had managed to shut the door. Thank God she had control of her wings.

"Talk to me bird, what's going on."

She took a deep breath. "I was out back eating when I heard the truck come back so I flew up to the porch to see what was up. Beth, but not Beth, was there with that thing she calls a boyfriend, shortly after that they had Izzy tied up and on the stand she used on you last night. He stripped her naked and has been saying things, I don't know what, but Izzy isn't fighting back and I don't know why and I don't know what's going on." All of that was one sentence, one breath. She inhaled again. "He's got magic, I don't know how but he's using it on her, and I don't know what to do, I couldn't abandon her, and when I felt you coming, I flew off to get you, and you have to save her, because a little while ago that hunter came, not the good one, the bad one."

Fuck, what the hell was Beth thinking? Why the hell had Izzy not fought back? As I drove, it hit me. I turned down a different road than I normally do and went down an access road.

Rain screamed. "What? No, we got to save her!"

"And we are, but I'm not walking into a trap." I stopped the car on the side of the road and got out. We were behind the house and in those woods less than 20 yards away was the edge of the property. As I got out of the car I said to Rain, "I think I know how this is being done."

She got out, and realized where we were. "How?"

"Liz revoked hospitality because we left a mess, Allen has hospitality because Liz gave it to him." What was it Kevin had said? Hospitality could render a fae powerless? That sounded right, felt right, the truth of it was its own steady source of power.

Rain's reaction confirmed that truth. "Shit, shit, shit." She took a deep breath. "But why would Beth do that?"

"Simple, she's not Beth, she's Liz." Beth was my best friend, and I think she's still in love with me. Liz is Allen's slave, and something tells me he's the kind of 'dom' who doesn't care what his property wants. "If he's using fae magic, he's renamed her." And he did. She hated the name Liz. She couldn't stand it.

He called her that all the time and Liz loved it. He'd done the same thing to Beth that I had done with Rain, only for a much darker intent.

"So how do we fix this?"

I headed off towards home through the woods. "I have a plan, but first we got to get inside."

Chapter 47

Our back yard slopes down and our back deck is basically on stilts. Sure, if they were looking out the back, they would see me coming, but that was a risk I had to take. Going in the front was not an option. Great, I was here, no one was yelling at me to stop sculking around, so I probably haven't been seen. Unless they were trying to sneak up on me.

Paranoia gripped me and I felt like bolting. A quick look around and I didn't see anyone. The door to what passes for a basement was right behind me, sadly it wasn't an option to get inside. One, it was locked, and two, passes for a basement because other than the furnace it was mostly used for storage. Storage in a geek and con going house. In other words, it was a mess. Not to mention the door squeaked.

Crap.

Whispering under my breath I asked Rain, "Are you sure that younger hunter is here?"

She nodded.

Great, that meant his dad was headed to the wrong place. Worse, it meant if he laid a finger on Izzy, I would find out what bad really meant. Pictures of what had started happening to Rain danced in my head. Unpleasant pictures.

I pulled out my cell phone and dialed.

"What?" I could hear the sound of him driving in the background.

"Change of plans. Your boy isn't at the shop anymore."

Kevin started swearing. "I know that. I turned on his cell phone tracer. Had it in case he or I got captured so we could find each other. But if you know that you didn't do what I told you and stay at that damn coffee shop of yours."

"How far out are you?"

"About ten minutes, why?"

"I'm under the back deck, just outside."

"Damn it woman, get out of there."

"Can't, they have Izzy." That let out a string of words that I found to be quite impressive. "Look, I'm still trying to save his dumb ass too. I got a plan, when you get here come paly holy hell on the front door until they let you in."

His voice got cold, scared, "Don't do anything stupid."

"Stupid's all I got." With that I ended the call.

Fuck, shit. I hit redial.

"Thank god. Whatever you're thinking, don't."

"Allen. Did Allen give your boy a new name, a new nickname, anything?"

Silence from the other end, then with an exasperated sign, "He started going by Tucker after his mom died. It's his middle name."

"Allen did the same to Beth, calls her Liz."

"Fuck."

"Yeah."

"So, that Ferris boy is a fae?"

"I don't think so." Him being fae didn't feel right. "I got to go. Get here when you can. Make noise," and ended the call again. Steeling my nerves, I walked out from under the porch and made my way up the back stairs.

The closer I got to the sliding glass of the back, the more I could hear.

"Man, just collar the trap already, come on Allen, what are you waiting on."

I could hear movement. "Something isn't right."

"What's not right my man? We've been working on this for months. You noticed it at your slits stupid fucking shop. It's powerful, we both know that. But it's just a fucking fae."

The sound of something hitting the wall stopped me at the top of the stairs. Through the back glass I could see that Allen had Tucker by the throat and pinned him up against the wall.

"But it's not just a fucking fae you stupid reject. The iron should be hurting it more, dragging its will down." He stepped in closer, "It's on her wrists, ankles, up her fuck hole ass and there's an iron bit in her mouth, and yet she is still able to defy me."

"But it is working man," He grunted out. "You saw it start to turn red as soon as it touched the skank. Plus you got hospitality and she don't, trust me my man if she was anything other than a fae none of that would matter."

"You sure your old man is right about this?"

"Dude, you're the one with a patron."

"You think they tell me what hurts them. Why do you think I want this thing? Its more power."

"It's mouth will look good waxing your..."

Whether that was as far as he got or as much as I heard didn't matter. Someone was pounding the hell out of the front door. "Ash, Ash I know you're in there son, open up the damn door."

That's when I knew that my idea would work. For just a second, Jacob, Ash, Tucker, whomever this kid was, his eyes flickered and he looked towards the door.

"What the fuck is your dad doing here Tucker?"

Tucker snapped his attention back to Allen.

"I don't know man. He turned into a pussy ever since we fought this thing."

"Well get rid of him."

"Ash, open this god damn door. You and that Ferris boy both need to get the hell out here right now." The two of them looked at each other. "If you fucking don't I will call the police and get them to help me get you out."

Allen's eyes widened. "He wouldn't."

"Like I said, he's turned into a pussy. He wants me to steer clear of both your bitch's roommate and the trap." Tucker started heading for the door, so did Allen. "Can't you use your mojo on him and make him go away?"

"It takes days to set up."

I waited until I heard the front door open, then slipped inside.

Chapter 48

As I opened the door, inside a nightmare greeted me. Beth was naked and standing beside Izzy who was suspended off the ground face down on her own swing set up. The leather straps had been replaced with iron shackles, her hair was tied with rope forcing her head up and her back arched. A Pear of Anguish was insider her and she was bleeding, and an iron bit gag was in her mouth.

That wasn't the worse part.

Beth was covered in bruises, her arms, legs, and body had stripes from a cane. Everything would be covered by clothing. I realized I hadn't seen Beth naked in months. As I crept in keeping an ear out for where Kevin was raising hell, Beth was stroking Izzy and talking to her.

"Don't worry, my love, it will all be over soon, and we will be happy. You are so beautiful." She walked around her, stroking her as she went. "If you hadn't tried to take my Lydia from me, I probably could have got Master to leave you alone."

I loved Beth, but Liz? Liz was sick.

I hear you little one. I hear you. You have to break this spell. Break it and I can do the rest.

Not quite sure how or if my idea would work, but I had to try. "Beth sweetheart, honey, what are you doing?" Start slow. Start quiet. God please let Kevin keep them busy. "Izzy doesn't look like she's enjoying herself."

Beth's head snapped around. "Oh, Lydia." She came over to hug me and then stopped. "No, no... this isn't right. You shouldn't be here yet." She backed up hugging herself and looked down at her bruises. "It's not ready yet."

I came a little closer and kept my voice down. "What's not ready yet Beth?" Remind her of who she is, keep her talking. "Talk to me Beth, what's not ready, what happened to you?"

"I..." She paused. "I didn't do good."

"What didn't you do good Beth?" I crept closer. "What's wrong?"

"I, I made you a partner and didn't ask. I... signed half the house over to you too. I didn't tell you, it was in the paper work." She looked away. "I wanted to surprise you. I love you." She got a faraway look on her face. "But I messed things up and now Alle...Master has to fix it."

"Beth sweetie, you didn't mess up." Just a little closer. "I love you too." A little closer. "Beth..."

"Stop calling me that. It's Liz, he likes Liz." The high pitched whine of her voice showed me how much pain she was in. It was also loud, loud enough to call attention.

I took my chance, grabbing her, I kissed her for all she was worth. As she pushed herself off of me, she fell. I went to pick her up only to hear the sound of a hammer being pulled back.

The men had arrived.

Chapter 49

"What the fuck did you do to Liz?" The Colt Peacemaker in his hand had to be an antique. It was single action meaning he was going to have to cock it every time. It was also a .45 caliber ball in the cylinder. I knew all of this because Izzy and Beth had been giving me the crash course on firearms for the Cyber Punk game. It was an evil thing to have pointed at me.

Behind it was Allen, and behind him 'Tucker' had something a little more modern pointed at his dad, a 1911.

"Ash, you don't have to do this son."

"God, shut up already, you fucking pussy. What the hell happen to your balls? It's a damn tranny and not even human on top of it. Why the hell do you care?"

The Peacemaker never wavered, "I said what the fuck did you do to Liz bitch?"

"Allen man, this is a bit much." Allen's gun wasn't wavering, but Tuckers was. "I mean it goes both ways, it's not even human, come on man, I ain't killing my dad over this and I know him. He may have turned pussy, but he won't let this go. Grab your slit and let's get out of here."

"Shut the fuck up Tucker." He walked forward and put the muzzle right between my eyes.

Izzy lost her shit at that. She started rocking, testing the shackles, shaking and what's more, screaming at him around the gag.

I, however, only had eyes for Beth.

Beth was slowly getting up, looking herself over, looked at Izzy, then looked at Allen. "What the fuck do you think you're doing Allen?"

"Shut up Liz. Are you ok?"

She stood up and looked around. "You know what? No, I'm not ok. I hate that fucking name, don't call me that again and get the hell out of my damn house."

I smiled. "Izzy, I invite you in and give you hospitality and clan rights." That last part seemed important.

With those words the world went dark. Shadows crept over everything, on everything. All reaching for Izzy. Darkness itself swirled around her and an icy wind blew off her naked form. Her eyes turned black and she started to change.

Allen stopped pointing the gun at me and opened fire.

Squeeze the trigger, pull the hammer, squeeze the trigger, pull back the hammer. Over and over again.

The first round hit her in the chest, not far from where the bolt had. The rest?

Blackness covered her body, and like that night at the restaurant, wings sprouted out of her back, wings of dark shadow. This time they didn't stop. Black gave way to something darker, something almost blue, and in that new, darker than black darkness, stars came out. The shadows kept creeping up her body over her, and I heard when the iron of the bonds snapped.

"Don't just stand there Tucker, shoot the bitch."

"She's in Iron, she can't be doing this, she can't." Tucker took the gun off his dad and that was all the opening Kevin needed. He sucker punched his son so hard I hear the boy's jaw break.

Better a broken jaw than whatever would have happened had he managed to point the weapon at Izzy.

Allen had seen enough and went to run out the still open back door, only to find it wasn't there anymore. It was still home, it was still our living room, but now? Now it was also my dark forest.

I knew every tree here, every stone, off to the left where my room was, where my room should have been was the briar thicket that hid the entrance to my den. I was home in more ways than one.

I also finally saw the beast that had been plaguing me, hunting me in my nightmares. It was all around Allen. It had arms longer than its lanky legs, its body was twisted and grey, black hair, Allen's black hair, cascaded down its back. Allen was human, but his use of the magic had twisted him, and on this side I could see him for what he was. A troll.

He looked at his hands in horror and let out a scream.

It was the last sound he would ever make.

Izzy was AWAKE!

When the clawed arm shot forward, I looked back to see what it was attached to, and see I did.

Izzy was a dragon.

She picked Allen up and threw him against the nearest tree. His body made the most satisfying crunch when it hit.

And just like that, we were back in the living room, Allen laying slumped against the wall, Izzy, naked, bleeding, standing over him.

Tucker was groaning on the floor with his dad standing over him, and Beth? She was staring wide eyed at Iz as if she had just been some huge, winged lizard. Funny thing? Those wings had been feathered.

Finally, she spoke. "Someone want to tell me what's going on?"

Izzy turned around, and fell forward.

Oh, right, she had been shot.

As I scrambled over to her, uniformed men came in through the front door followed closely by Rain. "I did it, I called them." She took one look at Izzy and squawked out a cry. "No, no be dead, don't be dead."

Chapter 50

"So let me get this straight, your roommate's boyfriend had been systematically abusing her for months, which she hid from you, but when you found out the guy who tried to rob you was friends with him, you knew something was wrong and rushed home?"

I rolled my eyes. "No, I tried calling first and got no answer, the first or the second time. When I called the third time and the phone was off, then I knew something was wrong and rushed home." I had been at this for an hour and a half. The noise of the hospital had long ago faded into the buzz of the background.

I couldn't blame the cop, not really. We had a body, an abuse victim, a sexual assault victim with a gunshot wound, a robbery perp with a broken jaw who was at the house of his victim, with his father, a 22-year-old with no ID, and a woman who had been driving a car with an APB out for it for reckless driving.

"And you didn't notify the police because?"

I let out a long sigh. I had answered that question already multiple times. "Because I was hoping like hell I was wrong." He wrote something down in his little book, what I had no idea, but he seemed quite intent on it. "And that's when you asked the homeless girl to call the cops while you went in, all by yourself."

That wasn't a question, so I didn't bother answering it. "Look, Rain's a local and she helps us out sometimes. I had no idea she was homeless, though she does describe herself as wild, so I guess that makes sense." Meanwhile Izzy was still in surgery and again, since I wasn't family, I wasn't being told anything. "Can we, like, hurry this up? I've got a headache and I'm tired."

With that he gave me a sympathetic smile, "Yeah, adrenaline dump. Sucks when you come down." He shook his head, "Just a few more questions."

"You said that half an hour ago."

"What was Mr. Gregor's father doing there?"

"After the attack, we kind of met up and he was trying to help us out. He felt bad for what his kid did and was trying to do right by us."

"You know the same night you got attacked the second time he brough his boy in to be stitched up from a knife wound, the same kind of wound you had given the guy who had attacked you outside the restaurant."

There it was, there was the reason I was dealing with a detective. "Look. I had no idea that Allen and Kevin's kid were in cahoots or what they thought they were going to do, ok? I was hopped up on so much adrenaline and fear that night that everyone looked like the guy who had just fucking robbed me. I was jumping at shadows." Which was the truth, kind of. "I wasn't going to falsely identify him as the guy I stabbed."

"It never occurred to you that the two events were related?"

"It never occurred to you that the guy who robbed me comes into the hospital on the same night I got attacked again and it might be connected?"

"Touché." He tapped his pen on his pad. "What I'm getting at is what was Mr. Gregor doing there?"

I let out a sigh. "Tucker or whatever his damn name is came into my store earlier and caused a scene. I had called him to come get his damn kid before I had him arrested for trespassing. When he was hanging up he said something about a Ferris boy and my paranoia hit overdrive. I ran home, called him back when I saw that bastard of his was there and well. He was trying to talk his kid out of being stupid."

He nodded, "I see, and he's the one who hit his son." I nodded. "But Mr. Ferris was the one who shot Mr. Dorcha?"

"Ms. Dorcha, and yeah."

He nodded, "So what was the younger Mr. Gregor doing at that point?"

"Trying to talk his buddy out of being stupid. I don't think he signed up for it going as far as it did." Everything I said was true, well, Jedi true anyway. As such, my story hadn't changed one bit.

He nodded, closed up his notebook, and said. "Thank you for your co-operation. We'll be in touch." With that he went to walk out, only to stop at the door. "Don't you want to know what's going to happen now?"

"With all due respect detective? I currently don't give a fuck. My girlfriend and best friend are both hurt, I feel like shit, the guy who did it is dead, and you got the guy who helped him. Hang him, let him out, take his word over ours that this was all a misunderstanding and that we were asking for it. I don't give a fuck, I'm numb."

"Not your first rodeo with a SA?"

I thought back to Shadow and all of the things that happened there. Kidnapping was the only thing that stuck. Everything else she did to me she swore was consensual and it was my word against hers. All the defense attorneys had to do was trot out that I was into slap and tickle games and played the field in college.

"Not by a long shot." God I was so damn tired.

"If it matters, I believe you. Even if your friend had agreed, with those injuries? No way was she still agreeing. Mr. Ferris's death is unfortunate, but we'll have to wait on the report of what caused it seeing as even being pushed into a wall as hard as he was shouldn't have killed him." He sighed. "I wish I could say this is over for you, but there's still a lot of questions."

"I know, I'll see you soon detective."

***

Izzy made it through surgery and recovered quickly. Beth and I both went into therapy; God knows we needed it. Kevin testified against his son, said he figured it was the best way to save his life. Ash stopped using the name Tucker and is working with the prison psychologist trying to figure out what happened. Seems he had some kind of break after his mom died and something, something. He shows signs of magical thinking and even told the prison shrink that him and his dad were vampire hunters or some such.

Izzy made a quick recovery and the Cafe was only shut down for a month for her to get everything done. She also moved in with both of us. Beth and I are working on us, because apparently there is still an us. She has a thing for Izzy, but the two of them are taking it really slowly. We still don't know what Izzy is, not really. Closest thing we can think of is a Dragon that somehow got itself a Sidhe title.

All in all, life's not too bad.

Epilogue

Our laughter rang out though the Cafe, it was after closing and myself, Izzy, Beth, and Rita were sitting around and shooting the shit.

"So let me get this straight, you been shot how many times?"

Izzy cocked her head. "Counting my brother or not?"

"Your own brother shot you?"

"To be fair that one was an accident."

"Fine not counting him." Rita said.

"Um, 6 times now. Only one cross bow though."

"What the hell you been doing to keep getting shot at?"

"Just popular I guess."

"Husbands?"

"Only two." That got everyone laughing again. "To be fair, I didn't know."

I got up and went to fix myself another coffee. It had been six months and other than finding out that a few of my regulars were very odd, life was great.

R. F. DeAngelis
R. F. DeAngelis

About the Author

R. F. DeAngelis is Trans Woman and activist with a chronic pain condition and dyslexia. She honestly believes that the story will set us free and refuses to give up despite the curve balls life throws at all of us. She has been in a committed relationship for 20 years and is a practice of BDSM as a top with a wonderful family and support structure she loves very much.